OUTTA NEWARK

A Tale of Love, Friendship and Payback

DAVID MALLEGOL

DEDICATION

This novel is about friendship. I would like to dedicate this book to my brother, Andre Mallegol, and my good friend, Al Henry. Both of them make my life better.

[signature]

November — 2017

Outta Newark

Also by David Mallegol

Historical Fiction Series
The Bronze Horsemen
Adventures of the Bronze Horsemen
Hunt for the Wolf Clan

CONTENTS

ACKNOWLEDGMENTS

Numerous people have helped me make this story into a novel worth buying with your hard earned money.

I was fortunate that Frank Bruno chose me to tell his "story." My wife, Irma Mallegol, helped more than a little over the 18 months while I was writing and reviewing this novel. I thank her for her input and patience. Editing and advice were professionally provided by Robert Bacon of The Perfect Write. For proofreading, I have to thank Sonia Lichtenberg.

CHAPTER ONE

Throop, Pennsylvania
July 4, 1954

BOOM... BOOM... BOOM!

My name is Frank Bruno. I'm fourteen years old and in seventh grade at St. Stephens Middle School in Scranton, Pennsylvania. Tonight my dad and I are lying flat on our backs on a big plaid wool blanket, watching fireworks. I'm happy to be here with my dad because we haven't spent much time together these last few months.

I hollered amid the noise, "Wow, Dad, these are the best fireworks I've ever seen!"

My dad put his hand on my shoulder and said, "Yeah, it is, Frank. It's some show."

I was really glad to see my father's having some fun for a change. Ever since my mom became sick, two years ago, all my dad has done is work and worry. I remember how thrilled I was to see him when he came home from World War II in 1945, but my mother says he's different from when he went into the service.

I asked her what she meant by my dad being different, and she says he's quieter and often lost in thought, and that he never wants to talk about what happened. She added, "When men come home from war, they're all changed."

Mom's had a bad cough for as long as I can remember. Dad took her to our old family doctor, who's about to retire. He's the only physician in Throop. At first he blamed her cough on smoking cigarettes, but everyone smoked, even some kids I knew in school, yet no one coughed like she did.

Mom stopped smoking but it didn't help with the cough. My parents continued to see the old doc, and every time it seemed they brought home a stronger cough medicine. Each was supposed to be better than the last, but none of them cured her.

A while back I'd looked at the dark-brown bottle of her "newest" cough medicine and read the label: "Contains Codeine." I wondered what codeine was, but when I also saw "Not for Children" I assumed it must be something strong. A month later, after finishing four bottles of the stuff, she was no better—and maybe even worse. Then we learned the truth about her condition.

BOOM... BOOM... BOOM! The ending to the fireworks would be coming soon. This was the best part. My mind wandered as I looked around and awaited the big finish.

Several kids I knew from St. Stephens Catholic School were here tonight. My buddy, Russell Brewer, had his arm around a pretty girl who was in seventh grade. I watched as he slid his hand all the way around her waist and under her sweater. I could see him grab a quick feel when the fireworks flashed. *Lucky Russell.* The girl smiled and didn't seem to mind at all.

I wished I was with my girlfriend, Mary Jo, who was here with her parents and watching the fireworks, too, but this was the first chance I'd had to do something with my dad since we got the news. The old doctor had told my mom what she really suffered from. He called it "The Consumption." Her cough wasn't from smoking, and the medicines wouldn't help. Our house would never be the same.

Dad and I generally ate breakfast together every morning: oatmeal or cereal, sliced apples and toast with strawberry jam, sometimes grape jam if we ran out of strawberry. And he read the newspaper aloud to me. I loved it when dad got to the sports page and anything about the Yankees. I wasn't too interested in world news, but I was scared of Stalin and the Russians. Bombing America might be next.

Dad said that Stalin was killing millions of his own people, and I was sure if he came to the U.S. he'd destroy us all. It seemed to me that the nuns were scared of Stalin too. In case there was an atomic-bomb attack, we practiced a safety drill on the first of each month. The nuns called the practice "Duck and Cover."

When the alarm bell went off, each of us got under a desk and covered our head with a book. Every time the drill started, I crawled one row over and got next to Mary Jo and held her hand. When the nuns turned off the lights to make it seem more like we were really under attack, I kissed Mary Jo on her lips. Wow, did that make my heart pound! No bomb needed.

No one squealed on me about making out with Mary Jo. My fourteenth birthday was back on February 28, which made me six months older than most kids in seventh grade. Not only that, I was taller than every other boy in my class, and I was friends with pretty much everyone. Russell and some of my other buddies kissed their girlfriends during air-raid practice, but the younger boys were too embarrassed to try it. Mary Jo and I mugged it up. She said she liked kissing but didn't want to get caught by the nuns—and neither did I.

The nuns scared all of us. If they saw me making out with Mary Jo, they'd raise holy hell and tell our parents, but for me it was worth the risk. Mary Jo had just turned fourteen, and she seemed quite different from when I first noticed her in sixth grade. Always pretty, with her short brown hair, blue eyes, and great smile, this year she really looked like a teenager and not just a very cute young girl.

On top of this, her body was more like a woman's, and I'll admit that her boobs were always on my mind. I often stared at her when she wasn't looking, especially when she wore a tight sweater. It seems that she always catches me when I check her out, but she just smiles. I can't help it, I think about her all the time. My palms become sweaty when I'm near her, and my mouth gets dry.

As for appearances, I look about the same except older. I did start combing my black hair straight back, and I use Brylcreem so it'll stay in place. I'm taller and my arms and shoulders are bigger compared to most boys my age. I'm getting hair under my arms and on my balls. The other boys my age say they're getting hairy "there" too. I wanted to ask my mom about it but was too embarrassed to bring it up, so I figured it must be normal. Maybe I'll ask Dad when I get the nerve.

Anyway, Mary Jo is so pretty that I sometimes wonder what she sees in me. After all, I'm just another boy in her class. Maybe it's that I get the best marks in the seventh grade, and that includes all the girls too. One thing she told me she likes about me was that I don't let the big kids pick on the little kids.

Russell teased me about studying and called me a bookworm and a study freak, but to tell the truth grades just come easy to me. Of course I pay attention in class, and I take good notes when I'm not looking at Mary Jo's boobs. I do my homework, and so far I have straight A's except for one B-plus. The B-plus came in a geography test when I couldn't find Persia on a map because the country's name was changed to Iran back in 1935. How the hell was I supposed to know?

In Catholic school, if you don't do your homework you're in big trouble with the nuns. Some nuns are worse than others, and everyone stayed clear of Sister Agnes, who carried her pointer and whacked you if she caught you not paying attention or with your hands in your pockets. Sister Agnes had a saying: "Hands in your pockets is like playing with the devil. If you play with the devil, you will go blind." All the boys knew what she called the devil. I'll bet she's never seen the devil.

BOOM... BOOM... BOOM... BOOM... BOOM! The grand finale of the fireworks display was underway.

Dad rolled on his side and said something about the last huge explosion. I was watching the fireworks but thinking about Mary Jo and her boobs, so I jumped at the sound of his voice, which must have seemed weird with all the other noise. I smiled at him.

My dad's family was big, with lots of relatives. They all came from Calabria, Italy. His father, who was my grandfather, moved here in the early 1900s. All of the men in the family worked in the coalmines. Miners dug anthracite coal, or as they called it "clean coal." I can tell you one thing, it was not clean when you touched it, but it was supposed to burn cleaner and pollute the air less than bituminous coal. My dad told me that even back in 1900, when his father arrived, a lot of people wanted less smoke in the air they breathed.

When the mining slowed, several of my dad's cousins moved to a big city called Newark, someplace in New Jersey, for better jobs. Dad had stopped working in the mines a long time ago because he'd developed a cough from breathing the coal dust.

So instead of mining he bought a truck and hauled coal to local businesses. It ended up that he made better money than he did when he worked deep below the earth's surface.

Dad also did odd jobs, as both an electrician and as a welder. He was a man who learned a new trade quickly. Seeing something once was usually enough for him. It seemed there wasn't much he couldn't do. After coal hauling dried up as a business, he was one of the first men to learn how to work with electricity. Right now he's employed with The Scranton Transit Company, building the first electric trolley, despite his having only an eighth-grade education. He's a smart guy. Maybe that's where I get it from, but I don't want anyone to think I'm not proud of my mom. They're just different people.

My dad is shorter than my mom, by several inches, but he has thick, strong arms, huge shoulders, and a broad chest. My mom is a big, tall woman. People say she's big because she's Hungarian. Her brothers and parents are big too. I guess all Hungarians are big people. I seem to take after the good things about both my parents. I'm taller than every other kid in my class, and I have bigger arms than the rest of them as well. Maybe Russell is almost as strong as I am, but he's the only other kid in my class who even comes close.

The fireworks didn't end as fast as I thought they would, and out of the blue my dad said to me, "Son, we may have to move to New Jersey so your mother can get the right kind of treatment for her illness. They have better doctors in big city hospitals because I need to find one who can help her. She's not getting any better here. All she does is sleep all day and hardly eats anything. I can't just stay here in Throop and watch your mother waste away. I have to do something, Frank. Your mom is special." He shook his head and turned away.

Dad took a while before he spoke again. He wiped his eyes

with a handkerchief and said in a choked voice, "I'm not sure what I'll do in Newark, but I can't lose your mom. She means everything to me." His body shook as he tried to hold back his tears.

The idea of moving away from Throop bothered me. I knew everybody in town and liked the school and of course Mary Jo. I played baseball and basketball in the Catholic Youth Organization or as everyone called it, the CYO league. The baseball coach told me that since I was a lefty I could play first base. I didn't know why he wanted me at first base, but if he wanted me there it was okay with me. I just wanted to play. Besides Mary Jo, sports, and school, I had my best buddy, Russell, and a lot of other friends. In New Jersey I had nothing. I didn't want to go, but I sure couldn't stay if my parents were moving.

I was thinking about moving just as the fireworks started up again. This time I was certain it was the end, as the night sky filled with color and the explosions were louder than ever. Some of it sounded like cannons going off, one after the other. I yelled to my father, "Dad, is this what World War II was like?"

Dad shook his head and yelled back at me, "These fireworks are just for show. The war in Germany was real. Instead of noise and flashes of light, there were bombs going off all around us. Real bombs with guys getting blown apart. Believe me, Son, I was lucky to come home. Talking about it brings back bad memories for me. A lot of really good guys were killed by those damn Nazis. I hate to think about it."

There was one huge final explosion and a great flash of light with all the colors of the rainbow high above us. Fourth of July fireworks were over for 1954. Dad and I picked up our blankets and walked with the crowd and headed back to our truck for the ride home.

———

Dad started our Ford pickup with the flathead V-8, and I said, "If we have to move to New Jersey, I hope they have fireworks as good as these." I wanted to cheer him up and added, "Thanks for bringing me. It was great."

We reached our driveway, and I hopped out like I always did. My father, whose real name is Dominic Bruno, asked me to get the mail. I reached into the mailbox as he pulled the truck up the driveway and went inside our house, calling out for my mom, "Irene, we're home." My mom's full name was Helen Irene Bruno, but dad liked calling her by her middle name, and often sang a few lines from the popular song "Irene My Dream" as they washed and dried the dinner dishes together.

I grabbed everything in the mailbox and climbed the steps to our house and opened the door. I glanced at the mail as I hung my jacket on a hook. There was never anything for me it seemed, but to my surprise this time there was something. Well, not for me—yet probably about me—from St. Stephens Catholic School.

The top left corner of the envelope had a man's name on it, and his title, which was Bursar, whatever that meant. I was glad it wasn't from the principal, but even the name with Bursar after it might mean I was in some kind of trouble, so I stuck the letter in the bottom of the stack and dropped it on the kitchen table, hoping dad would tire of slogging through everything before he finished the pile.

I twisted the knob to the "on" position and waited for our new 14-inch black-and-white Philco TV to warm up, which took a couple of minutes. I watched wavy lines scroll up and down as I thought about my mom and dad and moving from Throop.

With dad's many jobs, he told me he was making pretty good money, which is how he was able to afford the TV he bought last year at Sears and Roebuck. He'd paid cash instead of using something new called "revolving credit." Revolving credit was a type of payment system that enabled people to pay for a purchase over time and not all at once. Dad told me that if you buy on credit you pay "interest" which makes the price of whatever you purchase a lot more than if you paid cash.

The picture on the screen wouldn't stop rolling, so I adjusted the rabbit ears from one side to the other. The picture stopped moving but it was a bit fuzzy. My dad had wrapped aluminum foil around the antenna wires, so I slipped this up and down until the image got better. Now I could clearly see *Dragnet* and Sergeant Friday and his sidekick, Officer Frank Smith, talking to a woman who looked guilty of hiding something, probably murder. I loved Sergeant Friday when he said, "Just the facts, ma'am, just the facts." I knew Friday had her in his sights when he said that. After a half-hour of questioning and sifting through evidence, he arrested the woman for murdering her husband. Friday always got it right.

When the show was over, I checked to see if my dad had opened the envelope from St. Stephens, but the letter hadn't been touched. I noticed a lot of other mail from the previous week, and some from the week before that. All of it was unopened. There was letter from the county, with "Tax Bill" marked on the envelope, the electric bill, and something from the coal company. I thought it might be a check, so I placed it on the counter so Dad couldn't miss it. It seemed to me he was so worried about mom that he forgot to pay attention to everything else.

I headed upstairs to bed. As I passed their door, I heard my parents talking in their bedroom. I thought they might be talking about me so I listened for a minute. Their voices were low but I did hear them say something about Newark and dad's cousin, who I called Uncle Louie even though he wasn't really

9

my uncle. He and his wife, Aunt Marie, were always great to me.

I grabbed my toothbrush and shook out some Pepsodent tooth powder, most of which fell in the sink, and I brushed my teeth and washed my face. I jumped into bed and pulled the chain on the lamp on my nightstand and crawled under the covers. *Uncle Louie lives in Newark, so it can't be all that bad. Maybe there's a CYO league, and I can play basketball and maybe baseball too.*

CHAPTER TWO

Broken Eggs

For the next two weeks my parents hardly talked about moving, or at least they didn't discuss it in front of me. I was hoping that maybe they had dropped the idea.

During the summer, except for my paper route in the mornings, the days were my own. Some friends and I had used scythes to clear a field of brush, and we hauled off everything in wheelbarrows. We moved rocks to make an infield and used whatever we could find to serve as bases. After a week and a half of hard work, the field was ready for our first baseball game. The infield was rough but we were really anxious to give it a try, and it proved to be okay.

We often didn't have enough players for a nine-person team, so while one kid batted the rest of us played the various positions. When there weren't enough kids to cover all the outfield positions, we left some fields open, especially right, and even second base if we had to. I was a natural lefty, but I had to hit righty most of the time because we were without a right fielder. After weeks of batting this way, I got used to being a righty.

When there was no baseball game I rode my Schwinn bicycle the few miles to Scranton and met Mary Jo at her house. Her mom worked at a sewing shop and her dad was a conductor for the electric trolley company, so we had a lot of time alone. My mom and dad couldn't afford a phone, so I just took my chances and pedaled over to Mary Jo's house, hoping to find her home, and most often I did.

Mary Jo and I usually went to the Barre Sweet Shop on Jefferson Street and had an ice cream soda I paid for with money I earned from my paper route. If we didn't get whipped cream on the top, it cost 15 cents. Once in a while we went to a daytime movie, called a matinee, which cost 20 cents for two. If the usher wasn't watching us, when the theatre darkened we snuck up to the balcony and made out. Mary Jo was a great kisser.

Today, Mary Jo was home. We walked to the sweet shop and had a chocolate ice cream soda. She got whipped cream but I didn't. On the way back I told Mary Jo that my father was worried about my mom's health, and that he said we might have to move to Newark, New Jersey, so my mom could get better treatment for consumption. This was first time I mentioned that I might have to move away.

She stopped walking, grabbed my arm, and looked at me with sad eyes. "I'd hate it if you moved Frank, but my father and mother are talking about moving to Newark, too, not right away but maybe next year. I have an aunt and uncle who live there."

"Why would your parents be moving?"

"The trolley has fewer passengers each month because people are taking busses. I asked Dad why, and he told me that busses stop anywhere someone wants to get off, and trolleys can stop only at designated places. So the trolley might shut down and he would lose his job. But if this happens he has the promise of getting hired by The Essex County Bus Company in Newark, where my uncle works."

"Do you know where you might live?"

Mary Jo said, "The place we might move to in Newark is called The Projects. It sounds pretty nice to me."

I couldn't believe what I'd just heard. "Geez, Mary Jo, that's the same place my dad said where we might live. He'd be going to work in a shipyard as a welder or an electrician. I think my parents are pretty serious about it. Wow, if both of us moved to The Projects, you could still be my girlfriend."

Mary Jo and I jumped up and down together and laughed. She looked so darn good. She leaped into my arms, her breasts rubbing my chest, which made my dick get hard. I'm sure she felt me. Funny thing is, she didn't move away. Instead, she kissed me on the lips and pushed her tongue into my mouth. I slipped my hand under her sweater and touched her bra, not knowing how she might react.

To my surprise, she kept her body pressed against mine and smiled and said, "Your hand is okay. We might never see each other again if one of us has to move and the other doesn't." I kissed her and let my hand stay where it was, on her bra. It felt like cloth mostly, but it was my first real feel ever.

We walked back to her house, pulled down the shades on the porch, and we kissed each other for a few more minutes. I hated leaving Mary Jo, but it was getting late and without a light on my bicycle the ride back could be dangerous, so I had no choice except to get going.

I thought about Mary Jo all the way home. I also thought about how so many other people had moved from both Scranton and Wilkes Barre during the past few years. Jobs in the mines were mostly gone, and businesses had been boarded up everywhere. My seventh-grade classrooms contained a lot of empty desks.

With so many people leaving at the same time, it was hard for the owners to sell their homes, and many of the houses sat empty with hardly anyone showing any interest in buying. Luckily, my parents rented the house we lived in, so all we had to do was load up our furniture and clothes and kitchen stuff and Philco TV, and drive off.

I had to pedal harder, as the ride back to Throop was now uphill. I rested as I leaned my bike into a right-hand turn to enter my street. A short way down, I noticed that two more houses had just been put up for sale. Good luck. On the house across from where we lived, a for-sale sign had been staked out front for longer than I could remember.

This made me think even more about moving. Many kids in my class had no fathers; these men had died in mining accidents. Almost as bad, a lot of the dads had black-lung disease from breathing coal dust their whole lives. If the father had died or become too sick to work, the oldest son—or sometimes all of the sons—had to work in the mines to put food on the table and pay the family's bills. Now, even those jobs were disappearing. Some older kids I knew had quit high school and worked in the mines. They hardly looked like kids a year or two later.

I had another block to go and I'd be home. I spotted Russell waving to me from his front porch, and he walked out to the street to stop me. His head was hanging low as he said, "You might not believe this, but my dad is leaving his job as a chemist at Planter's Peanuts and going to medical school in New York City. We leave in seven days." Russell couldn't have sounded worse if Stalin had threatened to drop an atomic bomb on his house.

I said, "Don't be so sad. We'll always be friends, no matter where we live. Anyway, my dad says we might be moving too. My mom's health is getting worse. You and me can talk more tomorrow. Right now, I have to get home in time for dinner." I pedaled off toward my house when I saw a little boy lying on the sidewalk. He was crying. Another kid, a lot bigger, stood over him.

I got closer and recognized the bigger kid as someone I'd known since fifth grade. It was Jimmy O'Leary, who was a pain in the butt and always making trouble. He was holding a carton of eggs, and I watched as he dropped a raw egg on the boy on the ground. I stopped my bike and put down the kickstand and yelled, "Hey, O'Leary, what's going on here?"

Jimmy O'Leary looked at me and snarled his reply: "This little turd needs a lesson in respect. Here I am, walking on the sidewalk, and this brat comes along on his bike and yells at me like I'm a nobody. The punk told me to get out of his way. He wasn't asking, he was telling. My dad says the Irish don't have to take that shit no more. So I said to myself, 'Who the hell does he think he's talking to?' I figure the little dick needs a lesson in respect, so I took his mommy's eggs and busted a few on him. The little shit deserves it." He started laughing.

It was easy for me to see what was really going on. The smaller boy had ridden his bike, which had been shoved off to the side, to the grocery store, probably running an errand for his mom. On the way back Jimmy O'Leary had blocked the sidewalk and started the trouble. Jimmy O'Leary was known as a bully. So far he's gotten away with a lot of stuff because the nuns hadn't caught him. Today, there were no nuns around.

I was tired from my long bike ride and angry about moving

from Throop, so I wasn't in a good mood. I grabbed the egg carton from Jimmy O'Leary's hands and pulled the biggest egg from the container and smashed it on top of his head. It was a double-yolker, and O'Leary ran his hand through his now sticky hair as I pushed him backwards. Eyes wide, he appeared stunned. I pushed him again and said, "Now who's laughing. Next time, pick on someone your own size."

Jimmy O'Leary hurried away, walking backwards while he wiped at the yellow ooze running down his face. He yelled something to me about getting his brothers to settle this. I laughed and yelled to him, "Bring them." He cursed at me and spun around and ran off.

I helped the little kid up and handed him the carton with the few eggs that remained unbroken and said, "Quit crying like a baby and get the rest of these eggs to your mom. O'Leary won't bother you while I'm around. If he does, you need to punch him in his mouth before he starts anything. If you do that, he'll leave you alone and pick on somebody else." I was talking to myself. Obviously the kid was terrified of Jimmy O'Leary, and there was no way he'd ever fight him. *Trouble was, I wouldn't likely be around here to help him the next time.*

I got back on my Schwinn and pedaled hard for home. I doubted this thing with Jimmy O'Leary and the little boy was over, but there wasn't anything more I could do right now. As I reached my house, a large boxy looking truck was parked in the driveway, alongside my dad's Ford pickup. The big truck had a New Jersey license plate, and gold red letters on the side panels: "Bruno's Gym." And just below that, in smaller print: "Learn to fight like the Japs."

Wow, Uncle Louie was here!

Uncle Louie, like my dad, was thick through the chest and strong as a bull. Most men would not even think about wanting to mess with him. I bet he could break a man in half. He was drafted to fight in World War II soon after my dad was called up, but instead of going to Europe he was assigned to combat in the Pacific, fighting Japanese soldiers he called "Japs." He fought in caves and on odd-sounding islands with names like Guam and Iwo Jima, places no one ever heard of until the newsreels came out.

Many of his buddies died on these islands despite our planes bombing the beachheads before our guys landed. He faced brutal fighting, often hand-to-hand combat with bayonets on rifles. He also had to avoid flamethrowers and dodge hand grenades. Unlike my dad, Uncle Louie talked about the battles. He said that the Japs took no prisoners. Some of his buddies had no choice except to surrender, but they were shot by the Japs anyway. So he killed Japs whenever he could—even if they gave up.

These days Uncle Louie runs a gym in Newark and teaches people how to fight, not just box but how to street fight. If you want to know how to break bones, or how to kick or strangle someone, he's the guy to teach you. No doubt about it, his gym is the place to learn a lot more than self-defense, although that's what he calls it. He runs the gym fulltime now, but right after the war he took a job on the assembly line at the Budweiser plant in Newark.

All this made me wonder if war was worth it. My dad had fought against the Germans, and now Uncle Louie works part-time for Germans who own Budweiser beer, made right in Newark, one of the biggest businesses in America. We worry about Stalin dropping a bomb on us one of these days, yet he was fighting on our side against the Germans just a few years ago. It all sounds crazy to me.

Just then the front door to our house swung open and Uncle

17

Louie and my dad came out, carrying our couch. I yelled, "Hey, Uncle Louie, it's great to see you, but what are you doing here?"

He slid his end of the couch onto the back of his big truck and said, "Hello, big guy," and he ran over and hugged me. He lifted me off the ground, but he didn't swing me in a circle like he did when I was a little kid, probably because I was now almost as tall as he was. Not as big but as tall.

Dad said to me, "Son, we're going to Newark. Your uncle has lined me up with a job at the shipyard as a welder. Your mom needs a good doctor, so we're packing up today and leaving tomorrow morning. You can say goodbye to Throop and Scranton."

It was happening so fast I could hardly think. There hadn't been much talk about moving during the last few weeks, but now it was really happening. And right now! *Holy crap, we're actually leaving. I might never see Mary Jo or Russell again. Maybe if I woke up early enough tomorrow morning, I could get on my bike and say goodbye to both of them.*

I went inside the house and found my mom packing up her pots and pans and mismatched dishes and other kitchenware. She was weak and looked tired. Everything was hard for her these days. She coughed whenever she finished wrapping just a few knives and forks. I looked at the paper napkin she was using to cover her mouth, and it was smeared with pinkish phlegm. I made up my mind to stop feeling sorry for myself about the move and help her pack. If Newark could save my mom, I'd have to make the best of everything. Maybe it wouldn't be so bad. I grabbed some newspaper and helped her wrap dishes.

We worked until well after dark. Except for our clothes and the Philco TV, we'd be ready to go the next morning. Dad said we'd need to get an early start, so I dropped any plans to see

Mary Jo and Russell. *Damn*. I wrote Mary Jo a note and told her what was going on. I found an envelope and a stamp and mailed the letter. Dad and Uncle Louie and I shared a pepperoni pizza for dinner. They drank Rolling Rock beer and I had a sarsaparilla soda. My poor mom coughed throughout the whole evening.

Dad turned on the TV to a late program called *The Tonight Show*. The first guest was a guy with some animals he'd trained to do tricks. He was okay, but when a beautiful woman named Lee Meriwether came on the show, a Miss America contestant, I watched with greater interest. But even with her on the TV, I was tired and went to bed.

I passed the kitchen. The same bills were still piled high on the countertop—except for those now on the floor. What I thought might have been a paycheck from the coal company was gone, but the envelope from St. Stephens was still in the stack. *Whatever the problem was with that bursar person, it doesn't matter to me anymore. I leave in the morning. Who cares about the bursar?*

It was dark outside when my dad woke me. He said that the Philco TV, wrapped with a blanket and tied around it, was already loaded in Uncle Louie's truck. When I walked by the kitchen, all the mail that had piled up was now in the garbage. *Goodbye, Mr. Bursar.*

As I climbed into Uncle Louie's big truck, I glanced back at the house. I couldn't help but wonder what was written in that letter. I also thought about the young boy with the eggs and that damn bully, Jimmy O'Leary. *Sometimes little kids have to stand up for themselves. Maybe he'll learn to fight back.* I closed my eyes and thought about Mary Jo and how much I'd miss her. I felt the vibration of the truck as it bounced along a two-lane tarred road following a long line of summer traffic.

New Jersey, here we come was the last thing I remember thinking about before falling asleep.

CHAPTER THREE

The Silverman Family
Berlin, Germany

November 6, 1938:
Kristallnacht

Saul Silverman stood in the long inspection line, waiting to cross the border from Germany into Denmark. Everyone was stopped, searched, questioned, papers were argued over, and jewelry changed hands as guards were bribed. At a snail's pace, the line inched forward.

Dressed as an Arab woman, and covered from head to toe in the traditional garb of that culture, the burqa, Saul Silverman was confident he wouldn't be detained at the border. His reasoning was because Hitler had made it known that he wanted the oil-rich Arab countries as his allies and not as his enemies, and Muslims were not to be harassed in any manner. Hitler wanted Muslim countries to join him in his war effort and help him eliminate Jews throughout Europe and elsewhere. In Nazi

---

Germany, no one questioned an order from Der Feuhrer.

But Saul was certainly not a Muslim. He was one of the few remaining free Jews in Germany. Most had already been identified, their houses marked with the word "JUDE," their movements blocked, and their businesses either taken from them or burned to the ground. Tens of thousands of Jews had already been sent to concentration camps.

Saul knew very well that his people would be exterminated if Hitler took full control. His mother had been killed a year after Hitler assumed leadership of the Reich because she refused to give the Nazi salute. A military truck passed by, as part of a parade, with a Nazi flag attached to the back of the vehicle. Instead of saluting she cursed the Nazis. Two German soldiers in brown shirts heard her. They jumped from the vehicle, which was still moving, and smashed her head with their rifle butts. She died on the spot as the crowd cheered the cowardly act.

Saul, as the oldest son, inherited everything after his father died from a heart attack a few years later. His younger brother, Menachem, got nothing, which was the custom.

Since he was twelve years old, Saul had learned the jewelry business by working at his father's side. The Silverman's had always lived quietly and simply, and from what Saul knew of his family's finances, he expected to find a little money and a small quantity of jewels in the safe hidden behind dark-walnut cabinetry in the backroom of his father's workshop.

Saul had long known the safe's combination. He twisted the dial and listened as the tumblers clicked into place as he sat on his father's worn-out leather chair. He pulled the heavy iron door open, and he took a deep breath as he began opening small boxes he'd never been allowed to even touch before.

If he hadn't already been seated, he would have fallen over. What he found was an enormous store of diamonds, all of

22

outstanding clarity and color—and size. The stones ranged from one to six carats, and many were flawless. He also found thousands of German marks wrapped with rubber bands. One thing was certain: He had to move this fortune in diamonds and cash from Germany or lose it to the Nazis—and likely his life as well.

With the Nazis infiltrating all aspects of German life, Saul's father had counseled his son that sooner or later their family would be found out, and they must plan to leave Germany before this occurred. Saul didn't know that his father was referring to the family's immense wealth, and now he fully understood the implications.

Over the years, the elder Silverman had developed a personal relationship with many of his Muslim customers. One of the wealthiest Muslim women in the neighborhood confided with him; "Mr. Silverman, I have cancer. I need treatment and pain medicines, but these Nazi doctors only accept payment in German marks, or they demand some of my jewelry. If I pay the Nazi bastards with a diamond, this covers just one visit. The next time the doctor sees me, he acts as though he has never seen me before and demands another piece of my jewelry. I am no fool, Mr. Silverman, if I can make a fair trade with you for my diamonds in return for German marks, I can pay for many doctor visits and not go broke."

Saul's father offered to help her. At the same time he helped himself. He traded a hundred marks for the first diamond and the second and the third, and he continued to buy more from her as she continued her treatments. This woman bragged to Muslim friends about "her" jeweler, telling them that she had found a fool. "Marks are the only thing of value here in Germany," she had said. "Diamonds are useless except for showing off in public, but this jeweler offers cash when no one else will."

The business in German marks for diamonds flourished, and Saul's father had done this in relative secrecy. Saul himself knew what had transpired with the Muslims over the years, as he became friends with some of them and learned their customs and much of the language. But he had no idea how many diamonds his father had accumulated, as the boxes in the safe were always off limits. Only today after he inspected the contents of the safe did he learn the truth about his family's substantial wealth.

Now, however, if Saul was to escape the Nazis, his time in Berlin was limited. Without telling anyone in advance except Rose, his wife, he sold the building that housed the retail business to a local German jeweler, for almost nothing. The new owner was delighted with the deal and changed the name of the business to his German name immediately. Silverman's Jewelry was gone and soon the Silverman family would be a fleeting memory as well. But Saul wouldn't get out of Germany yet because he felt a responsibility to his people.

Saul and his wife and brother moved to Hamburg, in northern Germany. Rose wore a burqa at all times, and Saul and Menachem took Arab names, trimmed their beards, and dressed as Muslim men. They searched for a suitable location to open a new business, found a building to their liking, and had a sign painted on the front window: "Abdullah Jewelry Shop. We Buy Diamonds"

But just a month after the new store opened, the danger of his family's being caught was too much for Saul. A few minutes after dinner, Saul spoke to his wife and brother, "I have made a decision. I will stay here and help as many of our people as I can to escape the Nazis." He placed two rail tickets on the table. "You will see that both tickets are in the names of Muslim women. I have also purchased the proper paperwork to match your tickets. You will both wear burqas and act as if you are sisters. You will leave for Denmark in three days. From Denmark you will go to Sweden. From there you will travel to the United States by ocean liner. I plan to join you in three years." He sat back in his chair and held up his hand to Rose, who was about to speak. "There will be no argument."

Rose was distraught. She could not believe Saul was staying behind. She pleaded, "Saul, we have enough money, we have more than enough. If you stay here and try to help Jews, you will be caught and sent to the gas chamber. Please, let us all leave together. Please, husband, buy one more ticket and come with us." Her cheeks ran wet with tears. Menachem said nothing.

Saul refused to listen to Rose's pleas. "If I stay here in Hamburg, I can make many more trades in our favor, and we will live an even better life in America. There is little danger here for me, but both of you must go."

Three days later, Rose and Menachem left, each with a fortune in diamonds sewn into the seams of their burqas. They also had enough, more than enough German marks to cover bribes and travel expenses.

Because Rose and Menachem were small in stature and acted as though they were Muslim sisters, they were not suspected of anything and boarded the train without incident. Each carried only a small handbag and a single suitcase, as if they were going on a short trip. When the train moved from the station, Rose cried as she watched her husband standing on the platform, convinced she would never see Saul again.

Saul decided well in advance where Rose and Menachem were to live in their new country. It was a small community named New Town, in the state of New Jersey. He had learned that many Jewish families had settled there, and it sounded ideal.

With Rose and Menachem well on their way to America, Saul began a complete transformation. He changed his appearance from that of a man to that of a woman, dressed in his own black abaya, and wore a face covering. He shaved twice each day, and with practice he changed his voice from its normal man's tone to the higher pitch of a woman. He also wore black women's shoes, although he found them terribly uncomfortable. The change was complete, and by all outward appearances Saul was an Arabic woman.

He was relatively certain that Jews from all over Germany, Austria, Czechoslovakia, and Poland would travel the same escape route his own family had taken on their way to freedom. His instincts proved correct, as his people came from everywhere and stopped at Hamburg before boarding the train to Denmark.

Abdullah's Jewelry Shop was the only business that offered cash to Jews at a fair price. Saul bought only diamonds. He remembered his father's words: "Diamonds are the smallest object in size that carries the most value. When you need to get out of Germany, carry only cash and your very best diamonds. Use the cash for expenses and bribes, never use the diamonds. Sell your stones when you reach your final destination. There, you will make the most favorable deal."

Every day, Hamburg was busy with people of many religions and nationalities desperate to get out of Germany. Saul felt as if he was helping his people in particular by trading cash for stones at a decent price, and at the same time he would be helping his own family.

As an example of a typical transaction, when a harried Jewish couple came into Abdullah Jewelry, Saul of course was aware of what they wanted. He smiled knowingly and repeated his practiced speech: "One diamond will cover one bribe, but cash, my friends, will pay for many bribes, many fees, many meals, and many boarding passes."

The husband quickly pulled his wife's beautiful diamond ring from his pocket and handed it to the female jeweler known as "Abdullah." Saul looked through his jeweler's loupe, seeing a fine diamond, and he'd smile and say, "Here is my offer." His offer was always fair—but it was also the only one from anyone that involved marks.

Like the others before them, these people were in a frenzy to escape and took Saul's money as fast as they could grab it off the table. Saul heard the husband speak to his wife in Hebrew: "I am amazed a Muslim would make a fair trade when she knows we are desperate to leave. Most of them are dishonest, greedy bastards. This one is most unusual."

Saul said nothing, only watching as they ran for the waiting train, tripping over one another along the way. Saul felt good, knowing he had helped them as he had aided so many Jews before them. That couple, like the next, and the multitude after that, accepted the trades Saul offered. Yes, Saul profited—but the people he dealt with escaped with their lives.

Saul received a message from New Town and learned that Rose and Menachem had arrived safely. The letter came in Arabic, which was the only reason why it got through to him, and now he had the most important thing he needed for the rest of his plan to succeed, which was his wife's and brother's address in America.

From then on, each morning before opening Abdullah Jewelry for business, Saul went to the post office, which was just two short blocks away. Day after day he mailed his wife the same cheap blue-and-white salt and pepper shakers he'd purchased at a local German shop. Of course the first dozen or more packages were opened by Nazi mailroom inspectors. Finding nothing other than salt and pepper shakers, they smashed these condiment holders on the floor, to the amusement of the soldiers supervising the inspections. Saul never showed any anger. Instead, he simply sent another package the next day, and the day after and the day after that.

At first it was great fun for the inspectors, breaking the salt shakers on the floor right in front of the dirty little Arab. But they wanted things of value, not salt. One day, the head inspector, annoyed at the usual mess on the floor, told his workers, "Get to work. Open someone else's packages. This piece of camel dung has no money. I went to her shop when the Gestapo raided her store. All they found were diamonds so small they could barely be seen, like a grain of salt." This was true, and Saul was very proud of the way he'd handled the soldiers who'd rifled through his safe. They never found the massive diamond cache he kept in plain sight—in the sand at the bottom of his fish tank.

Saul continued to send his seemingly worthless salt and pepper packages. Well after the postal workers ignored him he placed his first diamond in with the salt in the salt shaker. From that day on he did the same thing, methodically mailing his highest-quality diamonds to America right under the noses of his worst enemies, the Nazis.

It wasn't long, however, before Saul started having nightmares because of seeing Jews turned in by so-called friends and shot on sight. He became deathly afraid of being found out. Finally, three years later, fear overtook him. He had seen enough. He headed to the post office, just as he did every day.

Today, though, he mailed his final set of salt and pepper shakers. When the package arrived in New Town, with no diamond in the salt shaker, Rose and Menachem knew Saul was on his way to America.

He boarded the same train his wife and brother had taken out of Germany. Saul left on November 6, 1938, just days before the Nazis staged a massive wave of attacks on Jewish homes and businesses. It was the same night Hitler's brown-shirts burned dozens of synagogues and killed over a thousand people.

The German's called this "Kristallnacht," or "The Night of the Broken Glass." The terror attacks continued throughout the next day, and for the next six-and-a-half years. It was the beginning of the end for six million Jews.

As the train pulled out of the station, heading for Denmark, Saul shook in uncontrollable fear, believing that he still might be caught. He dressed in his oldest frayed burqa, wore his worst shoes, and donned a full-face veil so as not to attract any attention whatsoever, because his inside pockets were sewn with false bottoms and filled with large high-quality diamonds.

When he arrived at the border, looking like a Muslim woman, he was not searched or told to undress by the Nazis because they were well aware of Hitler's order not to harass Arabs. Saul followed the same route by rail to Denmark, boat to Sweden and an ocean-going ship to a reception center called Ellis Island in the New York City harbor. Over the past three years he'd lived under tremendous fear of being caught. He had seen so many Jews murdered and sent to death camps that he had become paranoid.

When the boat docked in the New York harbor, Saul was up early and waiting near the front of the line, where he took deep breaths of fresh cool air after hiding in the hold of the ship for several days in a row, away from everyone else. He carried

29

only a gray cardboard suitcase with a wooden handle, once owned by his father. He still wore his dirty Muslim burqa. It was the garment that had saved him. He would never be able to throw it away because it might be found by the Nazi's.

Immigration took too many hours to clear, but Saul was finally free. He got off the Ellis Island ferry at the dock in New Jersey and walked on wobbly legs as he searched the crowd for Rose and Menachem. When he spotted them tears flowed down his cheeks. He waved and called to Rose, who returned his wave and nodded as if to say, yes Saul, we're here, your plan worked.

Saul trembled, cried and hugged Rose before he stepped into his brother's black four-door 1930 Model-A Ford. Menachem headed south toward New Town, New Jersey; his new home.

Throughout the entire voyage he'd imagined Nazi officers roaming the boat. In his nightmares, he heard them calling his name, but in reality, there were no Nazis aboard that ship.

Saul had defeated the Nazis and he had done it without a rifle. However, he would never be the same man or the same loving husband Rose knew before she'd left for America three years earlier. Hiding his identity and living in fear for so long and seeing so much brutality against the Jews had affected him profoundly. Saul couldn't help it, he was a changed man.

Their only child, Simon, named after Saul's grandfather, was born August, 3rd, 1940.

CHAPTER FOUR

Newark: Oh no!

I woke up in Uncle Louie's truck, my parents following behind in our pickup. None of us had eaten breakfast before we left, and my stomach was growling. I said, "Uncle Louie, I'm starved. Can we stop somewhere and eat pretty soon?"

"Sure, kid," he replied. "I'm hungry too. The next place that looks halfway decent and serves breakfast, we'll park it. I'm sure your mom and dad are ready to eat something too, so let's keep our eyes open for a good diner."

There weren't any places to eat on this stretch of road, so I decided to ask Uncle Louie about where I'd be living. "What's Newark like? Is it like Wilkes Barre or Scranton, or other big towns? Do they have a Catholic Youth Organization there, you know, a CYO? I hope I can play baseball and basketball. Are there a lot of kids around my age and..."

"Whoa, Frank, slow down. You have to ask one question at a time. So you want to know what Newark's all about? Well, let me put it like this, it's a big city, a real big city. Not as big as

New York, but it's sure a lot bigger than Scranton. There are big government buildings downtown, hospitals and office buildings, and wide streets jammed with cars and trucks of all kinds. And, get this, once in a while you might still see a horse pulling a wagon or a cop on a horse."

I was now more curious than ever about Newark. "Tell me more, please."

Uncle Louie smiled at me. "Okay. If you remember that tall Catholic Church on Washington Street in Scranton, there are plenty of buildings much taller than that in Newark. As far as basketball goes, you'll find courts in every park, with lots of kids playing. As a matter of fact, I think there's a basketball court right where you'll be livin'. No problem finding courts and kids who want to play sports in New—"

He slammed on the brakes and cut short whatever he was going to say. I slid forward on the seat and had to put out my hands to keep from hitting the dash with my head. Three deer stood in our lane of the highway! Drivers going both ways brought their vehicles to a halt, and only after some horn blowing did the deer trot off.

"Wow, they stopped in the road and just stared at us," I said, climbing back onto the seat. "Where the heck are we, anyway?"

"Poconos—we're in the Poconos—lots of mountains and lots of deer here." He wiped his forehead with his shirtsleeve and pointed to a billboard. "There's a place for breakfast comin' up ahead." He opened his window and signaled to my parents that we were going to make a stop. I was ready to eat anything.

We parked our trucks at a place called The Old Mountain Diner. I wondered if the sign meant that the mountain was old or that the diner was old, or maybe both. Uncle Louie and I went inside and got a table for four, knowing that my mom and dad would be right behind us.

———

There were a few truckers eating at a counter and some young couples sitting at tables and holding hands and smiling. "Newlyweds," my dad said and added wryly, "In another month they might not be holding hands and smiling at each other."

Mom laughed at my father and said, "They'll be holding hands for a while longer, but after that they'll be holding babies." Mom tried to laugh again but went into a coughing fit and had to leave the table for a minute.

Mom returned just as a cute waitress came over to us and asked, "Coffee, everyone?" We all nodded. "So you know, our eggs, potatoes, and Taylor ham make for the best breakfast around here." She was a year or two older than I was maybe a freshman or sophomore in high school. I liked the way she acted so sure of herself. She took our orders and brought us all coffee. I added two sugars and some cream to mine, and I watched as she reached up and pinned our order to a wire in front of the cook. *Nice.* Not as much up top as Mary Jo, but nice.

"Plenty more girls like that where you'll be livin'," Uncle Louie said to me under his breath as my mom started coughing again. "Newark is loaded with pretty girls. Mostly Italian where you're going to live. You'll have lots to pick from."

I liked hearing that. Dad got up and bought a Philadelphia newspaper for a dime. He looked at the front page for a moment and said, "Hey, Louie, it says here that Vietnam was just divided into two parts and President Eisenhower backed the move. The half in the south is a democracy, and the north is communist. I hope it stays that way."

Even though we'd ordered, Uncle Louie had continued to go through the menu. He put it aside and said, "I'd hate to see us involved in a war way over there for no good reason, but you never know. Seems the commies are always pushing into someplace where they don't belong."

———

Dad continued scanning the paper and said, "Here's something good. That new movie everyone is talking about, *On the Waterfront*, came out in Philly last night." He turned to Mom. "I hope we can see it, Irene. Marlon Brando's the star."

Mom's eyes brightened as she said, "Oh, Dominic, I might have to drink a whole bottle of cough medicine just to sit through it, but I'd love to see that movie. I hear it might win an Academy Award." Dad placed his hand on Mom's back and rubbed it gently.

"Dad," I asked, "anything in that paper about sports?" Right then another young couple entered the diner. The guy snuck a kiss and grabbed his girl's ass when he thought no one was looking. *Lucky bastard. I'd like to do that with Mary Jo again someday. But I might never see Mary Jo again. Too bad for me. I was just getting somewhere with her.*

My father handed me the paper and pointed to an ad. "Here's a new magazine you might like. The first issue comes out August sixteenth, and it's all about sports. Name is *Sports Illustrated*. I don't know about this idea. You can read all about sports everyday in your local newspaper, so who needs a monthly magazine?" He shook his head. "Probably be a flop."

Our cute waitress brought our breakfasts. Dad salted his potatoes and eggs and dug in. "Mmm, these spuds are good, and the pork roll is great," he said between bites and glanced at Uncle Louie. "Just like the Army, right, Louie? Great food at every meal!" Dad laughed and salted his potatoes again.

I'd eaten Taylor ham before, or as dad called it "pork roll," and it was really good, maybe even better than bacon. I ate everything, including some leftover toast and grape jelly.

After breakfast Dad and Uncle Louie and I stood by the gas pumps while mom got in the pickup. A gallon of regular gas was 19 cents, and it cost 3 cents more for high test. Dad said to

Uncle Louie, "Gas was 15 cents a gallon two years ago. I wonder what the hell's going on. Before you know it, regular gas will cost two bits a gallon."

Uncle Louie replied, "We're in a resort area, Dom. This is the Poconos, the honeymoon capital of the whole East Coast. Everything up here costs more, but gas in Newark will never hit a quarter a gallon, not in our lifetime. Nobody would pay that much for a gallon of gas."

I hurried back inside the restaurant and asked the cook, who I guessed was the owner, if he had any old newspapers so I could read them on the way to New Jersey. He laughed. "Sure, kid, right over there, plenty of 'em." He pointed to a pile off to the side of the newspaper rack. "Help yourself. I can't sell them once they're a day old. Some are a lot older."

I went through the pile and took all the sports pages and several front sections. I thanked the owner, and on my way out I took one more look at the waitress. She turned toward me and I caught her eye. I smiled at her and she smiled back. *Wow, I could get to like that beauty.*

Off we went, following a line of cars and trucks on a narrow two-lane blacktop road. We seldom went any faster than thirty miles per hour. Some cars managed to pass us, and these vehicles often dragged old shoes and occasionally tin cans tied to their bumpers. Most of the cars had white shoe-polish on the back window that spelled out "Just Married." The Poconos were indeed where honeymooners went for a week of fun, away from friends and family. Fun in this case was spelled S E X. And I guessed lots of it.

As we chugged along the highway, which was quite bumpy in places, I began reading some of the sports pages from the old newspapers. "Here's something about pro football," I said to Uncle Louie. "The Detroit Lions beat the College All-Stars thirty-one to six. Well, that's no surprise, the best team in the NFL beat the best college players. What would anybody expect to happen?" Uncle Louie make a scoffing sound but said nothing.

I read another article and said, "Darn, the Cleveland Indians beat the Yankees. Oh, and Ted Kluszewski just hit his fortieth home run for Cincinnati." I turned to the next page. "Wow, Rocky Marciano knocked out Ezra Charles in eight rounds."

I picked up the sports page from another old paper. "Listen to this, Uncle Louie. Yogi Berra, the Yankees catcher, played a game at third base, and Mickey Mantle, who usually plays outfield, played that same game at shortstop. The Yankees are so far ahead in the American League, that they're just goofing off."

After a while I finished reading all the sports pages, so I went to the front sections. "This is cool," I said in a raised voice to Uncle Louie, just to keep him interested. "Alan Freed is moving from Cleveland to New York City with his rock and roll radio show. He'll be on a station called WINS. Can we get that in Newark?"

Uncle Louie made a face, which made me laugh. "Yeah, you can get WINS, but rock and roll is garbage compared to the big bands we had when I was a growin' up." Just then I noticed steam rising from the radiator. Uncle Louie stared at the heat gauge and grumbled, "This is trouble. We have to pull over and let this thing cool off. Radiator must be leaking again." He found a spot to park the truck and shut off the engine right away.

Dad pulled in behind us and Uncle Louie told him what was wrong. "With this heavy load and these mountains, my old truck is havin' a hard time. Radiator is about shot anyhow." After letting it cool down somewhat, he took a towel and covered the radiator cap and removed it. Scalding hot steam rushed out.

"We need some water... bad," Uncle Louie hollered above the hissing from the radiator. Fortunately, Dad carried a five-gallon container of water in the back of his truck just in case we had trouble like this. We had to let the engine cool before he could refill the radiator, and it took an hour before we got going again.

Now it was Uncle Louie who carried on the conversation. "Frank, I can tell you some pretty interesting stuff about New Jersey if you want to hear it." Of course I nodded eagerly. "Okay, the first thing you should know is that New Jersey tomatoes are the best in the world. Second thing, there are more blueberries and cranberries farmed in Jersey than any other state. And the first Indian reservation wasn't far from where we are right now, in the Watchung Mountains."

I was impressed and told Uncle Louie that he sure knew a lot about New Jersey. That was all he needed to hear, and he went on and on, finishing with, "New Jersey has more diners than any other state in the country, and Thomas Edison invented the first light bulb here and the first record player at his lab in Edison." The more I heard about New Jersey, the better it sounded.

We passed Mount Pocono and Dingmans's Ferry, and a little while later our truck rolled onto a bridge with a big sign that read: "You are crossing the Delaware River." At the other side of the bridge another sign informed us: "You have entered New Jersey."

From what I saw, New Jersey was all forests, rolling hills, and green. It looked like a pretty nice place. I imagined that Newark must be like this, too, and I was getting excited about living there. Just as I was relaxing with my pleasant thoughts, a rush of steam shot out from under the hood, which caused another halt to our drive. Luckily, Uncle Louie and Dad had refilled the five-gallon can with water when they got gas earlier.

Uncle Louie had also topped off the water in the radiator, but it was obviously going to continue to overheat. This time we had to wait two hours for the truck to cool down. Uncle Louie was worried about pouring the water in too soon and the block cracking, whatever that meant. We finally got underway, and a short while later we turned onto a different highway. Uncle Louie said, "From here we head east, Frank. Newark isn't more than a couple of hours."

It ended up a lot more than a couple of hours, because the truck overheated again and again. We were lucky to come upon an ESSO gas station, and Uncle Louie bought some kind of fixit stuff for radiator leaks. Once more we waited for the engine to cool down before we took off, thinking we'd be okay now. But in another hour we had to stop or the engine would blow up. I got out of the truck to find rust-colored water dripping fast onto the ground, as if someone had left a faucet running.

We waited, filled the radiator, and since it was late we found a diner and ate our evening meal. Uncle Louie asked about a cheap motel. We were told to try the Sunshine Motel down the road. The sign in front of the motel read: $19.99 per night, clean sheets, air cooled. Uncle Louie said to me, "This place looks like a good deal. I don't want to get stuck on the road at night."

Uncle Louie got a room for him and me and another for my parents. He parked his truck, and my dad pulled in next to us. Mom waved at me. She was a great mom. Always sweet, caring, and loving despite her poor health. She always took good care of me and my dad, no matter how tough things were for her. Our whole family of uncles, aunts, nieces and nephews loved her. I said to Uncle Louie, "I hate to see my mom so sick.

If there's a cure for her in Newark, it'll be worth the move. If Newark is anywhere as good as what I've seen of New Jersey so far, I won't miss Throop." I paused to consider what I'd just said and added, "Well, maybe I'll miss some of it." *Of course I was thinking about Mary Jo.*

The next morning we ate breakfast at the same place we'd stopped for dinner the night before. Despite a couple of more cool-offs and water fill-up stops, we reached Newark before noon. My first look at the city made me want to cry. *Holy crap, this place is a dump.*

No doubt about it, this city was big. Lots of traffic, lots of people, tall buildings, and hardly any houses like those back in Throop or Scranton. Everywhere I turned I saw apartments and buildings of all kinds. There was hardly anything green except for a few parks I noticed as we rode by. But there were basketball courts, so that was one good thing.

Finally, our truck came to a halt. Uncle Louie jumped out and I followed him, now out of habit. "This is it Frank," he said and pointed to the building in front of us. "This is what they call The Projects." I didn't know what to think.

After Uncle Louie went inside and got the key from the office. The building appeared to be fairly new, but it had no elevators, so we'd have to lug our furniture and belongings up a flight of stairs to a two-bedroom apartment on the second floor, which would be our new home. The apartment seemed in good shape except for needing a good coat of paint.

As I was going down the steps to get my second load of stuff, a kid my age was coming up the stairs at the same time. I couldn't help but notice his huge right cheekbone, as if it might be a birth defect. He looked me square in the eyes and put out his hand and said, "Hi, you must be new. I'm Joe. People call me Cheeks. Welcome to the neighborhood."

I shook his hand and said, "Nice to meet you. I'm Frank Bruno… from Pennsylvania. I'm just moving in. Are there any basketball courts around here?"

The guy with the messed-up cheek said, "Yeah, at the other end of the building. Come on down when you get done here. There's usually a game every afternoon. If nothing else, there's always somebody to play horse with. I plan on going down later. Maybe I'll see you there?"

I smiled at him and he did his best to return the smile. A friendly face was just what I needed, even if the face didn't look too great. He continued up the steps and I yelled to him, "See you on the court."

Unloading everything and setting up our furniture required all afternoon, and by the time I made it to the basketball court it was early evening and no one was there. I took in my new neighborhood. This wasn't Throop or Scranton or Wilkes Barre. What a change from when first entering New Jersey. None of the blueberries Uncle Louie had talked about, no mountains, and definitely nothing green.

What have my parents and I got ourselves into?

CHAPTER FIVE

The Bursar

My parents were up and out early the next morning because they had an appointment at Newark City Hospital with a pulmonologist, a doctor who specializes in lung problems. My dad was told by the old doctor in Throop that this was the only kind of physician who could treat my mom any better than he could.

I had the day free and decided to explore the neighborhood. I wandered around The Projects and came upon a bronze sign with the following inscription: "Bradley Court: A Modernization and Asset Preservation Project built in 1940 as a Family Housing Development for Government Workers, with 10 buildings that provide 298 apartments. All units have electricity, natural gas, water and sewer services." Since I was born in 1940, The Projects and I were the same age—fourteen years old.

Mom and dad said they expected to be at the hospital for most of the day, so I didn't plan to see them until evening. I

---

decided to get some breakfast, and a couple of blocks down the street I spotted a sign for Pantello's Bakery. Dad had given me two quarters, and I bought a cup of coffee with extra milk, along with three jelly donuts, for thirty-five cents. As I was adding sugar to the coffee, I picked up a newspaper someone had left behind and read the sports page. The lead story was about Roger Bannister from England setting the record for running the fastest mile ever. "Wow," I said aloud, not even considering if anyone was listening, "Bannister ran a mile in four minutes flat, which means he ran fifteen miles an hour for the whole mile. Amazing."

Newspapers were piled in a corner, and I asked the man at the counter if I could look through them. He nodded, and I dug into the stack and found one from July, which had an article about something that happened back in 1945. A B-25 bomber, flying over New York City in heavy fog, hit the Empire State building. The plane was destroyed but the building suffered only minor damage.

I was eating my second jelly donut and reading another article when the same kid I'd met the day before on the stairs entered the bakery. He ordered a cruller covered in powdered sugar and a Boston cream and a cup of coffee. He came over to my table. "Hey," he said, "I'm Joe from yesterday. How did the move go? You all set up?" I didn't answer right away. I couldn't help but stare at his face because his right cheek was so much larger than his left one.

"Uh... the move went pretty well," I said, feeling my embarrassment and looking away. "My dad said he'd repaint the place when he started making money. But, yeah, it went pretty well. At least the TV is set up." I couldn't help it, I had to ask, "So what happened to your face, Joe?"

Between chomps of his donuts, the kid touched his right

cheek and said, "It was a sledding accident over on High Street, four winters ago. I lost control of my sled when it hit some ice, and I slammed into a pole and broke my right cheekbone. My folks didn't have the money to have it operated on, so it just healed up the way it did. That's why everyone calls me Joe Cheeks."

He told me his real name was Joe Giardello, but I was thinking about his face and the accident and I never really heard his last name. Joe said, "You look about my age. You going to Sacred Heart Catholic or West Side High, he asked?"

"Catholic school, but I didn't even know the name until you just said it. I went to St. Stephens in Scranton. I'll be going into eighth grade." I thought a moment. "You know where Sacred Heart is?

He slurped his coffee and laughed. "Sure I know where Scared Heart is. I go there too. Be in eighth grade, just like you. But you look older, so I figured you might be in high school."

"I probably look older because I'm bigger than most kids my age, and I'm close to fifteen."

He grabbed a paper napkin and wiped his mouth. "Sacred Heart is a bit of a walk from here, over on South Orange Avenue, but we can hoof it okay, and I'll show you how to get there. The principal is Sister Elizabeth Ann. I know her a little because I had the best marks in seventh grade last year, and she told me I could win a free education if I stayed at the top of the class. Sacred Heart is all boys of course and it has a special program that started four years ago. The top two kids from Scared Heart go to Stanton Prep for free."

"Wow," I said. I was also a very good student, so my mind was spinning with ideas.

"And, get this," Joe continued. "If my grades are good

enough after prep school, I can go to Stanton University, also for free. So I'm working my ass off to make it happen. I could never attend any college if it wasn't free. My parents just don't have that kind of money." He pushed his now empty cup aside. "So, Frank, how are your grades?"

"My grades are almost perfect except that I got a B-plus in geography last year because I couldn't find Persia on a map. How was I supposed to know the name was changed to Iran? Pretty stupid-sounding name for a country, I think. I had to take a guess, and I guessed wrong."

Joes responded, "I don't know where Iran is either. That was a bad break."

I shook my head. "Funny thing is, I never got my seventh-grade report card from St. Stephens. The homeroom teacher always handed them out, but this time the other kids got theirs and I didn't get mine. I thought it might come in the mail, but I never got it."

We left the bakery and started walking, with Joe asking mostly about my old home in Throop. I could tell he had a real interest in me as a friend. After many blocks we turned the corner and stood in front of Sacred Heart Catholic School, which was across the street from St. Mary's Orphanage.

Even though school was out for the summer, Joe entered the building like he belonged there, saying a big hello to a guard and to a nun we passed in the lobby. I walked beside my new friend as if I was supposed to be with him. Joe turned down a long hallway, with dark wooden floors that creaked as we walked.

At the end of that hall we came to a glass door. The word "Principal" was written in fancy gold lettering, and underneath was the name "Sister Elizabeth Ann," in the same style. I wondered why nuns never had last names like everyone else.

Then I remembered that all nuns were married to God and didn't need last names.

Sister Elizabeth Ann's secretary sat erect at a nicked-up wooden desk, looking as though she'd been placed there to guard the door to the principal's office with her life. The secretary was an average-looking woman, kind of chubby, thirty or so with goofy little glasses on her pug nose and dull black hair all tied up in a bun.

Joe Cheeks noisily said hello and introduced me as the new kid from Pennsylvania. I stepped forward to tell the secretary who I was, and that I had attended St. Stephens. I was about to explain about not getting a report card and that my mom was sick, but before I could say anything else a door flew open, and a nun who was obviously the principal came out.

She was dressed in her full black habit and headpiece, and she carried the usual angry frown expected of a head nun. An older woman with pale hollow cheeks, she wore wire-framed bifocals, which had slipped to the very end of her tiny nose. Her forehead creased, she snapped at me as she pushed up her glasses, "What is all the commotion about?"

I told her I was new and without my grades, and I related the rest of the story that had been cut short. Sister Elizabeth Ann held her frown throughout my explanation. After I finished, she said, "I know of St. Stephens in Scranton from conferences I've attended. They are as strict as we are about grades and student conduct. St. Stephens is not in the same diocese as we are, but we should be able to get your grades."

I managed to mumble, "Thank you, Sister Elizabeth Ann."

She folded her arms across her chest and stared at me. "We'll find out what's going on with you, Mr. Bruno." She pointed a bony finger at me. "But let me warn you, if I find one ounce of deceit in what you've said, you will not attend this school."

She instructed her secretary to get St. Stephens on the phone, which the woman did by dialing the operator. The secretary was switched to another operator for interstate calls. All of this took some time, so Joe Cheeks and I sat and waited until Sister Elizabeth Ann's secretary was connected to the St. Stephens Catholic School in Scranton.

The secretary was connected to the school but transferred to the bursar's office. Sister Elizabeth Ann told the bursar I was planning to attend her school and needed my grades. Her face became even more drawn as she listened to whatever the bursar was telling her. She finally said, "I see." She listened to more one-sided conversation before adding, "Yes, yes, Officer Bursar, I understand. We will definitely look into this, and I assure you we will take care of the problem from here. And, yes, please mail that item along with Mr. Bruno's grades. Yes, directly to me."

Sister Elizabeth Ann handed her secretary the phone and glared at me. "A letter from the accounting office at St. Stephens, in the name of the Bursar, was sent to your home in Throop, stating that you owed sixteen dollars for lunchroom fees. That bill was never paid, Mr. Bruno, so your report card is being held back."

"I... I didn't have the money. My mom is sick and..."

"There are rules, Mr. Bruno, and I must uphold those rules. The bill and your grades are being sent to me. Unless it is paid in full before the new school year starts, you will have to repeat seventh grade. No ifs, no buts and no excuses. The bill must be paid. And, young man, if not for your mother's medical condition, I would not even ask St. Stephens to send the bill. You would have to repeat seventh grade."

I tried to look as innocent as possible, and I meekly

responded, "Thank you, Sister. I'll get the money... somehow."
But how?

She turned her attention to Joe Cheeks, and she also used just
his last name. "Well, Mr. Giardello, if your friend here gets his
bill paid and joins you in the eighth grade, it appears you'll have
some competition for the best academics in this school. Mr.
Bruno's grades appear to be as good as yours, possibly even
better. My advice is for both of you to study hard and pray to
God for guidance. Stanton Prep is the reward for excellent
school work." She repeated what Joe had told me about the two
best students getting to attend the prep school each year—at no
cost to their parents.

I very politely thanked Sister Elizabeth Ann and her secretary
for their help and assured them, "I'll bring the money to you in a
few days." When I returned to our apartment no one was home,
so I left my dad a note that I was at the basketball court at the
far side of our building. With all the problems he was facing
with mom's illness, I didn't want to trouble him with my
problem at school, but I had no idea how I'd come up with
sixteen bucks.

One thing was for certain, as of this day I had a friend in Joe
Cheeks, a pal who knew his way around the area and had
something I didn't have: street smarts. At the basketball court,
Joe introduced me to his friends, Nicky the Boot, Mikey the
Moose, Ralph Nicosia, Bobby Ciccone, Mal Maltese, Vic Di
Silvester. All the guys were Italian except for a Greek kid
named Koutsis.

Bobby Ciccone was clearly older than everyone else, and by
his confidence he seemed to be in charge. Each of these kids
wore a black silk jacket with a Roman gladiator on the back.
The figure was embroidered in gold, as was "Romans A.C."
placed right underneath the symbol.

———

Bobby came over to me and said, "I see you looking at our jackets. There's a lot more of us Romans than just these few guys, another dozen or so, and a bunch of older guys who graduated high school and work fulltime jobs. Frank, you want to meet the rest of the guys, you come to The Paramount Sweet Shop and ask for one of us. Now, let's play some roundball, shirts against skins."

Most of the boys wore slicked-back duck's-ass haircuts, which made them look tough. Right away, I decided to let my hair grow longer.

I had a good day on the court, passing the basketball to the open guy and scoring under the hoop. The game was rough and the competition was better than I thought it would be, but that's the way I liked it on both accounts. After the game I drank water from a nearby outdoor fountain. The water was warm but wet. I joined my new acquaintances, who sat on wooden benches, and I carefully asked Bobby Ciccone about the Romans and street gangs in general.

He stared at me and said, "Look, kid, street gangs are against the law but athletic clubs aren't. That's why we call ourselves Romans A.C. Our gang was formed about fifteen years ago, for the protection of its members. It's a brotherhood. If you're not in a gang in this city, other gangs will rough you up or rob you if you're by yourself. But if you wear our colors, they know we'll do the same thing to one of their gang in return. So you'll be left alone."

"Do the guys stay in the gang forever?" I asked, now feeling more confident that I could ask questions.

"When Romans get out of high school, they usually aren't regulars anymore. They get jobs, marry somebody, have kids, and move on. But they help gang members with jobs when they get out of school. Some of our guys become city workers, like cops and firemen, or they join the union and work construction. Quite a few Romans have joined the military, and a few have even gone to college." Bobby gave me a quirky look. "To answer what I think you're asking, if one of us needs help at some point, believe me, the older guys will be there."

"How could I join the Romans?" I couldn't believe I was asking this.

"Like I said, we hang out at The Paramount Sweet Shop on Seventh Street. If you want to join us, get to know everyone. Then somebody has to nominate you. If that happens, we take a vote. If you pass, you're in. But you have to buy a Romans A.C. jacket and help out with whatever we need from you."

I didn't ask anything else, and Bobby Ciccone sat back on the bench. "Frank, if you live around here, especially in The Projects, you better belong to the Romans or some other gang. If you don't, you'll get your ass kicked on a regular basis. Even as big as you are, they'll come at you with three and four guys. It's your choice."

I thought about what Bobby said and asked him, "Why does the owner of sweet shop let you guys hang out there?"

Joe Cheeks smiled and answered for Bobby. "Owner's name is Luigi. Three years ago he had an *incident*. Three Falcons, another gang from around here, came into his shop and tried to rob him. They had knives and threatened to carve up the old Guinea. They didn't know there were four Romans in the backroom, playing pool. When our guys heard what was going on, they broke the legs off a chair and charged the Falcons. We beat the shit out of them, using the chair legs as clubs. Since then, we're always welcome at the sweet shop, and the pool table is free for us."

Bobby said, "On top of that, on the floor near the pool table sits a bucket with plenty of chair legs in it, just in case we need

---

them as Falcon repellent!" The guys laughed, but later I saw the bucket filled with wood and learned from Luigi that everything Bobby had said was true.

While Cheeks and Bobby and I talked, three hot-looking teenage girls walked over and sat on another bench across from us. Each of the girls had dark pony tails, cute faces, lots of eye makeup, and very nice bodies. They looked Italian, and they also wore black silk jackets identical to the guys', except with "Romanettes" embroidered on the back. It looked to me like there might be some side benefits to being a member of the Romans.

One girl, whose name I learned was Zan, a nickname for Alexandria, and was the sister of one of the gang members, a guy named Frank D'Orio. I was told that Frank was a senior and a huge guy, but since he had my first name, I was sure we'd get along. So I went over to his sister, and we talked for a while before the other girls wanted to leave and she went with them.

After the girls left, Bobby asked about me and my family. His eyes lit up when I mentioned Uncle Louie. Then I asked him what kind of *help* he was talking about."

He said, "We keep our territory safe. If someone wants trouble, we give it to them. So if you don't know how to fight, you better learn. Try your uncle's gym." He winked at me, which was a real surprise, but he surprised me even more when he continued by saying, "He was a Romans A.C. founding member, and he's the guy who taught most of us how to fight." Wow, there was a lot more to Uncle Louie than I ever imagined!

I said, "I'll come by the sweet shop and get to know the guys as soon as I can."

"Don't take too long. These streets are bad news if you're on your own."

Joe walked with me back to our apartment and told me more

about the Romans and who was important, Bobby Ciccone included. He also filled me in on the other gangs in the area. The Pontiacs had blue jackets with a fierce Indian on the back, the Falcons wore red jackets with a nasty-looking falcon on it, and the Snake Eyes gang had green jackets that showed a snake coiled around a pair of dice with a single black dot on each.

"There are a few girl gangs too," he said. "The toughest are the Pink Panthers. They carry what they call 'hat pins,' but those hat pins are actually ice picks. A couple of months back, one of the Falcons wound up stabbed to death by 'hat pins' on a back street not too far from here."

"Whoever did it, did they get caught?" I asked, now feeling a little queasy about the whole gang idea.

"A cop, who was an old Romans member, found the dead Falcon. He was wearing his gang jacket, and he had about twenty ice pick wounds on his chest and another dozen or so around his balls. The rumor on the street was that a bunch of the Pink Panthers got even with the guy because he raped one of their girls. So, Frankie, my advice is, don't fuck with the Pink Panthers. As far as anyone getting caught, the dead guy had a bad reputation, so the police said it was just another dead Falcon to them, and they let it go as an unsolved street crime."

Wow, nothing like this ever happened back in Throop. Not even close. If I wanted to survive here in Newark, it was pretty obvious that I'd have to become a Romans Athletic Club gang member.

CHAPTER SIX

The Stanley Theatre
South Orange Avenue

My dad came home that first evening—alone. Mom had to remain in the hospital if she was to have any chance of recovering. The pulmonologist told my father that she had an advanced case of tuberculosis, or TB as it's called, which is the modern name for what the old doctor in Throop called "The Consumption," but it was much worse than what he had diagnosed.

Since my mom was so much sicker than anyone knew, I'm worried about losing her. Dad said the doctor is treating her with a new drug with a long name I can't remember. Even with the new drug, dad said her chances for recovery aren't too good because her problem wasn't treated early enough.

But things weren't all bad. The very next day my dad landed a welder's job at the shipyard after taking a test that demonstrated his skill with the equipment. He immediately joined the union so we'd have medical coverage to pay for at least some of mom's hospital expenses.

I visited her today, and she didn't look too good. She'd lost more weight and had dark circles under her eyes. I hoped maybe it was because she just wasn't getting enough sleep, but in the back of my mind I pretty much knew she was getting worse. How terribly sad.

With dad working and spending all his free time at the hospital, I was left to do what I wanted which meant playing basketball and hanging out with Romans at the sweet shop. What I learned from the Romans wasn't all good, stuff like cursing, smoking, drinking beer and about other street gangs. I hadn't been invited to join yet, but I believed it would happen soon.

I played basketball every day it didn't rain. Zan stopped by often to watch the games, and I couldn't help but think it was really to see me. I talked to her quite a bit after we finished playing, and I was certain if the Romans let me join that she'd date me.

With so much practice and such good competition I became a better basketball player. I could score with either my left or my right hand, probably because back in Scranton I'd learned to hit a baseball from both sides of the plate. I played as hard as the other guys, and it was clear they respected me for it.

I still didn't have the sixteen bucks I owed to St. Stephens and I knew I'd be repeating seventh grade at Sacred Heart if I didn't come up with it. I couldn't tell my dad I'd spent the lunch money during the past year on ice cream and candy instead of good food, so I was in a real spot. School started in a month and a half and I was worried, so I went to my Uncle Louie and asked if I could borrow the money from him. His first question was: "Does your dad know about this?"

"No," I said, embarrassed. "I didn't want to worry him. He has enough on his mind with mom and all the doctor bills. He's even taking on more work. Last Saturday and Sunday, he helped with electrical stuff for the escalator at the new Bamberger's store. On top of that, he took an evening job at the M&M candy factory. Dad needs all the money he can get to cover mom's medical bills, so I didn't have the guts to tell him that I blew the lunch money on soda pop and other stuff."

Uncle Louie said that his other brother, Peter, the one he called "Cagoots," which means cucumber but we all knew it really meant "big dick," got my dad the job at the M&M plant. Uncle Louie became quiet and stared at me intently. While he was making up his mind as to how to agree to my "loan," or at least that's what I hoped he was doing, I watched through the window in his office door as adults and kids of all ages lifted weights and practiced self-defense. The self-defense part fascinated me.

Even though I was still shy of my fifteenth birthday, I was almost six feet tall and stronger than most kids even a year or so older than me. However, I'd never had a real fight in my life. Yeah, I'd pushed a few kids around who needed it, but it had never come down to an actual fist fight. Learning to fight and defend myself seemed like a great idea.

Uncle Louie brought me back from my daydreams, saying, "Here's what we'll do. I'll loan you the sixteen bucks, and you can work it off here at the gym. You come here after school for an hour each day, and after sixteen days we're even. You can start tonight. We have a deal?"

"Wow, Uncle Louie, we have a deal for sure!" A dollar an hour for cleaning up around the gym was more than I ever could have asked for, so I decided to push my good luck and asked,

---

"Uncle Louie, what can you tell me about the Romans? I think they're going to ask me if I want to join their gang. Bobby Ciccone said you were a member, and that I should ask you about what it's really like to be one of the gang."

Uncle Louie took a cigar from his desk drawer but didn't light the stogie, rolling it around in his fingers instead. "I'm still a member of the Romans—and always will be. Being a gang member is something that might be a little hard to understand. If you join the Romans, the gang comes first. It comes before the individual, which means before you. You do what the gang needs to get done. In this city, that mainly comes down to defendin' each other from other gangs. I can tell you one thing, if you don't join the Romans, you're on your own. That means takin' on a lot by yourself. Especially as you get older."

"Bobby Ciccone told me about being on my own. You think Dad will mind?"

"Your dad knows I was a member of the Romans, and he knows what happens in a big city like this if a kid isn't in a gang. I don't think he'll be upset if you join. If you want, I'll let him know you're thinkin' about it so you won't have to tell him yourself."

Uncle Louie stood and reached inside a closet. From the back I could see him pull out something, but I didn't know what. He turned to me and said, "Here, Frank, try this on." He was smiling proudly and holding a black Romans jacket to me. I tried it on and its length was just about right in the sleeves, but I had some filling out to do in the chest and shoulders. I looked in the mirror and found myself grinning from ear to ear. I looked cool. And I felt cool.

I removed the jacket and reluctantly handed it back to Uncle Louie. "The gang hasn't accepted me yet. For now, show me what I'm supposed to do around here. I've got a debt to pay off."

"Good boy," Uncle Louie said, and he took me around the gym, the locker area, and the restrooms. He handed me a push broom, told me what he wanted done, and where to get rid of the trash. I went to work that very afternoon.

When I was done, he said to me, "Why not stay an extra hour each night and learn self-defense? You'll need it in this city. That's why all those guys are training. By the time you start eighth grade six weeks from now, you'll be one of the toughest kids in the school. But only if you work hard at it."

I clapped my hands and said, "Great idea. How soon can we start." He laughed and walked me over to a heavy bag hanging from a thick rope. He told me to hit the bag. I swung my left arm with a much force as I could muster but it barely moved.

Uncle Louie laughed real loud. "You'll get better. And you need to, 'cause right now one of the Romanettes could kick your butt!" He showed me how to put my shoulder into a punch and how to rotate my hips to create power. Next came kicking the heavy bag. He demonstrated how to aim for different body parts, especially the groin. I was pretty bad and missed the intended mark by a lot. It looked easy but it wasn't. I needed a lot of practice.

"I'm not very good, am I?" I already knew the answer.

"It takes time. Tonight is just the start. In six weeks, you'll be a different person." Before I left for the night, Uncle Louie gave me a twenty-dollar bill, telling me to use the other four bucks for school supplies.

The next day, Joe Cheeks and I walked to Sacred Heart Catholic School and I paid my debt. I gave the chubby secretary the twenty, and she kept looking at the bill like it was phony. Then she glared at me as if I stole it. She took forever, but she went out and came back with four dollars and also wrote me a receipt. *Wow, what a load off my mind. I wouldn't have to worry anymore about repeating seventh grade.*

I jammed the receipt and the bills in my pants pocket and asked the secretary, "Can I see my grades?"

"Please, Mr. Bruno."

"What?" I didn't understand her.

"Always say please. And the correct way to ask that question is, 'May I please see my grades?'"

I wanted to whack her one, but I said, "May I *please* see my grades?"

She reached into a desk drawer and handed me my seventh grade report card, but she immediately turned her attention to Joe. "Mr. Giardiello, as Sister Elizabeth Ann said, you have some competition. Your friend here has all A's and one B-plus. Eighth-grade marks will determine who goes to Stanton Prep. Perhaps both of you will qualify. Just keep in mind that no one from Scared Heart has never gotten through and attended Stanton University on scholarship."

That made no sense. Why had no one who had excelled at Sacred Heart not done the same at Stanton Prep and gone on to the university? I wanted to ask but I wanted out of the principal's office more, so after a brief thank you I motioned to Joe and we left.

We were on our way back to The Projects when Joe said, "I have an idea. Why don't we go to the movies? *On the Waterfront* is playing at The Stanley Theater on South Orange Avenue. The matinee should be just about over, and we can catch the next show."

I was surprised Joe had even asked. "No way, Cheeks. I owe my uncle sixteen bucks, and that four dollars I got back from the twenty is for school supplies. Movies cost a quarter, and I'm not making the same mistake I made before, not with

---

the money my Uncle Louie gave me for school stuff. I'm not spending a penny of it on anything else."

Joe laughed. "You don't get it, Bruno. It won't be a problem. The show's free. Follow me." I shrugged my shoulders and tagged along with him.

The walk was a long one. I rested against the wall as we waited outside the exit door of The Stanley Theater. Soon the door flew open, and Joe held it as the crowd of mostly old folks left the building. When the line slowed, Joe motioned to me and we entered the movie house through the exit doorway. Joe said, "I told you, Bruno, no problem."

I remembered that the newspaper said that *On the Waterfront* was about an ex-prize fighter who has trouble standing up to a corrupt union boss. Sounded like a good action movie, the kind I enjoyed the most.

We quickly took a seat. Joe picked up a full waxed cup of soda with a plastic cover on it and a straw sticking out which he promptly tossed on the floor. A few minutes later two young kids, maybe fourth or fifth graders, began cleaning up. One gave Joe a good stare knowing that he and I probably snuck in but Joe turned to show he was wearing his Romans A.C. jacket and the boy hurried about his work, knowing better than to ask a Romans A.C. gang member if he'd paid to get in. Joe got up and took a clean straw from the kids vest pocket and inserted it in his soda. "Thanks kid." I sat there confidently. *Joe Cheeks definitely has street smarts.*

We watched the previews and a newsreel about the first Miss America contest, coming up September 11. The woman from *The Tonight Show*, Lee Meriwether, was highlighted. This was followed by a sports program about a pitcher named Hoyt Wilhelm and his knuckleball. A reporter used his camera to record Wilhelm's pitches in slow motion, and ball after ball moved around so much that the catcher dropped four out of five of his tosses.

After that there was a special about Jackie Robinson, who on April 15, 1947, had started a game at first base for the Brooklyn Dodgers and became the first colored guy to play in the big leagues. Some of his own teammates hated having him on the team because they didn't want any negroes in the major leagues. Robinson went on to earn "Rookie of the Year" honors, and he was named to the All-Star team in 1949. By now everyone knew who Number 42 was, but when Jackie Robinson came to bat, despite how good he was as a player, even now—seven years later—some people in the stands still booed him. I found this terrible.

The soda had run right through me and I told Joe I had to take a leak and I'd be right back. When I walked in the restroom, I was the only person in it. I stepped to the urinal and unzipped my fly and started to take a much-needed pee. I heard the door open but paid no attention to who came in, thinking it might be Joe. I just looked straight ahead.

I soon heard several feet scuffling, and as I was pulling up my zipper and turning to leave, four guys pushed me and one of them punched me in the ribs. I threw a wild punch and hit one of them, but three of the guys started pounding on me at the same time. I kicked at them but I stumbled against the wall and fell to the floor. I felt a hard kick to my ribs. I grabbed at a boot as another kick was coming my way. The boot had a Falcon drawn on it. If I survived, that was one symbol I'd never forget. The boot came free of my grip, but I'd seen the falcon clearly enough to make out that part of the drawing of the beak had worn away.

The Boot yelled, "Hey, yah piece of shit, stay out of our fuckin' territory or your next beatin' won't go so easy. Next

60

time, we bust up some bones."

The Falcons left just as fast as they'd come in. I sat on the floor, stunned at what had happened but happy to be in one piece. Everything had taken place in a rush, but I was mad at myself for not getting in a few more good punches. As I thought about it, I had to admit that Uncle Louie was right. I really didn't know how to fight.

I wasn't bleeding anywhere I could see, but my ribs were killing me. I threw some water on my face and tucked in my shirt. It hurt to take a deep breath, and when I got back to my seat and told Joe what had just happened, he smirked and said, "If you were wearing a Romans jacket, they probably wouldn't have touched you. If they did, we'd beat the shit out of every Falcon we came across." I didn't have to think about it any longer, if the Romans asked me to join I'd say yes immediately.

Joe and I watched the movie, which was pretty good, but I was hurting and my mind was on what had just happened. On the long walk home, which was painful every step of the way, Joe told me that getting attacked by another gang was no big deal. "If it wasn't the Falcons it would be the Pontiacs or another gang. Don't worry about it. Happens all the time. I'm going to sponsor you with the Romans, and we'll vote right away. I'm sure you'll be in. Then we'll get our guys together and find some Falcons and kick the shit out of them."

With considerable effort, I made it back to The Projects. I wouldn't let Joe know that my side was hurting as bad as it was, and this was one time I was happy my dad wasn't home, as he'd have known something was wrong with me.

I undressed and looked at myself in the bathroom mirror. I was black and blue all over my chest and stomach area. I ran the tub full of the hottest water I could stand and lay in it until the water got cold. I felt better, and the next day the Romans voted me in as a member. By the following week I was healed, and a half-dozen of us roamed Falcon territory until we found three of their gang near The Stanley Theatre. We beat the crap out of them, and let them know why, but the guy with the falcon on his boot wasn't one of them.

Over the next three weeks we had two more street fights with the Falcons. I held my own against them because of my continual training at Uncle Louie's gym. Bobby Ciccone said I had the makings of a hell of a Roman. I don't know when I've felt prouder about anything.

CHAPTER SEVEN

Simon Silverman: 1949
Inside the Pipe

Rose Silverman told her friends at the synagogue how her husband had helped so many of our people escape the Nazis. Those stories were passed on, from family to family. With Rosh Hashanah coming up, I was sure the tales would once again be told at our dinner table. My dad, Saul Silverman, had become a legend in our area, and he certainly deserved their respect, not only for what he had done but for how he'd accomplished it right under the noses of the dreaded S.S.

Everything took place back in Germany before I was born, and well prior to Uncle Menachem marrying my aunt, Frieda. I was the oldest child in our household and knew those stories by heart. I thought about them today as I was helping my mother set the table. We were expecting Uncle Menachem and his family, and another couple who were friends with both our families.

I placed a set of the cheap blue-and-white salt-and-pepper

shakers in front of each place setting, as I always did, but this time I studied the condiment holders under bright sunlight coming through the large window in our dining room. The salt-and-pepper shakers had traveled all the way from Hamburg, Germany, to a post office box in New Town, New Jersey and to look at them, they were certainly nothing special.

I opened one of the salt shakers. Appearing to be just salt inside, it must have seemed the same to Nazis inspectors in 1938. However, I knew that one flawless diamond was hidden amid the salt. I carefully tightened the cheap shiny metal top and placed it on the table in front of my father's plate. As in the past when he told the story, he would reveal the diamond.

Millions of Jews and non-Jews were sent to gas chambers. When I think about it, my dad could have been one of them, but he successfully masqueraded for three years as a Muslim woman and helped so many people escape the Nazis. He bought diamond jewelry at reasonable prices from those who wanted to flee Germany, and he gave them the only money that mattered back then: German marks.

However, by the time my father reached America, he was a changed man. Even today, he lives in fear of being caught—in New Jersey. The farm where we live, on the outskirts of Milltown, is actually many miles away from the closest town. It is really "out in the sticks," as people say. The previous owner died several years before my dad purchased the property. The place was abandoned and rundown, but my father liked it because it was isolated, with very few neighbors close by.

Several weeks after my dad acquired the property, he told me that he walked to visit Ted Nenninger, a farmer who lived over a mile from our house. Dad approached the farmer with caution and introduced himself. After a brief conversation, he asked him, "Mr. Nenninger, can I purchase a ride with you to

Milltown next Saturday?"

Ted Nenninger, a tall leathery farmer about 50 years of age, showed his friendship to his new neighbor, just as he would to anyone else, saying, "Of course you can ride along with me, Mr. Silverman. I make the trip every Saturday morning to sell my chickens and eggs, so there's no need to pay me. I'd welcome your company."

Saul was distrustful because "Nenninger" was a German name, and he suspected there were Nazis lurking behind every tree, ready to pounce on him at a moment's notice. He'd learned, however, that the farmer made the trip to Milltown every Saturday, in a wooden cart pulled by a big draft horse. The wagon was loaded with eggs that Ted Nenninger sold to the grocers in the small town. He'd take his chances that this farmer was not part of the Nazis.

The following Saturday morning, Saul arrived in Milltown. From there he took a trolley to New Brunswick. After that, he boarded a train to New York City. He remembered seeing New York City off across the water after disembarking the ship at Ellis Island, but today as he got off the train he was overwhelmed by so many tall buildings, the crowds of people rushing everywhere, hearing so many different languages, and the frantic rush of traffic.

He stood with his back to a building for a few minutes before he placed his yarmulke on his head and walked to 47th street, where he observed several young Jewish men with black curly braids and unkempt beards go about their business. These men were street buyers, and the area was known as "The Diamond District." Saul was in the right place. He had diamonds to sell.

Saul watched as desperate people sold stones for what he knew were ridiculously low prices. The young buyers working the street bought everything they could from any seller, whether a recently divorced woman needing cash, a burglar or a pickpocket.

Saul was far more experienced than these young men, and he certainly did not intend to deal with this level of "trader." What he carried in his money belt were excellent high-quality diamonds he would sell only if the price was right.

Saul approached the buyers and asked to speak to the "boss." After several minutes of conversation, with Saul's knowledge as a diamond merchant now clear to these young men, he was directed to the second floor of a building a few doors down the street. He climbed the stairs, knocked and waited. Two burly fellows, their holstered pistols quite visible, opened the door and walked him to an inside office.

Saul handed him a diamond of such high quality that, by the look on the man's face, they buyer was quite surprised to be holding such a gem. This "boss" asked, "Where did this diamond come from? Is it stolen?" Saul said nothing, letting the man's interest build.

As he viewed the stone through his loupe, turning the diamond so he could see it from several angles, he said, "I rarely see such size and with this quality. When I do see those types of stones, they are often illegally acquired." After some hesitation, and complaining about the risk of buying such a valuable stone that might be stolen, he made an offer that was not nearly enough for a diamond of that size and caliber.

Unlike other sellers, Saul was far from desperate. He rose from his chair, folded his arms across his small frame, and with an angry look on his face, demanded, "Give me my diamond and tell me, who is your boss? I will deal with him. Now, direct me to the right person or I'm leaving."

The man made a phone call, accurately describing the diamond, which he carefully returned to Saul when he finished talking, making it clear he didn't want to give it up. Saul was escorted by the guards to another door down the hall. An elderly man with very thick eyeglasses made a careful analysis of the diamond, weighed it, and made an offer. It was not overly generous, but after some negotiation of the price, Saul accepted.

The head diamond buyer handed Saul the cash and said, "If you have more stones of this quality, I am interested."

Saul said, "I may return one day," and nothing more.

The cash was counted out in front of Saul, but he counted it again, nodded when finished, and left. He went to a pawn shop and purchased a pistol that looked similar to what the guards had carried in their holsters. He returned by the same means he had taken earlier that day, except when he got to Milltown he took a taxi home. Saul felt the pistol in his pocket during the entire trip back. The gun gave him comfort. If someone waited in ambush when he arrived at his home, that person would pay the price. No one was hulking in the shadows except his dogs.

A month later, Saul again rode with Ted Nenninger on his horse cart loaded with eggs, only this time the farmer had a dozen squawking chickens in wooden cages for sale too. Saul met with the same elderly buyer in New York City and sold him several diamonds this time. With the proceeds, Saul purchased a recently unoccupied store in Milltown and named it Silverman's Jewelry, with additional lettering: Specializing in High-Quality Diamonds.

****

I'm Simon Silverman, Saul's son. I've known Andre and Dave Nenninger as long as I can remember. Dave and I have always been in the same grade and in the same grammar school. The two of us have been friends even though we're a lot different. I'm more studious whereas Dave and his older brother are what people call, rough and tumble farm kids.

In August, with one month of summer left before eighth grade started, Dave and I often took long walks on trails that ran for miles. We explored the woods and looked for long-abandoned stills. Milltown was famous for its farms, but it was also known for moonshiners back in the 1920s. One afternoon we followed a path we had never taken before. After a considerable distance, the trail got wider. Someone had definitely made a road here a long time ago!

Before long we found what we only imagined had existed: several broken oak barrels, copper tubing, and some weird-looking metal contraption with what looked like bullet holes in it. We also found a string of tin cans, still hanging from wires, which we assumed had been set up to warn the moonshiners that someone was approaching. By the appearance of everything, no one had been back here for years, but we were scared, so we gathered up the copper tubing and raced back to the start of the path. The following week, the junkman bought the copper for two dollars and a quarter. We felt like we were rich.

A new rule for the '54-55' school year was that if you lived more than a mile away from school, a bus would pick you up at an assigned spot, some of which had small shelters built by a farmers' association called The Grange. I lived a little more than a mile away, so now I'd be riding a bus along with Dave and Andre.

I knew everyone at McGinnis School, where I'd been going, and the kids knew me. They were used to me being the smallest boy in the school, and they were used to my thick glasses. I was shy and not even close to being good looking. Every boy and most of the girls were taller. My father was a small man, and my mother, Rose, was tiny, so that was probably why I was so small. I had knotty hair, and I wore knickers that my mother bought at the second hand-clothing store. No one wore knickers anymore and I hated them. I pleaded with my mom to buy me regular pants, but my father wouldn't spend the money even though I was certain we could afford any kind of clothes for me. With my yucky clothes, thick glasses, and small size, girls stayed away from me, acting as if I had a disease of some kind. I often heard them whispering and giggling when they turned up their noses at me.

I'd tried to make friends with most all the kids, but it just didn't work. One boy I hoped might be a pal told me to stay away from him or he would stick his hairbrush up my butt. I was awful at sports and always the last player picked when teams were chosen. It was embarrassing to stand by myself until the very end, knowing all along that no captain wanted me on his team.

Once, at recess, the playground teacher named Dave as captain for a game we called Red Rover. Dave took me as his third pick, but I knew it was out of friendship and probably not because he really wanted me on his side. No matter, I stood next to him, my hands on my hips, feeling proud. I was really happy, but that was the only time he was captain, so I never got chosen like that again.

One thing I did do right was get good marks, actually the best scores in every grade so far. I beat Sam, Billy, and Dave, and the twins, Sandy and Susan. I also beat Clifford Hanson and that pretty girl Pat with the blond hair and Jane Vanderhoof who wouldn't look at me twice in the same month. I even got better grades than the Fielders, brother and sister twins, who were total bookworms. So, even with the other issues I had to deal with, I was okay with McGinnis School. And Dave was my buddy.

A couple of weeks before eighth grade began I met up with Dave and his brother on a familiar trail that went through a hilly section of old oak trees, some so big that four of us kids holding hands couldn't get our arms around them. Dave's grandfather told him that no one had ever cut down any of these trees, with some growing here since the Lenape Indians hunted these woods.

Dave said to me, "Have you seen what's going in the woods below our house, Simon?" I shook my head. "Workmen with saws and axes are all over the place, and they're cutting down the old trees grandpa said were almost sacred."

Andre said, "One man told me there's a highway coming through here, and a Negro man with an ax told me it's going to be called the New Jersey Turnpike. So we're checking it out."

"Why get near these men?" I asked.

Andre, being older than Dave and me, seemed as if he was smarter than us at times. This was one of them. "Because, genius, we're going into the soda business. These guys will be working their butts off. They'll be thirsty. Dave and I are going to carry soda to them and sell it at a huge profit. My grandfather is making wooden crates that will hold ice so the soda will still be cold by the time we reach the men." Andre had to catch his breath before adding, "Our dad said he can bring a trunk load of soda home from when he goes to Milltown this Saturday."

"What a neat idea," I said, really impressed. We live way out in the country, and my friends were going into business. I had to ask, "Can I help?"

Andre gave me a smirk and said, "Okay, maybe you can help a little."

That summer Dave and his brother made two cents profit on a small bottle of soda, mostly orange and grape, and five cents for a large bottle. The way these men worked, they mostly bought large bottles and drank half of it in one gulp and then stuck the bottle in the ground—with just the neck showing to keep the rest of the soda as cold as possible.

I hated to watch those huge ancient oaks being cut down, and it saddened me in a way. Dave and I counted the rings on one tree to see how old it was, but we lost count at 175. I guessed there must have been another 50 rings, maybe more.

The trees were sawed down and my friends sold plenty of soda. If Dave and Andre didn't have to go to school, they could have gotten rich selling soda to those workmen. The guys with saws and axes were followed by men driving bulldozers that pushed and pulled the giant stumps out of the ground. The stumps were piled high and doused with kerosene and set on fire. We didn't know it then, but we'd see the stump piles smoking and smell them burning for weeks. What didn't burn would be buried.

The bulldozers were followed by enormous earthmovers that scraped off the tops of hills and dropped the dirt in the valleys. Late one night, well after the workmen were gone, one of the older high school kids figured how to start the motor on one of the earthmovers. Black diesel smoke belched as the engine roared to life with a mighty rumble. I backed away, as did the rest of us, and we watched in awe and fear as the kid turned on the lights and fumbled with the gearshift. He pushed levers forwards and backwards until the giant machine started moving.

Everyone yelled with excitement, but we were all terrified, and as it turned out for good reason. The kid didn't know how to stop the earthmover, so he jumped off and let it roll along on its own. We weren't going to wait around for what might happen next, so we all took off running. No one went down there the next day to see what had happened with the earthmover, but that was the most exciting night I'd ever had in my whole life, at least so far.

Two other things happened that summer before school started; things I would never forget. I was at Dave's grandmother's house when a muscular Negro man came to her garage. He was carrying a bloody ax, and he asked Dave's grandma if she had any coal tar oil. Grandmother Nenninger asked the man, "What do you mean by coal tar oil? You looking for kerosene?"

He politely replied, "Yes ma'am, kerosene. I needs it for my foot." He pointed to his heavy leather boot on his left foot, which had a big cut in it. "I missed with the ax, ma'am." It was then that I saw that his boot oozed blood.

Dave's grandmother said, "You better get that boot off so I can take a look at that foot. You probably should see a doctor."

The man said, "Thank you, ma'am, but if'n I take that boot off, I lose my job. I have a wife and children, and I need this here job. Black men like me can hardly get good work these days that pays anything." Dave's grandmother handed him a bottle of witch hazel instead of kerosene, and the man asked Dave to please hold his axe. He filled his boot with the solution, thanked everyone, and went back to work. I never knew what happened to him.

The second event involved an earthmover again. And since no one got caught the first time, we were back watching what was going on, just a smaller group of us, by this I mean the high school kid, Andre, Dave, and me.

Long drainage pipes were installed under the roadway, from one side to the other, a distance of one hundred yards. The high school kid who'd started the earthmover said, "Who's a chicken shit here?" He looked at me and Dave and Andre. Andre snapped, "What do you mean by calling us chicken shit?"

The older kid said, "Okay, which one of you will crawl

behind me through the drainpipe while an earthmover goes over top. Or are all of you chicken shit?"

"That's crazy," Andre said.

"I know it's scary, but I did it yesterday," the high school kid said. "So you're a chicken shit?"

Andre balled up his fist at the older kid but relaxed his hand and said, "We'll all follow you."

I wasn't so sure I'd follow. I stuck my head in the pipe, which was just big enough for a kid to crawl through, and the light at the other end appeared as a tiny dot. I was scared. I could tell Dave was too, but I knew Andre wasn't about to be called a chicken shit.

I still had my head in the pipe, my eyes fixed on the tiny light at the other end, when a fully loaded earthmover rumbled across. Dirt stirred inside the pipe. I swore the pipe bent while I watched, and I wondered if I could breathe if I were inside it. Now I could hardly see any light at all at the other end, and I dreaded the thought of crawling through it. I quickly stood up.

Then I heard Andre say, "Dave and me and Simon ain't chicken shits. We're going with you to the other side."

Holy crap! We're really going to do this!

The high school kid said, "Here's the deal. I go first, Andre goes next, Dave behind him, and you, short stuff with the glasses, you follow Dave if you've got the guts. No one can stop in the middle, and you can't go backwards." He gave me a snide look. "You can stay here, and we can just call you chicken shit for the rest of your life. Your choice."

Nobody, including me, wanted to be called chicken shit, so in our assigned order we began crawling inside. The first few yards started out okay, but when an earthmover went over the pipe, the ground shook. I was certain I felt the pipe move, and thought it might collapse on us and we'd all die.

It was dark, dusty and hot. I couldn't stop or turn back, so I kept my eyes on Dave's behind as he moved on ahead of me. It seemed as though we'd crawled for a mile and still hadn't reached the other side. My eyes and nose were full of dust, and sweat ran down my face. My arms and legs ached something awful, but I finally smelled fresh air and saw a flicker of light.

I was covered with dirt and grit and my knees were scraped and bloody, but I was almost free of the pipe. Then, crap, I had to stop at the end until the other kids could get out. Finally it was my turn. I was so scared and exhausted that I fell to the ground as I crawled from the pipe. The high school kid pulled me to my feet and said, "Hey, four eyes, nice going. I thought I might have to go in there and drag you out."

I didn't say anything. Instead, I stood up on wobbly scraped-up knees and smiled as if it was nothing. But I never wanted to try something like that again. Being called chicken shit would be fine with me.

Eighth grade was starting in three days. I'd know most of the kids from last year, but not all of them. I knew our homeroom teacher was a guy named Mr. Dickerson. Kids who'd already had him for homeroom called him Mr. Dickhead because he had a reputation for picking on kids who weren't considered cool. I knew I wasn't even close to being cool. I had a feeling eighth grade could be a bad year for me.

CHAPTER EIGHT

Frank Bruno: 1954
Eighth Grade
Sacred Heart Catholic School

Today was the day. It wasn't about basketball or Zan, who by now was my girlfriend or about the Romans. This was the first day of eighth grade, and it started an hour from now. I hurried through my breakfast of oatmeal and sliced apples, and a cup of sugary coffee. Finished with my meal, I ran down the stairs, two at a time, and hurried to Sacred Heart Catholic School.

As was her routine each morning, Sister Elizabeth Ann observed what was going on outside from a window in her office on the second floor. She carefully watched the arriving students just like a predator hawk marking its prey from high atop a tree.

Sister Elizabeth Ann knew all too well, even though this was a strict Catholic school, there could be trouble. Serious

---

behavioral issues with students had occurred in the past. She folded her arms across her chest as the first school bus arrived and watched intently. Almost every student on this bus was familiar except for transfers from other schools.

There was little Jeffrey, making his way from the bus to the safety of the school. He wore an old dark-blue Navy pea coat. Sister Elizabeth Ann was aware that the poor child had been bullied ever since he'd first attended Sacred Heart two years ago. She spotted a bigger boy, that kid, Mikey, who was a constant menace. Thankfully, his older brothers, each of whom had created plenty of problems in the past, were off to high school—and now were someone else's problem.

Mikey approached little Jeffrey, and Sister Elizabeth Ann witnessed the smaller child's books being knocked from his hands. The big kid grabbed Jeffrey's lunch bag and searched inside it. He found a piece of candy and tossed the rest of the contents of the bag on the ground and smiled as he crumpled the empty sack and tossed it to Jeffrey.

Sister rushed from her perch in a panic, but she was intercepted by her secretary, who had a problem of her own that needed attention. Unable to ignore her secretary, Sister had to stop and listen to the issue before deciding she'd handle the matter later. Right now, she had to rescue poor little Jeffrey.

My first day at Sacred Heart began as I saw a little boy being picked on by a much bigger kid. I was a different person from when I'd first arrived in Newark several months ago. For one thing, I was no longer a kid with no fighting skills. I'd spent the last six weeks with the Romans, working out at the gym, lifting weights and learning how to punch and kick and use my elbows and knees to my advantage.

After all my practice, I pounded the heavy bag as well as

---

even some of the adult men who trained at the gym. Uncle Louie told me, "Frank, you'll be fine at your new school. My advice is, don't take no shit from nobody. If anyone thinks you're afraid to fight, it'll never stop. Since you're new at Sacred Heart, trouble will come your way, whether you're a Roman or not. So be ready."

I was ready, more than ready, and I had a total dislike for bullies. When I saw the little kid crawling on the ground, crying as he gathered together his scattered lunch, and the bigger kid standing over him and slobbering while eating a piece of candy, I ran up and yelled, "Hey, asshole, give that kid his lunch back."

The bigger boy chewed with his mouth open and laughed at me. I could see the candy in his mouth was a piece of caramel. "And who the hell are *you*?" he snorted. " What do you think you are, this little punk's guardian angel?" He spit what was left of the candy on the ground, right near my new lightweight shoes that Uncle Louie had bought for me to wear when school started. Uncle Louie had said, "These shoes give you an advantage when you get in a fight. Your kicks will be like lightning."

The chewed-up candy on the ground landed right next my new shoes. Without saying anything else, I spun and kicked the bully in the ribs. When he grabbed at his side, I punched him in the gut so hard that he went down on one knee and gasped for air. "Spitting that candy at my shoe was a bad mistake on your part." The little kid retrieved his lunch, a sandwich and bag of chips, and put everything in his now very crumpled bag.

I started to walk away but turned around and pointed at the kid I'd just clobbered. "Don't ever pick on that little kid again or I'll bust you up good next time." He said nothing, only nodding and whimpering, but I had a good idea this wouldn't be

---

77

the last run-in I'd have with him.

I was already in the school when Jeffrey got to his feet and Sister Elizabeth Ann arrived. "Young man, are you okay?" she asked and helped him brush himself off.

Jeffery pointed to the bully, who was still on one knee, and said, "That kid took my lunch and ate my candy. There it is on the ground, where he spit it out Sister Elizabeth Ann. But God sent me a guardian angel. I have my lunch back now, so everything's okay except for the candy."

"I saw what happened. You go on to class, and if you're hurt at all, you come to my office." Jeffrey thanked her and ran off.

Sister Elizabeth Ann held a quizzical look. Yes, she knew what had happened to Jeffrey and his lunch bag, but nothing explained why this bully was on one knee and winded. There were no guardian angels in Newark, no matter how much she prayed for them. She also knew all about Mikey because he was no different from his troublesome brothers. No matter how severe their mischief, the boys' father would speak to Father Joseph and make a donation to the church. This made it so his sons escaped expulsion. The worst they ever got as punishment was an hour of detention after school.

Once safely inside the school building, Jeffrey told his friends what had just happened: "The new guy saved me from Mikey. Anyone who messes with him will regret it." Word spread like wildfire.

After school was over, this Mikey kid, whose name I now knew, was standing a good distance from me and yelling my way, "I have two older brothers in high school. You'll hear from them, tough guy."

I smiled. I wasn't concerned about big brothers. I wasn't the same kid who had been roughed up at The Stanley Theatre a few months back. And, if I needed them, I had a few friends of my own in the Romans.

Without fail, I attended Sacred Heart Catholic School every day and visited my mom at the hospital on Tuesdays, Thursdays and most Saturdays. Sometimes she seemed better; sometimes not so much. I continued working at the gym even though I'd long since paid back Uncle Louie. He generally ordered a pizza for lunch but never ate the whole thing. I always devoured the cold leftover portion as if I were a hungry wolf. Uncle Louie began ordering two pizzas and saving one for me. I always finished off every bit of it.

Today was a new step for me at the gym because I'd be training with men. This evening's lesson was on how to defend against someone wielding a knife or a club. Uncle Louie approached me with a wooden knife, and I jumped backwards. He said, "Ah, Frankie, you had the natural reaction when I showed my knife. Everyone has the tendency to move away from a threat like a knife, but the better approach is to close the gap and attack when you have an opening."

It required many practice sessions, but I developed the confidence to move closer when under attack and spin on my heel and slam an elbow or a foot into my opponent's head. I got whacked by other guys, too, and often, but I also learned how to ward off blows. After a while, the moves for both offense and defense became fast and natural. On top of everything, by the middle of October I'd put on eight pounds of solid muscle and was fully six feet tall.

As for the Romans, every October they added a block or two to their "their territory." This year it involved taking over two blocks ruled by the Pontiacs, who were also called the

"Medigons," meaning non-Italian gang. Twelve Romans, with Bobby Ciccone at the lead, walked the two Pontiac blocks. I was in the second row.

The Pontiacs were a tough gang. They dressed in red satin jackets, with the image of an American Indian warrior embroidered on the backs. They knew the Romans were coming. One older Pontiac, who I was told was their leader, wore heavy sideburns and a duck's-ass haircut, He stepped forward and shouted, "Hey, assholes, get off our street if you know what's good for you."

Bobby yelled back at him, "This block is no longer yours. As of right now, it belongs to the Romans." We didn't give the Pontiac time to respond and charged instead. One of their gang held up a bicycle chain. When twisted sideways and swung, a bicycle chain becomes no different from a steel bar. We expected they might have bike chains, so we carried chair and table legs, courtesy of Luigi, and went at them. Some of our guys took off their heavy garrison belts and doubled them over our fists.

The guy with the bicycle chain was right in front of me. I raised my table leg and stepped forward, closing the distance between the two of us, just as Uncle Louie had taught me. The Pontiac swung the chain at my head. I ducked and slammed the guy's ribs with my club and kicked him hard in the knee. Something snapped and he went down. I kicked him twice more in the ribs. He was done and screaming in pain.

It was soon obvious that we were winning the fight, and Joe Cheeks yelled, "Kill 'em all!" I guess that scared the crap out of the Pontiacs, because those who could run did so. A Pontiac helped Bicycle Chain limp off. The whole thing hadn't taken any time at all, and the two blocks were now ours.

The following day we walked our new territory and paid a

visit to every store owner. We asked one simple question: "How would you like to rent one of our Romans A.C. stickers for your front window? It's five bucks a month." Most store owners knew what we were talking about, and they couldn't give us the five bucks fast enough. However, the owner of a deli, a huge Slavic guy, refused and told us to get the hell out of his store.

It ended up that he was the only one who said no in the entire two-blocks of storefronts. Somehow, his front window, a big one, got smashed later that week. The next day we approached him again, but he still wouldn't pay, cursing at us and having the window replaced instead.

We waited until he had the glass installed and his store's name painted neatly on the new window. Four days later, in the early hours of the morning, Bobby and I broke the deli window for the second time. The next day was a Saturday, and late in the afternoon the deli owner came to The Paramount Sweet Shop and asked to see the leader of the Romans.

I was in the backroom, shooting pool, when I heard the man's distinctive accent. He was talking loud and I suspected trouble. None of my older gang members were around, so I told the kid I was playing pool with, who was barely thirteen, to get ready for a fight. We had no choice but to take on this moose of a man by ourselves. I grabbed a table leg from the umbrella stand, handed one to the other kid and yelled to Luigi, "Bring him in here! Tell him he'll be talking to one of the leaders!"

I braced for a battle. The kid with me would be of little help against a man this size, especially a guy who was obviously used to physical labor. Instead of trouble, however, the deli owner squared up to me and pulled some bills from his pocket. "Here's thirty bucks, my payment for the next six months. Now give me my damn sticker, and leave me the hell alone." Luigi

---

kept a supply of our Romans A.C. stickers, so he handed him one and that was it.

Whenever we had money from "renting" our stickers, we generally used it to buy beer and snacks for a party. Luigi let us use the backroom and as usual the Romanettes never missed a party. Being teenagers, it didn't take too many gulps of Schlitz before we all felt the alcohol.

Zan and I danced, drank beer, mugged it up and held hands. During one dance she kissed me with an open mouth which made me hot as hell. I slid my hand down her behind and we ground out bodies into each other, but that was it.

It was a little after 11 in the evening when I got home from the party, but my dad was still away. He pretty much stayed at the hospital with my mom until the nurses made him leave. I began watching *The Steve Allen Show*, which was new to television. The guy the show was named after was really funny, and I was laughing out loud, when I heard the front door open.

Dad locked the door behind him, and I got up and gave him a hug. He grabbed some leftovers from the fridge and warmed the food up quickly. He sat down to eat and watch TV with me, but he had no spirit. "Your mom isn't doing very well," he said. "She's on oxygen and pain medicine fulltime now, and she can hardly breathe. I'm afraid we might lose her, Son." He sounded about to cry. "It doesn't look good, not good at all."

Since I'd visited my mother twice a week and often on weekends, I was sadly aware of her condition and not surprised to hear that she wasn't doing any better. I wondered what would happen to us if she died. How would our lives change? Dad was quiet for a few minutes, while I, too, was lost in deep thought. He finished his meal of lasagna and garlic bread that Aunt Marie had made. She cooked often for us lately.

Dad got up and took his plate to the sink. As he rinsed it off, he asked me, "So what have you been up to, Frank, other than working out and being a member of the Romans?"

I took a deep breath. This was the first time he'd mentioned anything about the Romans in a while. At first I didn't know what to say, but I realized he knew all about my joining the gang because Uncle Louie said he was going to tell him, so now I decided to get right to it. "Dad, if you're not a member of a gang here in Newark, you're pretty much on your own." He'd seen me after the attack at the theatre, so I was pretty sure he understood.

I watched him swallow his food and waited for his reply. "I hope you'll continue to see your mom. She loves it when you visit."

"I promise, Dad, I'll be there Tuesdays and Thursdays and Saturday mornings for sure. Just like always."

It was the following Tuesday when I visited my mom next, and as I walked the two miles home from the hospital, that damn kid, Mikey, along with his brothers this time, were waiting for me.

I was alone and there were three of them. Not good odds. I needed to improve my chances, so I ducked into a local grocery story on my side of the street and bought a raw cold potato that was hard as a rock. I paid the owner a nickel. "I used to eat them raw when I was a kid too, the man said." Before I left, I took off a shoe and a sock and put the potato in the sock. I tied a knot in the sock right behind the big spud so it couldn't move around. By the time I put my shoe back on, the three brothers were right outside the door.

I knew they came to fight so there was no sense in talking. Without saying anything, I charged the biggest kid and hit him flush on the side of the head with my potato sock, and he fell to the sidewalk. He was down and seemed out of it so I wasn't worried about him for now. The second of Mikey's older brothers came at me with his fists raised and rotating them as though he were some kind of professional boxer. I kicked him in the balls so hard that he threw up on his shoes. He gagged and choked and bent over to throw up again, and I slammed the potato sock into the side of his head. This flattened him.

With his two older brothers out of the fight, Mikey turned and ran. I wasn't going to let him get away. I ran after him and tackled him from behind. He fell to the pavement and scraped his cheek pretty bad. I flipped him on his back and climbed on top of him and pounded the piss out of him. He screamed and cried like a baby, so I got up and stood over him. I held my foot on his chest and said, "I warned you to back off. Now you know I meant it. And If I ever hear that you're picking on that little kid with the lunch bag again, I'll knock your fucking teeth out." I kicked him hard in his side for good measure.

His older brothers were just getting to their feet. I started after them, swinging my potato sock over my head, but they began running as best they could and I let them go. "Not bad," I said aloud to myself as I chucked the potato and put on my sock. "Not bad at all".

Over the next few days the story about the three brothers getting their asses kicked was all over school. Joe Cheeks said to me, "I hear they're calling you 'Fast Frankie' because of how fast you can kick. Pretty cool nickname for a new guy." He laughed and slapped me on the back.

I smiled but said, "I don't feel so new anymore."

Time flew, it seemed. Christmas passed and we never even put up a tree. Dad bought mom some perfume so she could smell good even if she was in bed all day. The last time I saw her, two days ago, she looked worse than ever. Yet regardless of how sick she was, I knew by her smile that she was glad to see me. To entertain her, I'd brought several old newspapers with me that I'd picked up from the bakery. I read articles to her about stuff I thought she might like.

"Mom, it says here, back on October 26th, Walt Disney's first television program aired. Too bad they don't have a TV in your room. I turned the page and read the next paper. "On October 28th, the Nobel Prize for Literature went to Ernest Hemingway, not that I've ever read a book by him, but I might read one someday."

I picked up the another old paper and read from the sports section: "The Philadelphia Phillies baseball team is moving to Kansas City, and listen to this, Mom, Ellis Island closed on November 12th of last year."

I read her several articles about the Yankees, but she was almost asleep, so I quickly pulled out my report card.

My mother's hand felt odd, colder than usual, but I didn't know why. "Mom, I have a surprise for you. This report card is for the first half of eighth grade. It's the best Christmas present I can give you. My grades are perfect, all A's. I'm tied with my friend Joe Cheeks for the best grades in the whole school. If I keep this up, I'll go to Stanton Prep and maybe Stanton University, all for free. Mom, I'll get that education we always talked about."

Her sweet face told me how much she loved me and I thought about how much I loved her. I saw her smile briefly as she closed her eyes. I called the nurse just to be sure everything was okay. The nurse came quickly and felt my mom's wrist for a pulse, but there was none so she yelled for the doctor who hurried into the room and checked for her pulse too. I was stunned into silence as a medical team tried to revive her. But she was gone! My mother died just as I had showed her my report card.

In a whisper, I spoke to her again after the doctors and nurses left, thinking she might still hear me, "Mom, I promise I'll go to Stanton Prep and make you proud."

The funeral was awful. I didn't realize until after she was buried how much I would miss my mother and her sweet face. My dad handled her death worse than I did. His grieving went on and on. In order to pay off mom's medical bills, he worked every extra hour he could at all three jobs. I saw him far less than ever, which I wouldn't have thought possible. I spent my time hanging out with the Romans and Zan. I liked her a lot, but not the way I liked Mary Jo.

I was jolted awake by a coal truck which arrived at The Projects. The driver let his load of coal slide down a steel ramp and into the basement. The noise of that rumbling coal sounded like a freight train rushing past my window. No one could possibly sleep through the monthly delivery.

I looked at the calendar hanging from the kitchen wall. Today is March 28, a month after my 15th birthday. I got up, showered and dressed, and walked to breakfast and hummed the number-one song on the radio: "Davy, Davy Crockett, King of the Wild Frontier." Of course everyone watched Fess Parker, the actor who played the lead role on the show, and the song was stuck in my head. Pantello's Bakery was my favorite place for breakfast, and where I was usually joined by Joe Cheeks.

The bakery was busy and crowded as usual. I spotted a customer reading a section of The New York Daily Mirror. The headline proclaimed in large bold print that *On the Waterfront* was the favorite to win the Academy Award for Best Picture and

Marlon Brando the Academy Award for Best Actor. The ceremony was to be broadcast on TV in just four days.

I ordered a cup of coffee and my usual three jelly donuts, but today I was starved and added a Boston cream. As I headed for an open table, I grabbed a discarded newspaper and sat at the rear of the bakery. I wanted to see what was in today's news.

February 3, 1955, President Eisenhower sent the first U.S. military advisors to South Vietnam, the country my uncle mentioned to me back when we moved from Pennsylvania. The President also said, if necessary, he would approve the use of nuclear weapons in war. I wondered if that meant a war in Vietnam, where he'd just sent advisors, or as Uncle Louie said, those advisors were really soldiers. *Enough about war.* I tossed the paper on the next table.

An old copy of the New York Daily News had a story about a polio vaccine that was proving to be effective, developed by a scientist named Jonas Salk. If this were true, the March of Dimes wouldn't be needed anymore. Just like every other kid, I feared getting polio.

I flipped a few pages and read an article about a guy named Ray Kroc who had just opened his first hamburger joint in Illinois, calling it McDonald's. *Who needs another burger joint when we already have White Castle? McDonald's, I predicted, would probably be a failure.*

I was finishing reading about McDonald's when I heard a voice that sounded vaguely familiar, and I lowered the paper to see what face delivered the words. *Oh, yeah, I remembered the voice now, and the words: "Stay out of our territory or your next beatin' won't go so easy."*

Damn, there he was, the same Falcon who beat me up at the movies, sitting just two tables away, eating donuts and drinking coffee, with his back to me. His jacket emblem confirmed he was a Falcon. I checked his boots. There it was in plain sight, the same falcon drawing with the damage to its beak! My heart pounded as adrenaline pumped through my veins. This was the guy who kicked me while I was down. Now I'm I going to return the favor, and this time it's just the two of us.

I stood up calmly and walked up behind the guy as he sat on his chair, munching away on his donut. I tapped the Falcon on his shoulder. He turned and looked up, probably not recognizing me. I cupped my hands behind his head and rammed my knee into his face with such force that it knocked him to the floor. None of the customers in the bakery seemed too surprised because there were gang fights all the time. I jumped on the guy and pounded the hell out of him.

He covered his face as best he could, but I had no mercy after what he and his gang members had done to me at the theatre. I grabbed his two jelly donuts from his table and smeared one on his face and crushed the second donut in his hair and spread the filling around as kind of a jelly shampoo. I poured his hot coffee on his boot, the one with the falcon on it, just as Joe Cheeks came through the front door.

Joe could see what I was doing and smiled at me. "You need help, Bruno?"

"Nope, not with this piece of crap." The Falcon staggered to his feet, and I pushed him toward the front door, which Joe held open. I gave the kid a hard kick in the ass to make sure he made it outside. He fell face-first onto the pavement. "That's for what you did to me at The Stanley, you punk. Now we're even, unless you want more?"

I'd been the talk of the school, but now I was the talk of the neighborhood as well. Frank Bruno was not someone to mess with. I was later told the Falcon had some kind of problem with his jaw, and maybe it was broken. Bad blood between our gangs was not about to end anytime soon.

At the end of the school year my grades were at the top in the class, and as I'd promised my mom just before she died, I received a full scholarship to Stanton Prep. Joe Cheeks finished just behind me and was awarded the other scholarship.

CHAPTER NINE

Simon Silverman: 1954
Eighth Grade: Milltown

One more year to go and I'd be in high school—that's if I survived eighth grade. Harold Higgins, picked on me from the first day. He was a big kid and a bigger bully. Everyone knew him by his red hair. He'd failed fourth grade, but after two years with the same grammar-school teacher, rumor had it that she passed him just to get him out of her class. The following year he failed fifth grade, which didn't seem to bother him at all.

On the first day of school I heard from Dave that Mrs. Warnsdorfer, our principal, demanded that Red Hair's father meet with her before the boy would be allowed back in school. Since he was sixteen and still in grammar school, Mrs. Warnsdorfer had the right to refuse his attendance.

In a rush, Higgins's dad drove a mud-splattered pickup into the school parking lot. He got out, spit, and displayed a disgusted look. He was wearing dirty overalls. I listened in the hallway outside the principal's office, and there was a lot of arguing and yelling going on inside. Mrs. Warnsdorfer was a tough old German lady, and she'd been in charge of McGinnis School for as long as anyone could remember, maybe from the time the place was built. I knew she was friends with Dave's grandmother, because one day I was at her house with Dave when the two ladies were playing pinochle with friends.

Mrs. Warnsdorfer took no crap from anyone, even when it came to Higgins's father, who was as big as a house. As for Red Hair, his best grades were D's. He never studied or did any homework. He was also absent on a lot on Fridays and the following Mondays. Kids said they saw him working for his father on construction jobs when he was supposed to be in school.

Higgins bragged to anyone who would listen: "Getting good grades is for bookworms and jerks. I've got a job. I make real money. By the time I get to my freshman year, I'll have a car and you dopes will still be walking. So who's stupid now?" He cursed a lot. "I don't give a shit about school. I'm quitting in a year or two anyway. Maybe sooner." I could only hope it would be sooner rather than later.

I tried to avoid Red Hair, but he would routinely wait for my school bus to arrive in the morning. When I got off the bus, he'd mess-up my hair and push me around. He liked to knock my books to the ground, especially if it was raining. He often took my lunch bag and helped himself to my peanut-butter-and-jelly sandwiches, and he took my candy if I had any.

As soon as I tried to gather up my books, he'd kick them and send everything flying. One of his favorite pranks was to tear up my homework and hold it over his head and let the wind blow it away. I'd scramble to pick up the pieces, and I had no choice but to Scotch tape everything back together as best I could. This happened so often that I carried my own roll of

Scotch tape.

He called me Four Eyes and Fag Boy; also Bucky the Beaver because of my front teeth. There were kids who followed him around, not because they liked him but only because they were afraid of him. They laughed when he laughed and repeated what he said when he called me names. Hate isn't a good enough word for how much I despised Higgins. I wanted to kill him, but there was nothing much I could do. He outweighed me by sixty pounds, so there was no chance I could handle him in a fight.

Other than satisfaction with my studies, sixth and seventh grades had been generally miserable for me, so I expected eighth grade would be bad too. Higgins was proving this to be true, and on many Tuesdays, Wednesdays, and Thursdays I feigned illness, but my mother always took my temperature and made me go to school. I knew the damn kid would be waiting by the bus stop, so sometimes I got off the bus early by running up to the driver and telling him I was going to throw up. Once off the bus, I'd hide behind some hedges until school started. Yeah, I was late for class, but it was better than facing Higgins.

I begged my parents for help. My father told me he couldn't do anything because we weren't citizens and the authorities might arrest us and send us back to Germany. I asked my mother to hire someone to beat Higgins to a pulp, but she said that was against the law. I begged my father to get a lawyer to make Higgins stop bullying me, but my dad refused to get involved. I even thought about taking a kitchen knife with me to stab Red Hair, but I was afraid I'd go to jail. Eighth grade was plain awful.

My mom often gave me money to buy ice cream in the school cafeteria, and Red Hair had seen me paying for it. So the next day he turned my pockets inside out and took the money he found on me. I began hiding coins in my shoes. The whole thing became so unbearable that I again pleaded with my father for help. Instead, he yelled at me, "Just bear it, Simon, it can't be all that bad. You'll get through this grade and go to high school next year. By then the kid will forget about you."

Higgins was bigger than every other kid except Donald Moore, and he never tried picking on him. A month after school started I asked Donald to help me. I offered to give him my ice-cream money every day for a month if he would punch Higgins in the nose, but he told me, "I can't fight your battles, Simon. You have to learn to fight them for yourself." What could I say to that?

One day Higgins messed-up Dave Nenninger's hair and my friend kicked him hard in the shin, which started a fight. When Higgins bent over to rub his shin, I have to say that Dave got in two good punches. He also managed to get Higgins in a headlock, but Red Hair soon overpowered Dave and threw him to the ground. He was just too big, and he moved on top of Dave and started swinging away but Dave bit his hand. The fight ended a minute later because a couple of teachers broke it up and took both boys to the principal's office. Red Hair's eye had started to swell up, and some of the kids who'd watched thought that Dave had won. But on the way home my friend showed me the bruises under his shirt. He'd taken a good beating.

Dave told me what happened in the principal's office: "She demanded to know who started this fight. I'm positive Mrs. Warnsdorfer likes me because of the way she talks to me when she's at grandma's house playing cards. I answered her questions before Higgins could say anything. I said, 'Look how big this kid is compared to me. Do you think I'm crazy enough to start a fight with him?'"

"What happened then," I wanted to know.

"She told me to return to class. I got out of her office as fast as I could but I listened outside her door. She scolded Red Hair, telling him that she was sick and tired of his behavior. She finished by yelling at him, 'You are expelled for a month.'"

"I hope Red Hair quits school for good," I said to Dave.

"He's going to be gone for a month, this means he'll probably fail eighth grade. I just hope the piece of dog shit has to stay here in grammar school. That way we won't have to see him until our sophomore year of high school." We talked about it some more and decided he'd likely quit school and we'd never see him again.

Even though Red Hair wasn't at school, my troubles weren't over. In the few remaining weeks of eighth grade, Mr. Dickerson, the homeroom teacher everyone called Mr. Dick Head, became my new problem. I couldn't avoid him because I had to report to homeroom every morning. Luckily, because I was in the advanced college programs, he didn't teach any of my classes. He only taught basic stuff, like spelling and geography.

Mr. Dick Head, like Red Hair, never stopped harassing me. From his remarks, it was clear he hated me because I was Jewish. "Where's your little beanie hat?" he ridiculed me by asking. "Why do all Jews have buck teeth? Why are all Jews little shrimps like you, with no backbones? Why do your people marry your cousins?" His comments continued from one day to the next. A few kids found him funny, which seemed to inspire him to be even meaner to me.

I ignored his taunts and refused to answer him. I just half-smiled and looked straight ahead. With a month to go, I figured I could tolerate anything. What he seemed to hate most was that I was about to graduate eighth grade at the top of my class and would be the valedictorian at our commencement ceremony. There was nothing he could do to prevent this, as I'd earned straight A's in every class I took.

With only a couple of days left in the school year, I sat in my homeroom seat and waited for the bell to sound. Final exams were tomorrow, and I had been studying during every spare minute.

My good buddy Dave was not quite so academically inclined. He was always flirting with the prettiest girl in school, Pat Dohn, a really cute blond. He had a big crush on her, and lately she was all he talked about. But Pat was six months older than Dave, and it seemed to me she was too mature for my friend. That didn't deter him though, and he couldn't take his eyes off her and her bulging bust. I had to admit she was awesome-looking, but just like all the rest of the girls in my school, she wouldn't give me a second glance even if I were dying.

Classes started in a few minutes, and my desk was covered with my study notes. I crumpled everything together and walked over to the wastepaper basket in the front of the classroom and tossed them in but one piece missed its mark and fell on the floor. I bent down and picked it up, but Mr. Dick Head yelled out, "I saw that, Simple Simon, now pick it up."

Since I'd already snatched the scrap off the floor, I wondered why he was making such a big deal of this. Yet nothing surprised me when it came to Mr. Dick Head. I dropped the errant piece of paper in the basket and went to sit down. Dickerson sprang from his desk and rushed toward me. He grabbed the full wastepaper basket and dumped the contents on the wooden floor and screamed at me, "Pick it up Simple Simon... all of it."

Everyone in the classroom stopped talking and watched what

was happening. I felt like a fool, but I put everything back in the basket. When finished I turned to go to my seat, but Dickerson stepped in front of me and shouted, "Stop right there, Simple Simon." I froze, scared of what the prick would do next.

Same as before, this rotten excuse for a teacher dumped everything on the floor. "Try it again, and this time do it right," he said, strutting back and forth in front of the classroom, arms folded across his chest, glaring at me the whole time. I was so embarrassed that I started to cry. A silent minute passed as I knelt on the floor, shaking with tears running down my face as I placed the trash back into the wastepaper basket.

Dave start booing. Donald Moore joined him, as did Billy, a kid I knew somewhat, and the rest of the class began sounding off as well. The girls, including pretty Pat and her friend, Alice joined in. Wow, Dickerson had acted like a jerk and the class was taking up my side. They were booing him, and were on my side! After the bell sounded Dickerson rushed from the room, and a lot of the kids came over and said they felt bad for me. I thanked everyone and all of a sudden I felt great

There was really nothing to do on the last two days of school, no more studying and no more tests, so we took long recesses, playing a game called Red Rover that had us all running back and forth. The boys liked it because they got to watch the girls—and their boobs bounce around when they ran. As luck would have it, Dickerson was in charge of recess for the entire day. A small man, he was 5 feet 5 and 135 pounds soaking wet.

He stood there, his arms folded over his chest, as if he were a big deal. Dick Head held a stern look on his face as he watched the game. He seemed to be watching Pat as she ran past him. Suddenly, my friend Dave snuck up behind him and locked his arms around Dick Head's body, pinning his arms at his side.

Dave was pretty strong for fourteen, and he was a few inches taller than Dickerson. He lifted the teacher off his feet and held him there. This wasn't supposed to happen to teachers, so the Red Rover game came to a halt as the class turned its attention to Dave and his hold on Dickerson.

He struggled to get away but Dave continued to keep the teachers feet from touching the ground. Dickerson's face turned red, and all the kids, Pat and Alice included, started laughing at him. Dick Head didn't look so authoritative as he kicked and twisted and turned, trying to get loose. His efforts were to no avail. Finally he screamed, "Put me down, dammit! Let me go! I demand you let me go!"

Dave released Dickerson, pushed him away, and said, "How does it feel to be picked on, Mr. Dickerson? Next time, try someone your own size." I noticed that Dave had balled up his fists. I was surprised that any kid would take on a teacher knowing he would be punished by the principal, maybe even expelled. Dave Nenninger was a true friend.

Dickerson cursed and straightened his suit jacket and tie. He glared at Dave but ran his hand through his crew-cut and quickly walked toward the safety of the school building. I'm sure he was angry as hell, but if he'd taken a swing at Dave, the entire class probably would have helped Dave, as everybody in the eighth grade hated Dick Head.

But it wasn't over. Not yet! The boys wanted to get even with Dickerson for what he had done to me with the waste basket. We were still on the playground when Donald Moore called us together and said, "I've got an idea for how we can get Dick Head real good. He loves his new MG. If we work as a team, we can embarrass him in front of the whole school. Here's the plan. We'll meet after school...."

Dickerson's shiny new red MG was parked in the teachers'

parking lot, which was considered off limits for students. But not today. Four of the strongest boys hurried to the front of the tiny car, four more of us went to each side, and four kids went to the rear, including Donald, who might have been able to pick up the back end all by himself.

We lifted the car, turned it sideways and placed it so it now sat between the two cars in the adjacent parking spots. The space was so tight that the MG couldn't be driven away without one of the other cars being moved first.

One of the kids had made a perfect cardboard copy of a New Jersey license plate that read: "Mr. Dick Head." He screwed it in place over the real tag. Our school busses left without us, and we all sat on wooden benches near the parking lot and waited.

The secretary from the principal's office walked to her car and saw the MG turned sideways. She laughed and held her fingers to her lips and went back inside. In a few minutes a slew of teachers came out, all apparently wanting to see what Dickerson would do. It wasn't just our class who didn't like Mr. Dick Head, it seemed everyone thought he was a jerk.

Finally Dickerson appeared. He strutted toward the teachers' lot carrying his brief case and jacket and noticed us sitting there. As he got closer, he saw what we had done. He stood there with one hand on his hip while we laughed and pointed at him. We started letting go with catcalls, the noise attracting even more teachers.

He did his best to threaten us: "If you have damaged my car in any way at all, I'll sue each one of you." We yelled louder and laughed as he raced around, flapping his arms, needing to find one of the teachers whose car was parked next to his so it could be moved and he'd escape his humiliation.

Word spread throughout the school, and soon almost every teacher and staff worker was standing in the parking lot. Most laughed at the situation. I wondered why Mrs. Warnsdorfer never appeared, which could have meant big problems. But she never showed. Maybe she secretly despised Dickerson, too, and wanted to let him suffer. Finally, one of the cars was moved and he sped off, never noticing the "Mr. Dick Head" license plate.

Weather was perfect for graduation day. Parents sat on folding chairs on the front lawn of the school. And here I was, at the head of the first row because I'd earned the best grades. I was the only student scheduled to speak. I wanted to come up with some clever remarks but just spoke about "going forward" and left it at that. It wasn't very special or inspiring, but I smiled the whole time. At the end of my brief speech, every person in attendance stood and cheered. My mom stood and clapped her hands as hard as she could, but my dad, fearing Nazis might be there waiting for him, stayed home.

The only teacher who wasn't there was Mr. Dickerson. Little did Mr. Dickerson know that Dave's father was recently appointed to the school board when another board member resigned.

Dave had told his dad about the wastepaper incident, at dinner that night and about Dickerson's constant slurs against my religion. Dave's father, a German who hated everything the Nazis stood for, was furious about the ethnic remarks and my being forced to pick up wastepaper multiple times. The president of the board looked into the charges and agreed with Dave's father. Mr. Dickerson was fired the morning of graduation.

I was happy. No longer did I have to contend with Red Hair's physical abuse or Mr. Dick Head's insults. *New Town High School, here I come.*

CHAPTER TEN

Frank Bruno: September 1955
Freshman Year: Stanton Prep

I never liked opening the mail because it seemed that it never brought any good news. Mostly it was bills, stuff about sales at Sears or Bamberger's, or coupons for discounts at the grocery store, but this morning I opened a letter addressed to me that Dad had left by the coffee pot. It was from Sacred Heart Catholic School.

It said that I was to come to the principal's office. Since I had already graduated from eighth grade, I figured it must be about my scholarship to Stanton Prep. And if I got a letter, Joe must have received one too. I gobbled down a bowl of Cheerios with banana slices and hurried to the bakery, where Joe and I met almost every morning.

He was on his second Boston cream. He dropped his letter on the table and grinned with his crooked jaws. "I assume you got one of these too."

'Yeah," I said, "mine is right here." I pulled the letter from my Romans jacket and showed it to my friend. "Sister Elizabeth Ann wants to see us. I figure it has to be something about prep school because we're the two scholarship winners."

"*After* I finish my donuts, *then* we go see Sister Elizabeth Ann. By the way, I hope this meeting with her doesn't take too long. I landed a job at the RKO Theatre as a cleanup guy. People are still coming in droves to see *On the Waterfront*. The next movie, *Marty*, is supposed to be a big hit too. Ernest Borgnine is the star. Anyway, today's my first day and I have to be at work by noon." Joe tilted his head and smiled. "They need more help, if you're ever interested, Frank."

"You got to be kidding. The RKO is a dump. The carpets are stained and worn out. The kids call it 'The Scratch' because of the cockroaches and fleas. The place is so filthy they should give out free tickets and lice combs. One of our guys worked at the RKO last summer. He told me the balcony was known as 'Condom Heaven.' Why would you want to work there? Anyway, I got a job at my uncle's gym, so I'll stay where I am."

Joe shrugged his shoulders. "I need the job, and it's all I can get right now that's steady. You're lucky to have a job at your uncle's gym. You get free pizza and self-defense training by one of the best. Look how much bigger you are than last year. You must be ten pounds heavier, maybe more. And it's all muscle."

"Actually, closer to twelve pounds." I picked up a paper from another table and read that the Yankees had clinched the pennant on Mickey Mantle's 50th homerun, but my mind was on the letter from school. We finished our food and headed out.

The secretary was expecting us, so after buzzing Sister Elizabeth Ann she led us into her office. Arms crossed, and dressed in black as always, Sister remained the ultimate figure of authority. She motioned for Joe and me to take a seat and said, "This will take a few minutes, so you might as well get comfortable."

Sister Elizabeth Ann started her instructions by saying, "I want to talk to you about preparatory school. You should know that Stanton is a Roman Catholic university started by Archbishop James Roosevelt Bayley, who was a cousin of President Theodore Roosevelt. He named the school after his aunt, Elizabeth Ann Stanton, who by the way is no relation to me. The goal for the school is still the same today as it was back then, which is to bring young Catholic men into higher education. Do either of you have any questions so far?"

Joe and I looked at each other and shook our heads in unison.

She continued, "Stanton Prep started this scholarship program four years ago. We send our two top students with the best marks every year, but there's been an issue. Not one young man has made it through the first year, and for this reason no one has ever attended Stanton University. I am quite sure I know the reason why this occurs, and I am going to share that information with you. But you must keep this to yourselves. Do you both understand me?"

This time we nodded in unison.

"The school is run by the Irish, and they *do not*, I repeat, they *do not* like Italians, especially Italians from Newark. They don't want any of you getting a free education to what they consider to be *their* school. Irishmen are on the board, and the Irish make up more than half the faculty. On top of that, the headmaster is Irish and—"

"That doesn't seem very fair," Joe said. I thought that Sister might snap at him for interrupting her, but her tone even softened a bit.

"Nothing about this is fair. Wealthy Italians boys from other areas don't have the same problem students from Newark have experienced. The headmaster is Father O'Brien. He has seen to it that all six of the young men from Sacred Heart have been pushed out, one way or another, before their freshman year was completed. So I am warning you, Father O'Brien will be looking for any reason to dismiss you permanently."

Joe asked Sister Elizabeth Ann why she didn't take this problem to the Trenton archdiocese and ask the Cardinal to talk with Father O'Brien. "I have done that," she said, maintaining her somewhat subdued tone. "Several times in fact, but it seems that the word of a priest carries more weight than that of a nun, even a nun who is in charge of a major Catholic school like this one."

She rose from her big leather chair and stood over me. "Mr. Bruno, you have quite a reputation on the street. I know more about you than you think I know, and I'm telling you that no matter what they do, no matter how many times they call you names, no matter what they say about Italians or about this school, you have to maintain self-control. You must ignore them. That also applies to you, Mr. Giardello." Now she raised her voice, and it was piercing. "Do you two boys understand me?"

We both replied in unison, "Yes, Sister."

"Good," she said and retook her seat. "After the first week at Stanton Prep, the two of you are to come here and report to me. I want to know everything that happened. I will expect to see you next Saturday morning, in this office, at around this same time."

We nodded.

"There are some additional things you need to know. Your tuition, books, and cafeteria meals are paid for. You have to wear a blue blazer and a white shirt and a tie every day. You must take the Number Nine bus on South Orange Avenue, and you will have to pay for that. It is only a matter of a few blocks from here, but I strongly suggest you do not walk to school. If you walk, there are too many opportunities for trouble along the way." She paused and looked from one of us to the other.

"We understand," I said, speaking for Joe as well as myself.

"I'm glad you do," she said. "You are to arrive early, before the rest of the students, and stay in your homeroom until class starts. Sit together at assemblies and try not to be noticed. Absolutely no gang jackets are allowed, and avoid getting into fights, no matter the provocation. Do you both clearly follow what I'm saying?"

Again, our response was the same: "Yes, sister." But I thought about it a moment and asked, "What are we supposed to do if one of them starts a fight? We might have no choice but to defend ourselves."

"You have to learn to do what Jesus did, and turn the other cheek,'" she said, without the slightest hesitation. "Then you must walk away. Mr. Bruno, this is your one chance for a free education at the top prep school in New Jersey. If you graduate, the prep school is your opportunity to get out of Newark forever. But you have to avoid trouble."

I closed my eyes for a moment, took a deep breath, and said, "Sister, I'll do my best, but it's not my nature to run from trouble. It just doesn't work. Bullies get worse if they think you're afraid of them. But I promised my mother I'd get an education, and I'll take your advice."

We stood up to leave, but Sister Elizabeth Ann raised her hand to stop us. "One more thing. Stay away from a senior by the name of Jack O'Brien. He's the nephew of Father O'Brien, and the boy's a trouble maker. Young Mr. O'Brien is a big part of the reason why the all the boys from Sacred Heart have been expelled."

———

"All of them?" I asked.

"Yes. Every one of them. So you must always keep on your toes." The O'Brien kid has a huge protector in the headmaster. This could be a real problem.

As we walked home, I said to Joe, "Even though we just got this warning about not starting a fight, hearing what that O'Brien punk did to the other Sacred Heart guys makes me want to kick his ass."

Joe nodded but said, "Frank, from what Sister said, that's probably just what the good priest wants you to do."

Something else was bothering me about what Sister Elizabeth Ann had said. "What do the Irish have against Italians?" Joe had no response.

Stanton Prep School opened on Tuesday, September 3rd, the day after Labor Day. Joe and I boarded the Number 9 bus on South Orange Avenue and arrived at the campus early, as instructed. We paused to admire the Immaculate Conception Chapel and read the plaque that told us that construction on the Stanton University campus had started way back in 1863, during the height of The Civil War. There was no such plaque for the prep school, so I assumed it was built much later.

Other students began arriving. They were dressed the same as Joe and me but in better-looking blue blazers than we had on. Dad got mine at the Goodwill store, the same as where Joe's parents found his. Our ill-fitting, frayed coats weren't our only differences, as our duck's-ass haircuts, scuffed shoes, and ties an old man would wear also set us apart. But at least we were here.

We were directed by signs to the gymnasium, where we took a seat on the bleachers and waited for instructions. Banners hung from the rafters, displaying Stanton University's many basketball championships. I had never been in a gym this large or one with such perfect hardwood floors. Being a boy's school, of course there were no female students, and the few colored guys I noticed sat huddled together, similar to Joe and me.

The bell sounded at exactly 8 a.m. and a man in a dark-blue suit came to a podium on the temporary stage set up in the middle of the gym. He mumbled his name, which I couldn't understand, but he cleared his throat and began speaking clearly: "All classes start on time, and lunch is served in the cafeteria from noon until two." He babbled on about the usual stuff before adding, "Stanton Preparatory School is based on the strict doctrines of the Catholic religion and its principles, and we are renowned for providing the best high-school education in New Jersey. All freshmen must take the mandatory courses, which are biology, algebra, English, math, American history, and religious studies. Only upperclassmen can take electives, which means courses of their choosing. If you do not have your schedule yet, when this assembly ends form a line to the right of this stage and one of our staff will help you."

A half-hour later the man finished, and Father O'Brien, wearing a most impressive purple and gold gown, took the stage and introduced himself and said, "I have a few simple words of advice for all new students: I strongly suggest you obey the rules and study hard. But I have to warn you, one third of you will not graduate from this school. Don't be one of the third who doesn't make it."

The first week went by quickly, and Joe and I had no problems with anyone. On Saturday morning we reported back to Sister Elizabeth Ann as she'd requested and told her that the week went very well. The only complaint Joe and I had involved the amount of homework.

She smiled at that and reminded us again that we were always to arrive early for school. Then she said, "Avoid the student union." She must have read my mind because she added, "It's where the upperclassmen congregate, and trouble can start there in a hurry." *The boys who'd been kicked out must have told her this.*

That Saturday night, with my dad's permission, I invited Zan to our apartment to watch Elvis Presley perform live on *The Ed Sullivan Show*. Zan and I thought Elvis was great. "The King," as his fans called him, sang "Blue Suede Shoes" and "Hound Dog," but the TV cameras never showed him below the waist because he swiveled his hips to the music, which was considered obscene and not for a general TV audience. By the end of September, Elvis had sold ten-million copies, and his *obscene* hip movements were all anyone talked about, which I'm sure boosted his sales a lot.

The month of September passed and Joe and I still had no problems, and we certainly hadn't looked for trouble. On the first of October, signups for walk-on basketball players were posted around the campus, so I tried out for the team. My neighborhood games had gained me a lot of good experience, and I more than held my own against many of the guys who had athletic scholarships called "full-rides," which paid for everything.

Joe didn't try to make the team because his job as an usher at the RKO and required working Fridays and weekends. Joe often got me free tickets to shows. On Saturday, compliments of Joe, Zan and I saw *The Ten Commandments*, which starred Yul Brenner and Charlton Heston. Zan and I liked the movie, but the theatre was still a dump and we wished we'd brought towels to put over our stained seats.

Monday came fast, and after classes I continued my tryout

for the team. The colored kids I'd seen at the assembly were all basketball players and guaranteed a place on the roster. Practices were hard and the play rough, but I was used to shoving and elbowing, and most of the other walk-ons stopped showing up before the first week of tryouts was over.

The following Monday, Coach put me in against a tall, skinny Negro. I had the ball and backed him toward the basket, gave him a well-placed elbow that knocked him off-balance, and I scored. This was nothing new for me, and neither was the hard play. But Coach blew the whistle because of my elbow, and for every elbow I threw after that. He also whistled me for pushing or grabbing the man I was guarding. But he seemed to like me, and with his advice my game became smoother. Three weeks later, Coach told me I'd made the team, along with another walk-on.

Just one other player on the team had an Italian name, a young guy named Chuck Gallopo. He and I became friends, both on and off the court. Chuck was tall and slender, and he'd gone to a private grammar school before coming to Stanton Prep. He was a serious student, and joined Joe and me in the library as study partners. We all avoided the student union.

It was still early in the school year, but I liked Stanton Prep more and more as the weeks rolled on. Sister Elizabeth Ann was pleased with what Joe and I continued to report, and I could tell she was surprised that we had encountered no problems with any other students.

Once I made the basketball team, a lot of classmates said hello to me in the hallways, calling me by my first name. I found it a little odd that they knew who I was but I didn't know them. Oh, well, it felt good. Our first game was against St. Benedict's Prep. I didn't expect to play much, if at all, but one of our starting forwards turned his ankle just before halftime, and Coach called my name. I was excited, and when I stepped on the floor the whole thing seemed natural to me. I was back in the neighborhood with the guys.

Chuck was the other forward. Time was about to run out for the half, and he passed the ball to me and raced toward the basket. It was a classic "give-and-go," and I passed the ball right back to him and he scored. Chuck's basket put us up by four points just as the buzzer went off, and the students in the stands stood and cheered.

Chuck and I dominated the scoring in the third quarter, with Calvin Jones, our center, getting almost every rebound. By the end of the third quarter we were ahead by twelve, and we won by double digits.

Three days later I started the game against St. Peter's, a school in New Brunswick, and we beat this team too. Our forward with the bad ankle sat on the bench, in street clothes. For the time being I was a starter, and it felt great.

In our third game we played St. John's Prep. Going into this game both teams had the same record, three wins and no losses, but the "Redmen" were ranked ahead of us in the polls.

St. John's led by three at the half. At the start of the third quarter I scored two baskets in a row. I turned to go on defense when the guy who'd been guarding me pushed me into the stands. I was back on the floor in an instant and shoved him so hard that he landed on his back. I clenched my fists and circled him, challenging him to a fight. I was about to kick him in the ribs when Coach grabbed me from behind, pulling me away as the refs went crazy, blowing their whistles and waving their arms like wild men.

Referees and coaches kept both teams apart as players shouted, threatened, cursed, and tried to grab each other. The kid who'd started it was thrown out, but I was tossed, too, for

---

challenging him to fight. My getting kicked out of the game hurt us more than the other guy's leaving harmed St. Johns, because he was second-string. Not having my scoring was bad enough, but late in the fourth quarter Calvin Jones fouled out and we wound up losing the game.

On the bus ride back to our school, Coach gave our team a lecture, which was clearly aimed at me: "This isn't the playground. You lose your cool and we lose the game. If they commit a foul, go to the foul line and make them pay. Fighting will get you kicked out every time." He was right about everything. I'd lost my cool and it cost us the game.

Our next game was against Delbarton, which we won. I did okay scoring-wise but fouled out in the fourth quarter. Chuck and Calvin played well, and our guards had just three turnovers in the second half. I started the next game against Fordham Prep, but I got into foul trouble early, and the kid I'd replaced now took my spot in the lineup. He hit a few jump shots and was four for four from the foul line. I sat on the bench and watched. We won barely, no thanks to me.

The next day, Coach called me into his office and told me to sit down. He paced back and forth. "You're a definite starter, Bruno—if you can stay out of foul trouble, and you have to control your temper better." He stopped pacing and sat on the edge of his desk and half-smiled at me. "I need you on the floor, not sitting on your ass, riding the bench with fouls. You're one of the best walk-ons I've ever coached. If you're on the floor, we can win the league championship. If not, we might not even make the playoffs." He took in a big breath and exhaled slowly. "Think about it. Not many freshmen walk-ons ever make this team, but with you we have a shot to win it all. But you have to stay on the floor."

I got the message. I had bad habits I would have to change.

What was okay on the playground wasn't working here.

CHAPTER ELEVEN

1956: Stanton Prep
Good Days and Bad

Stanton Prep against Madison Prep was an easy win for us. Calvin Jones and Chuck played well, and so did I. I started the game and scored in double figures by the end of the third quarter. Coach pulled me and played the other forward. After the win, we celebrated in the visitor's locker room, and Coach gave a rousing pep talk. We were really coming together as a team. The only problem was a kid named Bobby Murphy, a second-string guard who I'd learned was a friend of Jack O'Brien's. Bobby had always kept his distance, as if there was something wrong between the two of us.

It was Thursday afternoon, and our game against The Hun School was at home. Since our record was five wins and one loss, the stands were full. Coach started me. The guy trying to guard me was too frail to keep me from going wherever I wanted to go, and he fouled out by halftime. I was too strong for his replacement as well, and at the end of the third quarter

Coach gave me a breather.

We were up by sixteen points when someone yelled from *our* stands, "Go home, you Guinea grease ball." I don't know why, but I had a feeling Jack O'Brien was behind it, and that he'd introduce himself sooner or later. For now, however, I didn't even know what he looked like.

With a month to go in the first semester, I was tied with Chuck Gallopo for the best grades in the freshman class. We were just a notch ahead of Joe Cheeks, who got a B in a biology exam because he couldn't identify the location of a frog's liver. I knew the answer because Uncle Louie had trained me to kick a guy in the liver, which was on the right side of a person's back. It didn't dawn on me that some animals might be different, so I'd got it right.

As for the rest of school, I kept my nose in my books. Other than classes, basketball practice, and the games, I tried my best not to get noticed. Weeknights were spent at Uncle Louie's gym, with Zan and the Romans. Zan was fine, but she wasn't Mary Jo.

I saw my dad less than when my mom was alive, and at times I missed him almost as much as my mother. Thanksgiving and a short school week were coming up, and we had a game on Tuesday. I met Joe at the bakery before we hopped on the Number 9 bus. The financial section from The Star Ledger had been left on an empty table so I grabbed it and read the headline. The Dow Jones industrial average had hit 500 points for the first time ever.

Since I didn't know anyone who owned stock, I turned the page. There was a story about the average family income for 1956, which was projected to be $3,532 dollars for a typical household of four. I wondered how much my dad earned, even with working three jobs. If he earned that average, he probably owed a lot more than that for mom's medical bills.

I found the entertainment section stuck inside of the financial pages. I said to Joe, "I guess you already know that *Around the World in 80 Days* with David Niven will be opening soon. It looks to me that you'll be busy at the RKO." He groaned, no doubt unhappy at the prospects of all the theatre's seats being filled at every show and how much extra work that meant for him.

When we got to class, a folded-over piece of paper with the word "Bruno" was the desk where I usually sat. It read: "Hey guineas get out of our school." I handed the note to Joe, who sat in the desk in front of mine, and I said, "Looks like trouble is coming our way. If not for my promise to my mother to get an education, I'd skip this class and go find Jack O'Brien and kick the shit out of him right not, even if he didn't send the note."

We played Lawrenceville Prep on Tuesday evening and won by twelve. Coach was really happy with me and said, "Only two fouls, Frank. Nice work. You're looking a lot better."

A sock hop was scheduled for the next evening in the Stanton Prep gym. I asked Zan to go with me but she said, "No way, I hate those snobs up there. I don't think you should go either. Trouble always starts at dances."

I was going to take Zan's warning and skip the dance, but Chuck stopped me in the hall on Wednesday morning and said he had a cousin visiting his family for Thanksgiving. He wanted to know if I'd take her to the sock hop. He said that Camille, who was almost eighteen, was "experienced." At that remark I couldn't resist, and I readily agreed to Chuck's offer. He said he'd bring Camille to the dance, along with his girlfriend, and he'd drive me home afterwards. Everything seemed perfect, and the best part was that Zan would never know.

When Joe and I took the bus home after school, I told him what was going on. When I mentioned the "experienced" part, Joe said, "Frank, my friend, it could be your lucky night."

I showered and put on my only good slacks, which I'd worn just a couple of times, polished my shoes, and put on a light-blue shirt of my dad's and rolled up the sleeves. After a quick bite to eat, I headed back to the campus on another Number 9 bus and waited outside the auditorium for Chuck. It was early evening when I saw him drive up in a car I assumed was his dad's.

He held open the car door for his girlfriend and introduced her to me, but I didn't hear her name, I was so occupied by his cousin in the backseat. The dark-haired beauty stepped out and gave me a kiss on my cheek and said, "I'm Camille. I'm your date. I hope you're not disappointed." I almost fell over, this girl was that good looking.

"Wow, how could I be disappointed! You look terrific!" I stood back and admired her dress— and of course the tall awesome body that filled it out.

The four of us headed inside, and before long we all got a bit drunk on punch spiked with what I guessed was whiskey. I'd been told that this dance would be well supervised, but I guess not *that* well. Camille and I danced one jitterbug after another. Finally the DJ played a slow song. Camille was a great slow dancer and sexy as hell. I took a deep breath and inhaled her light perfume. She smelled good as we danced together. I thought I could feel her heartbeat, or maybe it was my own.

After the dance ended, she was right at my side and we both got another cup of punch. The booze was really hitting me, and I could tell by her giggles that she was feeling it too. Later, when there was another slow dance, we were in a tight embrace and moving slowly on the dance floor when someone bumped into me. I turned to see who it was but didn't know the guy. I was going to ignore him, thinking it was an accident, when he said, "That was from Jack O'Brien. He says hello."

The guy was older than me, probably a senior and about my height. I got a few inches from his face and rammed the heel of my shoe down hard on his toe and smiled. "Tell Jack, as soon as he finds his balls, to come and say hello for himself. Or maybe Jack is just a chicken shit who sends puppies like you to do his yapping."

The pain on the guys face showed how much I'd hurt him. He said nothing but hobbled off. Camille asked who the guy was, and at the same time said she wanted one more drink. I'd had enough, so I grabbed a cup of punch for her. She wanted to go outside for some air, and I was all for this. I spotted Chuck and his girlfriend smooching on the far side of the dance floor, so I don't think either of them saw us leave.

Camille and I looked at the stars, which were twinkling in a cloudless night sky. With no hint she was going to do this, she gave me a long, deep French kiss while a slow song played in the background.

With her next breath she asked me to show her the campus. As we walked, she took my arm and placed it around her waist. A short while later she stopped, kissed me passionately again, and said, "Frankie, let's go see the dorms."

"I think they're all locked up tight for the holiday," I replied, not knowing what to say.

"Some of them must be open so mommy and daddy can see where their little boys are living." She gave me a devious smile that made my heart pound even faster than it was already racing.

We headed into the first building with a light on, and we

—————

117

climbed the stairs to the second floor. We tried one door after another until one of them opened and we stepped inside. Camille said, "Lock it, but don't turn on the lamp or someone might find us. Put the light on in the bathroom and just crack the door enough so we can see. Then hurry up and take your clothes off."

I took care of the lighting situation, got undressed, and sat on the bed—but I wasn't sure what she wanted to do next so I waited. Camille reached in her purse and handed me a condom. "Frankie, you've done this before, right?"

I tried to sound confident, saying, "Sure, more than once." She had to know I was lying, but all she did was laugh softly.

I tried to put on the rubber but I fumbled with it. Camille smiled and said, "Here, let me help you." She held my dick in her hand and almost made me cum before I did anything. Then she pushed me on my back and got on top of me and whispered, "Let a woman show you how she likes sex."

Camille was certainly "experienced." She rocked back and forth on me so enthusiastically that it was over way before I wanted it to be finished. We lay on the bed for a few minutes, kissing each other and saying little, when she began rubbing me. After a cleanup with a hand towel and a fresh condom, we started making love again, this time for much longer. She was smiling at the end, which made me think I'd done okay. We dressed and hurried back to the dance before Chuck and his girlfriend might miss us.

On the way back to my dad's apartment, Camille and I whispered to each other in the backseat while Chuck drove and his girlfriend rested her head on his shoulder. I promised Camille, if she visited Chuck's family for Christmas, I would definitely be her date.

We were one of four basketball teams to make the playoffs, and we won our first game. We were now in the championship game, which was on our home court because of a coin flip. But the team we faced was St. John's. Coach lectured us before the game: "St. John's beat us earlier this season. But that was then. Right now, we're the best team. Let's show them and everybody else who we are. Play defense, keep your cool, no stupid fouls and we'll win the championship." I wouldn't lose this game for us by getting egged into a pushing match again.

We started strong. We hit from the outside against their zone defense, and when they switched to a man-to-man Calvin Jones scored in the middle. He also grabbed almost every rebound on both ends of the court, which was nothing new for him. In the second quarter, Chuck continued to score from the outside, and I muscled my way to the rim a few times. Bobby Murphy was now playing guard, which I never understood because a colored kid was way better. At the half we led by a single point.

As we walked from the locker room to start the second half, Coach motioned me to his side and said, "They'll try something so you'll lose your cool like last time. You'll have to take it. Okay?" I nodded.

But nothing happened as the third quarter got underway, other than we scored first and had a three-point lead. We scored again and St. John's called time out. The horn sounded to begin play again, and the same St. John's player who'd shoved me out of bounds in the first game came to the scorer's table. Coach pulled me aside and said, "That kid will foul you, and it'll be a hard foul. If you take the bait and go after him, you'll be ejected like last time and we'll probably lose the game. Be smart, Frank." He slapped me on the behind.

I trotted onto the court and heard familiar voices yelling my name. I took a quick looked in the stands. It was my dad,

Uncle Louie, and my Uncle Cagoots making all the noise. Wow, I didn't expect them to be at the game, but it was great seeing them up there.

Coach was right, a few minutes into the fourth period, with the game's outcome very much up in the air, I drove to the basket and the kid who was their enforcer knocked me to the floor with a "forearm." The ref's blew their whistles, but the guy fell on top of me and pushed hard on my chest to get up. I didn't react, and he made a fist. More whistles blew.

I got to my feet and laughed at him. He was ejected, and I calmly walked to the foul line and sank the technical foul. After that I made the two free throws for being fouled on my drive to the basket. The score remained close, but in the end, Stanton Prep won the championship. The people in the stands rushed onto the floor and celebrated.

But not everyone cheered. When things quieted a bit, a few students, including the kid who bumped me at the dance, and a couple of others chanted, "Go Home, Guineas."

Coach heard it, my father and my uncles heard it, and of course Joe and I heard it. Chuck Gallopo heard it too, and he shook his head. We'd just worked our butts off for the school, won the championship and had to hear that. I was pissed off. It was obvious to me that this thing with the O'Briens wasn't over. I say "O'Briens" because the headmaster was sitting nearby in the stands but he ignored the name calling as if it had never occurred. I figured that the good head priest and his nephew were behind it all along.

It was late May, and my freshman year was just about complete. I studied hard for final exams despite working at Uncle Louie's gym and hanging out with the Romans. Camille had cooled my interest in Zan, but we continued dating even though the relationship was going nowhere.

Depending on what happened with final exams, my grades would be near or at the top of the freshman class. Chuck or Joe—or both—might beat me out, but it would be close. Report cards were supposed to be in the mail by the Friday after school had ended.

With two days left in the school year, Coach asked the team to meet him in the locker room and we said our goodbyes to one another. I was especially going to miss playing with Calvin Jones, who was graduating, and I let him know my feelings. For whatever reason, Bobby Murphy wasn't around, but I didn't care about him and nobody else seemed concerned with his absence either.

Chuck waited until everyone left before saying his personal goodbye to me. I wasn't much for hugging guys, but we gave each other a bear hug. My friendship with Chuck extending beyond the basketball court and I'd never forget him for setting me up with his cousin, Camille. She didn't visit his family at Christmas, and as it ended up I never saw her again. But I'd always remember her. Always!

Chuck walked with Joe and me as we headed for our bus. He told me that since Italians weren't welcome at Stanton Prep he'd be transferring to Lawrenceville Prep. "They're breaking ground for a gym on a new campus in Lawrenceville. Maybe you should think about joining me there, Frank."

I didn't have to think for very long for an answer. "I wish I could, but there's no way that will ever happen. Dad's still paying off my mom's medical bills, and we don't have the money." I glanced Joe's way and he gave me a knowing look. "It's Stanton Prep or nothing for me and Joe." The three of us shook hands, and Chuck walked off as Joe and I headed toward our bus.

———

We turned a corner to find Bobby Murphy and five guys blocking the sidewalk. One older guy said, "I'm Jack O'Brien. I heard you wanted to meet me. Had to wait until school was over for the year to make it *official*." His crew laughed.

He stuck out his chest but this didn't scare me in the least. O'Brien came across more like a spoiled rich kid, all pretty and neat, with nice clothes and shiny shoes.

I shuffled up to O'Brien, but as a diversion I spoke to Bobby Murphy as I got closer. "I'm disappointed in you, Bobby. Looks to me like you're a little boy tugging at his mother's apron, and your mommy is this asshole."

Bobby replied in an oddly remorseful tone, "Too bad it has to be you, Bruno, but I have no choice. You see, I'm Irish, and so are they."

With two quick steps I closed the distance between Jack and me. Without saying a word, I kicked him in the balls and he went to his knees, holding his crotch and screaming in pain. The fight was on.

Jack wouldn't be able to do anything for a while, but Bobby and the others came at Joe and me. Bobby was a tough, strong kid, but I was trained for street fighting and he wasn't. I spun and landed what Uncle Louie called "a spinning back fist," to the side of Bobby's head. He went down like a brick.

Joe kicked and punched wildly trying to fight off three guys. I purposely threw a clumsy overhand right at a kid who ran at me. He ducked as I expected he would, and I kneed him in the face. I might have broken his jaw, as I heard a crack just before he began howling. The three other guys backed away just long enough so I grabbed Joe by the shirt. We took off, as the odds of six against two would eventually catch up with us.

Two blocks down the street, we ran into a soda shop and I rammed a chair under the front door so it couldn't be opened from the outside. An old man in an apron yelled at us to get the hell out of his store, but when I turned toward him, with my fists balled, he begged off, saying he didn't want any trouble.

I hollered at him, "Where's your damn phone!" He pointed to the wall in the back of the store. I put a dime in the slot and dialed The Paramount Sweet Shop. Luigi answered on the second ring. I told him about our trouble, and that Joe and I were holed up in a soda joint two blocks south of Stanton Prep, on South Orange Avenue.

He said, "You're in luck, Frank, a bunch of the Romans are working on a construction site at Ivy Hill Apartments. That's not more than a couple of blocks from you. I have a phone number. Hold those guys off as best you can, and the Romans should be there in a few minutes."

Jack and Bobby and the rest of their crew arrived faster than I thought they would, considering how badly I'd hurt three of them, and they started jostling the front door to try to open it. The shop owner grabbed the phone from me, saying he was calling the police. I yanked the receiver cord from its box and threw it on the floor. I was in no mood to apologize to the old man. Instead, I looked for something Joe and I could use as weapons, but the only thing I found was a set of salt and pepper shakers, as the chairs in the shop were all metal and of course so were the legs. Joe and I filled both our hands with pepper and readied ourselves.

A minute later a rock came through the glass in the front door. Someone reached in and knocked the chair away, and the six guys charged inside. We threw pepper in the eyes of a few of them, but with six against two we were getting our asses kicked even though I'd flattened one guy and he didn't get up.

Suddenly the odds changed!

Two truckloads of Romans arrived. Bobby Ciccone, Mickey

the Boot, Vic DiSilvester, Frank D'Orio, Tony Tadessa, Joe Carcusa, Koutsis the Greek, and Ralph Nicosia charged into the fray, all swinging pieces of wood like clubs.

The spoiled rich kids were no contest for our guys, who had been in so many street fights that this was second nature to them. I personally took care of Jack O'Brien, the so-called bad-ass of the bunch, ramming an elbow into his face. He stumbled backwards and felt his eyebrow as blood ran from where my elbow had caught him. I landed a hard punch to his stomach and knocked him backwards.

A good left hook and he went down and cut his face on a piece of broken glass from the door. He squealed like a girl, but that didn't stop me from punching and kicking him a dozen times. I backed away, knowing he was finished, and said, "Don't be such a baby, Jack. You sounded a lot tougher when you were yelling names at us from the stands."

Joe Carcusa and Nicky the Boot took on Murphy, who to his credit still had fight left in him after what I'd done to him earlier. They beat him and I kicked O'Brien one more time in the ribs for good measure. It wasn't long before none of the six were standing. Blood was everywhere, and it looked like a couple guys had broken arms. I heard the sound of police sirens in the distance—and getting louder.

Bobby Ciccone yelled to the guys to get to the trucks. They were used to cops coming and were gone in no time. Joe and I hurried to the sidewalk but then we slowed down as if nothing had happened, and we made it in time to catch a Number 9 bus. I said to Joe, "O'Brien and his bad-asses, right? What a joke." We laughed all the way back to Newark.

That evening, before my dad came home, I heard pounding on our front door. I looked through the peephole and recognized Dominic Spinelli, a detective from the Newark police department. My dad knew him from church and the Italian-American Club, neither place he made it to very often. I let the detective in, and he got right to the point. "So what's your side of the story, Frankie? And don't tell me you don't know what the hell I'm talkin' about."

I told him the truth, or at least the part that mattered to me: "Joe and I were heading home from prep school when we were stopped by six Irish kids. The leaders were Jack O'Brien and Bobby Murphy." I shrugged. "They started the fight, but they lost, so now they complain because we beat the shit out of them. They had six guys, we were two."

I smiled slightly, knowing that Detective Spinelli was a member of the Romans. Even though a very long time had passed since he'd been active with the gang, once you were a Roman you were always a Roman. I was sure he'd heard about the rest of our guys joining in the brawl, so there was no need for me to lie. But I didn't have to say anything more because he confirmed what had happened, no different than if he'd witnessed the whole thing with his own eyes. I guess he wanted to know how much I'd tell him, and if what I said was true. When he finished he asked for a beer, which I found for him in the refrigerator.

Dad arrived home a few minutes later, and I repeated the story for him. He asked the detective if I was in trouble, and he replied, "I think I can cover this one as self-defense, especially with six against two." He glanced at me and came back to my dad. "You might want to think about getting your son out of Newark, before it's too late. Frank's next stop could be jail."

My dad, who was also drinking a beer, put down the bottle and said, "Maybe you're right. I'm looking at a good job about twenty-five miles from here. I'm supposed to hear about it by the end the month. It'll pay as much as what I'm making now with all three jobs combined."

Four days later, I got a letter from Stanton Prep. It was a carbon copy of the original addressed to my dad, and it read: "Frank Bruno has been permanently expelled from Stanton Preparatory School for fighting. Because he has been expelled, he has failed the second semester of his freshman year. Grades will not be forthcoming." The letter was signed by Father O'Brien. The next day Dad showed the letter to Dominic Spinelli. In two weeks I had my grades. Later that summer, Dad told me what the detective and he had done to get those grades.

Detective Spinelli, dressed in a regular cop's uniform, and my dad, paid a visit to Father O'Brien, after normal school hours. Without knocking, they entered his private quarters on the campus. Spinelli stood guard while my dad pushed the priest against the wall and screamed in his face, "You're the damn devil dressed in another man's clothing. Some fucking excuse for a priest, you are. If my last name was O'Malley or Riley or some other Irish name, my son would not have been kicked out of this lousy school. Your nephew started the trouble, not my son, and you know it. Now hand over my boy's grades."

Father O'Brien was not one to be intimidated, even at a time like this. He yelled back at my dad, telling both him and the "cop" to get out of his office.

Dominic Spinelli was also not easily intimidated. He grabbed Father O'Brien by his priest's collar and hollered back at him, "Have it your way, but you'll give up those grades, one way or another. If you don't, and you set foot in Newark for any reason at all, even for the St. Patrick's Day Parade, I'll arrest your holy ass, put you in cuffs, and parade you in front of the newspaper reporters. I'll tell them you're accused of child

---

abuse. You can try to sort that out over the next five years." But even this level of threat didn't affect the tyrant, as my dad and the detective left without my grades.

That next morning, Detective Spinelli made a call to a longtime Italian friend who worked in the South Orange Avenue police district. That same afternoon, Father O'Brien was stopped and ticketed for speeding, doing 33 in a 25 miles-per-hour zone. "Oh, what the hell," the cop said with a smirk, "I'll round it off to a nice even 35 MPH. Easier to calculate the fine with a nice round figure." As the cop handed the priest his ticket, he smiled and said, "See you in court, Father."

The next day, Father O'Brien was stopped by a different Italian patrolman. In this instance he was ticketed for a broken taillight after the cop smashed it with his baton. A day later he was ticketed for running a stop sign. The cop who wrote this citation said, "If I've got the facts right, that's three tickets in three days, Father O'Brien. Obviously, you're a hazard on the street. I'll ask the traffic judge, who's Italian by the way, to pull your license. Have a nice day." The priest cursed the patrolman as he was walking away.

The cop quickly went back to the car, ordered Father O'Brien to step out, and he placed him in cuffs, accusing him of resisting arrest by disobeying a direct order. He shoved the priest into the back of his patrol car, no different from if he was a common criminal, and he called a reporter friend at the Newark Evening News on his police radio and said to meet him at the jail. He also said to bring a photographer.

At the jail, the cop ushered the priest into a holding cell and said, "Once we get you booked, you'll enjoy the company in your next cell. There's a schizophrenic guy who hates God. He's been off his med's for a few days, so it should be a fun night for you."

———

A filthy drunk in the holding cell got up off the floor and staggered over to the priest. He put his vomit covered arm on Father O'Brien's shoulders and slurred his words and threw up all over the priest's gown. He wiped puke on the priest's shoulder and asked, "So who the fuck are you, man, the Pope or Jesus?"

The priest pushed the drunk away and yelled for help. The cop slowly walked over to the priest, the drunk still at Father O'Brien's side and standing in his own upchuck. "Okay," the priest said and turned away from the stench, "I'll send the kid his grades, but get me out of here now—and before the newspaper people see me."

"You'll give me the report card when I drive you back to the school."

The priest took one more look at the drunk, who was smiling at him while displaying a gross mouth of missing teeth. O'Brien nodded as if to say yes, appearing as though he might throw up himself.

The cop replied, "Have to get the keys to the cell. Might take a while. Ten minutes later the cop unlocked the door and drove the priest back to his office at Stanton Prep, and stood over Father O'Brien until he handed over Frank's report card, which was in the top middle drawer of his desk.

Before the officer left, the priest demanded, "What about my car?"

The cop replied, "It's probably in lockup. Cost a hundred bucks or so to retrieve it. You'll have to go down and sign for it yourself. Can't be done by anyone else or it stays put."

As everything ended up, Jack O'Brien was not reprimanded in any way for starting the fight, but Joe and I remained permanently expelled.

Both Joe and I had our grades. I edged out Chuck Gallopo for the best marks in the freshman class, but it hardly mattered anymore. My promise to Mom, to get a college education, was gone. I didn't even know what high school I'd be attending for my sophomore year, only that it would be in a new community, as Dad had gotten the job. I think he said the place was called New Town.

Sister Elizabeth Ann was crushed by what had happened. Tough as she was, when Joe and I met with her one final time, I thought she might break down. I hated it as much for her as for Joe and me. I swore that one day I'd get even with Jack O'Brien.

CHAPTER TWELVE

Street Brawl with the Falcons
Summer 1956: Newark

Ten days after being expelled from Stanton Prep I was in trouble again, as the Romans and the Falcons had fought. And this time is was no minor tussle. The afternoon following the battle, Uncle Louie and my dad sat me down in the office at the gym, wanting to know the whole story. After being expelled from Stanton Prep, I was in a dark mood and didn't care what happened to me.

I shrugged. "They got what they deserved. What else can I say?"

Uncle Louie shook his finger at me and said, "Enough smart-ass answers, Frank. The cops are all over this. Your story better make sense. Now start from the very beginning."

I scoffed, but Uncle Louie and my dad were giving me very hard looks, so I said, "Okay, okay. Here's what happened. One of the Romanettes, who's a bit loose and has probably slept with half of our older guys, was grabbed by three Falcons and dragged into The Holy Sepulcher Cemetery, where they were going to rape her."

"You heard this directly from her own mouth?" Uncle Louie asked and shifted his big body on a boxer's stool.

"Yes. She said that two guys held her down while the Falcon with the crest on his boot, the prick who'd kicked the hell out of me at the theatre and the same guy who I returned the favor to later, pulled out his dick. Lucky for her, she got one of her hands free, grabbed an ice pick from her boot, and stabbed one of the guys holding her. She was able to get up and run away. The Romanettes are part of us. No way could we let this go. Bobby Ciccone sent word to the Falcons to face us in front of The Paramount Sweet Shop, or we take them out one by one. They accepted the challenge and we set the time."

"Does this stuff ever work; all these fights? It keeps going on month after month son," my dad asked, obviously worried about me.

I let out an angry sigh of my own, knowing trouble seemed to be following me. "Anyway, we knew they'd be carrying weapons, and not just bike chains or clubs. Another gang member told us they had zip guns." I'd learned that most zip guns were made from toy cap pistols, with a steel barrel fashioned from a car antenna. They could fire a single .22 caliber bullet, but they were made of such poor-quality metal that they'd often blow apart in the hand of the person pulling the trigger. Gang members would wrap their zip guns in duct tape to prevent injury to themselves, but even this wouldn't always work.

"Zip guns can kill yah," Uncle Louie said, his face long, as if he'd seen someone die as the result of being shot by one of these makeshift pistols.

I nodded and said, "We weren't going to let any Romans get

shot if we could help it. We knew they were coming, so we put the Romanettes on the flat roofs of the pastry shop and on the building across the street. We'd stolen a load of bricks from a construction site on Chelsea Street, and we hauled dozens of them onto each rooftop."

Serious as this was, Uncle Louie let out a laugh, apparently knowing what would happen next. I especially liked telling the next part of the story. "The Falcons got out of their shiny cars and trucks and rushed toward us. The guy with the Falcon insignia on his boot was in the lead waving his zip gun. Several other Falcons displayed them too, and the gang looked real confident. There was no reason for them to expect we had anything but clubs and garrison belts." I got excited relating the story and had to pause to catch my breath. "Advancing fast, the Falcons weren't too far from us when the Romanettes and a couple of our young guys on each roof started screaming: 'Rapists. Falcons are rapists.'

The Falcons stopped and looked up at the Romanettes just as our girls started pummeling both them and their vehicles with bricks. Our girls had won the fight for us before it got started! The Falcons ran to take cover and move their rides, but we chased them down and clobbered them with our clubs. The whole thing was over in no time, and not a single shot was fired. We found a couple of their zip guns and later threw them in a sewer drain a few blocks away."

"Is that it?" Uncle Louis asked.

"Some of the Falcons had been hit by bricks and gone down. A couple of them didn't get up, including their leader, the guy with the insignia on his boot. His head was bloody as hell, and he wasn't moving last I saw, not that I feel bad for the bastard. By the time the cops arrived, all Romans and Romanettes were nowhere around." I shrugged. "Like I said, they got what they

---

deserved."

Uncle Louie sat back on the tiny round stool and put his hands behind his head. "Maybe you're right, Frankie. They got what they deserved, especially for tryin' to rape a girl, and it wouldn't matter if she was a Romanette or someone else. Maybe the cops don't care this time, and maybe they'll treat this as just another gang fight, but eventually you'll get caught when someone gets hurt bad. When that happens you'll go to jail." He glanced at my father. "Your dad and I don't want to see that day come."

I said, "Maybe you're right. With Bobby Ciccone graduating from high school and going to college, and Nicky the Boot entering the Army, plus Joe Carcusa taking a job in construction, even though I'm only sixteen, and one of the biggest kids, I'm fourth in line with the Romans. The gang is looking to me as a leader."

My dad rose from the chair he was sitting on. "Son, it sounds like we're moving at just the right time—for both of us."

Uncle Louie got up too, and he smiled at me. "Frankie, don't worry about cleaning the gym tonight. I'll take care of it."

I thanked Uncle Louie for all he'd done for me. I knew he was right. It was time to get out of Newark. I was very lucky that I'd never been arrested. As my dad and I headed out the door, Uncle Louie said, "Oh yeah, one more thing, Frankie. With all that's going on, I almost forgot to tell you. A girl stopped by the gym this afternoon. Nice looking too. She said she just moved here and she lives in The Projects. She said she went to your apartment. You weren't home, so she asked around and was told you worked here."

Wow, a girl asking for me! Now that was good news! But it wouldn't have been Zan, so my immediate thought was Camille. Yet that didn't make sense either. I asked Uncle Louie if she'd told him her name, and he said, "Uh, let me think." His big dark eyes got even larger. "It was... ah, Mary Jo. Yeah, Mary Jo. Got the idea she knew you from Scranton."

I couldn't believe it! Mary Jo, here in Newark! She hadn't told Uncle Louie her apartment number, and The Projects were huge, so if I didn't find her, she'd find me.

The next morning I woke up thinking about what had happened at Stanton Prep. I was still angry and felt sorry for myself after losing my chance to go to college. I heard a knock on the front door, and my mind immediately shifted to the street fight with the Falcons and Uncle Louie's warning. I thought about the Falcon leader, who appeared to be hurt pretty badly. Could it be the cops? I slipped on a pair of trousers and a T-shirt and checked the peephole. What I saw could not be further from the police. I opened the door and a tender voice asked, "Remember me?"

I smiled. "How could I *not* remember you?" I said as Mary Jo stood in front of me, so fresh and clean. All I wanted to do was squeeze her tight, which I did. Compared to the girls I'd known in Newark, girls like Zan, she looked so innocent, wearing hardly any makeup except for faint pink lipstick.

I invited her in, and after all sorts of telling how much we'd missed each other, she explained what had taken place back in Scranton: "My dad finally gave up on his job with the trolley company and took the offer from the department of transportation here in Newark, and we were given a break on an apartment in The Projects. I'll attend West Side High School this fall. Maybe we'll be in some of the same classes." She smiled and hugged me and added, "It'll be just like it was before you left."

I didn't tell her about going to Sacred Heart and that I'd earned an academic scholarship to Stanton Prep and made the

135

basketball team and we'd won a league championship—and I'd already been expelled. And I didn't have the heart to tell her that I'd be moving any day now. Instead, I told her I'd show her around the neighborhood. We went to Pantello's Bakery, where I had coffee and two Boston creams, and she had hot chocolate and a jelly donut. A half hour later, Joe came in, wearing his Romans jacket, and I introduced him to Mary Jo. His cheek and his jacket led to a lot of questions.

Mary Jo and my buddy kept gabbing. After some time she turned to me, appearing rather shocked. "Frank, is this true? You're in a neighborhood gang with Joe."

I tossed aside the sport page I was reading while they were talking. "It's not only me and Joe. There are eighteen Romans. We take care of each other. Sort of like the brothers in a college fraternity." I didn't tell her about the Romanettes—Zan in particular—or the street fights. I figured she'd find out about all of this soon enough.

During the next week Mary Jo and I spent a lot of time together, going to movies, roller skating, and walking in the park and talking. Lots of talking, and what she didn't hear from me she learned from others. She'd always made friends quickly, and soon she knew it all, even about Zan and me.

On the night before my dad and I were going to pack everything in Uncle Louie's truck and move, Dad was at the Italian-American Club with Dominic Spinelli. I heard a light knock on the apartment door, and it was Mary Jo. I don't know why, but I thought she might want to give me a sendoff I'd never forget, but when I tried to make a serious move on her she backed away.

She was the same girl she'd always been, still sweet and innocent except for being a great kisser. I was the one who had changed. It was all different now. Newark wasn't Scranton,

———

and I wasn't the naïve kid she knew back then. Not even close.

CHAPTER THIRTEEN

Sophomore Year
New Town High School
Frank Bruno meets Simon

The Spitball

At this time in history, the Soviet Union held control over most of Eastern Europe. Living conditions in those countries were brutal. Tens of thousands of people who could find their way out immigrated to the East Coast of the United States, where jobs were plentiful.

The New Town community contained sand and clay pits that were used in the manufacture of bricks. The work was hard, but a nice paycheck made the aches go away. And in nearby New Brunswick, Johnson and Johnson, in its many manufacturing facilities, employed a wide range of engineers and scientists, as well as those who worked on assembly lines and operated machines.

There were also numerous small clothing factories in or near

New Town, in which women with sewing skills could immediately find jobs. While these women worked, they spoke their native languages. Romanian, Polish, Russian, Hungarian, and Czechoslovakian were most common.

At New Town High School, the student population was no different. Most kids found English difficult, and they spoke what they could with heavy accents. Attending classes was a huge problem for these kids because they often couldn't understand what the teacher was saying, even when a genuine effort was made.

A Hungarian boy named Peter had recently enrolled in school and knew little English. During his very first class, in his broken tongue, Peter made the mistake of asking Harold Higgins, "What is name of teacher?"

Higgins smiled and responded slowly to be sure this new kid understood what he was saying: "Her name is Miss Virginia, but she likes to be called Miss Vagina. Can you say Miss Vagina?"

Peter thanked Higgins and raised his hand and asked, "Can I make piss in boys' room, is okay with you, Miss Vagina?" The teacher shot up from her chair, and with her arms on her hips screamed at him at the top of her lungs, ordering him to the principal's office. He soon learned that the principal's name was Franny Large, or as the kids called her, Fanny Large. This woman had a huge butt, which made the name a given. I soon learned that Peter had a good sense of humor, and when he'd heard her name he thought it was another joke and couldn't stop laughing. Oh, well.

Franny Large was a stubby woman, in her late forties, with fat legs and almost no bosom. Rumor had it that she held the position of principal without any administrative training or compensation beyond a teacher's salary. The story was that extra salary was promised but never paid. Some said this was because she'd been caught with a student, but, looking at her, I doubted this was true. No kid could be that desperate.

Franny Large wasn't the only person at the school with accreditation issues. New Town High School was staffed by many teachers without teaching certificates, and in some cases the instructors had never gone to college—or even graduated high school. Auto-mechanics class and carpentry shop were taught by men with experience in these fields, but neither of these teachers had earned as much as a high-school diploma. New Town High School was a mess from top to bottom.

The physical structure was old, built over 80 years earlier, and falling apart at the seams. Doors didn't open and windows wouldn't close. Toilets malfunctioned and ran over all the time. The lights would flash on and off for no apparent reason, and school bells often rang sporadically and without meaning. Two years ago, New Town High had lost its accreditation with the state of New Jersey because of overcrowding, part-time classes, and a lack of teachers with certificates.

Loss of accreditation had caused many of the best teachers to leave. Students, whose parents could afford it, transferred to private institutions or Catholic school. I begged my father to send me to a private school, but despite his diamonds and all our wealth, which I knew about to some degree, my father refused my pleas. In his increasingly paranoid state, he whispered to me once, "We cannot let you go to a private school. The Nazis might notice our success." None of this made sense to me. But I couldn't do anything about my father's hearing voices and imagining things.

My freshman year at New Town High School had been my worst year ever. Red Hair was back, bigger and meaner than ever. The bully was finally pushed through grammar school by Mrs. Warnsdorfer, who was tired of him and the trouble he caused. Flunking him again would have kept Higgins in her school for another year, so he "passed."

Higgins had started and easily won four fist fights in his freshman year, earning a reputation as a terrible bully and someone to avoid. He smiled whenever one of his lackeys told him that another boy said he feared him. It was exactly the reputation he wanted—to be known as a mean, tough sonofabitch and being called a bully was fine with him.

Whenever he could get at me, Red Hair knocked my books to the ground and stomped on them, as if his actions were some kind of religious ritual. His "followers" cheered him on. Since I was the smallest boy at New Town High, my size didn't help me.

On the way to school one day, my friend, Dave Nenninger, told me, "Simon, if you don't stand up for yourself, it'll never stop. Punch the bastard in the nose and see what happens. Maybe he'll leave you alone and pick on someone else." But Simon was told over and over by his father to stay out of trouble, and I feared Higgins might kill me if I ever took a swipe at him.

Higgins's wicked behavior toward me never let up. If stealing my lunch wasn't enough, once in the boys' restroom, two of his friends pushed me into a stinking, yellowed urinal, of which the porcelain extended almost up to my head, and they hit the flush handle. To make it worse, with just a week to go until my freshman year was over, I was in the restroom and Higgins tossed a cherry bomb into a toilet stall next to mine. I couldn't get up to leave before the teachers arrived, who of course thought I'd been the one to set off the explosion.

Another trick Red-Hair enjoyed was to have his buddies steal my clothes and tie my socks in knots when I went to P.E. class. They hid my underwear and shoes in different empty lockers.

When I arrived late for my next class, my teachers scolded me for being tardy. Even the girls snickered. I hated high school, but despite Higgins, I still managed straight A's in everything.

But the worst day of freshman year happened while I waited for the school bus to take me home. Harold Higgins snuck up behind me and yanked my pants down around my knees. Somehow, my underwear stayed up, but everyone laughed and pointed at me and called me cruel names.

Dave Nenninger and Donald Moore both told me the same thing, which was that I had to fight back. But my father's warning rang in my ears: "Above all else, Simon, don't fight with anyone." As I walked up our driveway feeling miserable that day, I thought about what one kid yelled at me from the window of our school bus: "Hey Simon, why not just hang yourself and get it over with."

This time I did fight back, but what I fought was the tears streaming down my face. They all hate me. I hate this school. And right now I hate myself. But what can I do? The only good thing is that I'll soon be a sophomore and one year closer to graduation and getting away from Red Hair for good.

****

Every student was instructed to gather in the gymnasium, the same as orientation day at every school in America. Someone always droned on and on about rules. Frank sat with his head down, bored stiff and feeling angry at his situation, when he felt something hit him in the back of the head. And there it was, on the floor right on front of him: a spitball. *Here we go again. Assholes are everywhere.*

A large woman awkwardly waddled to the podium. The guy doing the speaking said that the lady was the principal and that her name was Franny Large. She took over the microphone and rambled on about more rules. Kids talked loud, laughed and flirted, doing everything but paying attention. A short while later Frank felt a second spitball hit him and saw it fall nearby. This time he looked around to see who might be smirking, but no one apparently wanted to take credit, as everyone seemed preoccupied. Frank picked up the wet, chewed piece of paper and stuffed it in his pocket.

When the assembly ended, Simon eased his way through the crowd to guy with the slicked-back hair and whispered to him, "Spitball. Harold Higgins threw it."

Frank peered down at Simon and asked, "Which one was he?"

Simon whispered, "Huge guy, red hair, dungarees, white T-shirt says, 'Bad News' on the back. He's always picking on me—has been for years. But... be careful, he's one of the toughest kids in school, and probably the meanest."

"I hate bullies," Frank said. "Why don't you get word around school that I'm looking for Higgins. Say I want to meet him at the bus stop after classes are over. Then you can watch me kick the shit out of Bad News, and I promise you, he won't bully you anymore."

Simon smiled and almost giggled. He could hardly believe it. Someone was actually going to take on Harold Higgins. But he still kept his voice to a whisper, saying, "I'll be there. My name is Simon, by the way. Simon Silverman."

"I'm Frank... Frank Bruno, Outta Newark. Now go spread the word that I'm looking for Higgins."

Five minutes later Simon went up to some guys he knew who were sitting together in study hall and announced, "A new guy from Newark is going to take on Harold Higgins after school. At the bus stop. Tell everyone."

It didn't take long for word to get around and Higgins to be made aware of the challenge by some new kid. He bragged to

---

his pals, "If this jerk-off knows what's good for him, he won't show up."

Classes ended for the day, and Higgins and a bunch of his toadies headed to the bus stop, cheering on the bully as they walked beside him. One of his pals looked around and said, "I don't see anybody we don't know. The new guy won't show. Like you said, he's got a big mouth and that's all he's got. You'd kick his ass if he did show."

Just then someone yelled, "Hey, there he is, the new guy, over by the bench."

Franks took a couple of steps forward and stopped, sizing up Higgins as he strode his way. He was linebacker big and likely the type who preferred to charge headfirst into an opponent to knock the guy off his feet and then get on top and pound him. Frank knew how to handle just such an assault.

"You looking for me, jerk-off?" Higgins said and scoffed.

"Yeah, I have something for you," Frank replied calmly.

Higgins stepped closer, and without saying anything more, he lowered his head and charged, as Frank figured he would. But just as Uncle Louie had trained him many times, Frank stepped back three steps, left-right-left, and planted his rear foot. Harold Higgins ran into the best left hook Frank had thrown since decking Jack O'Brien back at Stanton Prep. The punch stopped Red Hair in his tracks. He managed to stay standing, but he his eyes rolled in his head and he wobbled.

With his back now facing Frank, Higgins began staggering around in a slow circle. Frank kicked Higgins hard in the liver, and he fell face-first onto the sidewalk. He moaned loud as everyone watched him writhe on the cement and grab at his back.

Someone yelled, "Get up, Harold, he was lucky. Get up." But Harold Higgins didn't get up. Instead, Frank turned him over on his back and climbed on his stomach.

Frank talked to the bully in a calm voice, but Higgins was in so much agony he couldn't respond. Frank slapped him across the face and looked up at Higgins's pals and laughed at them, "This is like beating up a girl. You follow this piece of shit around?" Frank slapped Higgins over and over. Not punching him, just slapping his reddened face to embarrass him.

Higgins twisted from side to side to try to avoid the slaps, his cheeks now covered with red streaks. Finally, he pleaded, "I give... I give. Okay... I give up." Higgins's "friends" couldn't believe he didn't fight back, and some walked away so they wouldn't be seen rallying around such a loser.

Simon and the those who stayed watched with their mouths' agape as Frank kept at Higgins, not showing the slightest mercy. Slap, slap, slap. The bully's nose began to bleed. But it wasn't over yet.

When Frank did quit slapping Higgins, he dug into his pocket and pulled out the paper wad Higgins had hit him with at orientation and said, "Here you go tough-guy, it's your spitball. The same one you hit me with. Now it's a bit juicier though because I pissed on it. So, you have a choice, you can swallow this wad of paper soaked in my piss, or I can knock your fucking teeth out while the few of your asshole friends who haven't left watch me."

Higgins yelled for help, but his pals who remained wanted no part of the new kid. Frank squeezed open Higgins's mouth, and he dropped the yellowed spitball on his tongue and held his mouth closed. Higgins gagged and choked, but after a few more hard slaps he started chewing the paper. Finally, Frank made him open his mouth and stick out his tongue so everyone could see he'd swallowed the whole thing.

Frank stood and warned Higgins, "Do something stupid

around me again, and you'll have no teeth next time. And, leave the little kid alone. Touch him and it's like touching me." Frank stared down the few of the bully's followers who'd stayed. "Anyone else want a piece of me?" No one said a word. Instead, Harold Higgins's remaining "friends" all backed away. It was over.

Frank left Higgins on the ground, the punk not even trying to get up, many of the kids just staring at him. Frank walked away and Simon ran up to him. "Thanks for beating the crap out of that asshole. He's made my life miserable since fifth grade."

Frank nodded and said, "No need to thank me. I didn't do that for you, I did it for me. I hate bullies." He paused and said, "Nice to meet you but I have some advice for you."

"What's that?" Simon asked Frank, who was now his hero.

"Fight back the next time somebody bothers you. Doesn't matter if you win or lose, you'll gain respect."

That night, Frank's father brought home a pasta dish from a local Italian restaurant. While eating their dinner, his father said, "Son, you seem to be in a better mood. I take it your first day at school was a good one?"

Frank smiled to himself. "School was okay. Nothing unusual. But I did make a friend, a little guy but it's nice to have at least one pal. Nice kid. Seems to be pretty smart too. Oh yeah Dad, the school building is falling apart, the teachers don't gives a damn about anything." He scoffed. "I don't give a damn either, since my chances for college are over. I can tell you this, Dad, New Town High is a long way from Stanton Prep. Even West Side High was better that this dump."

Dominic Bruno said, "I'm sorry to hear it's that bad. Maybe we can think about a transfer to Catholic school when I get your mom's medical bills paid off."

Frank knew that would never happen, at least not by the time he'd be ready for college, in just three years. He picked up the newspaper, and instead of his dad's reading to him like he did when Frank was a kid, Frank now read to the father: "Listen to this. The Dodgers tried to trade the great Jackie Robinson, but instead of accepting the trade, and more money, he retired from the game. Even baseball is crummy these days."

That same night, Simon was so excited when he got home that he could hardly wait to tell his mother what had happened. With Saul Silverman in another room, Simon described Higgins's beating, adding, "Mom, kids steal my lunch most days. I hardly ever have anything to eat at school. I'm always starving. Look how skinny I am. Mom, I need a lunch account at The Hilltop Sweet Shop. That way Higgins and his goons won't be able to take the sandwiches you make for me. I know Dad will refuse, but I also know we can afford it, so please do this for me."

Rose hugged her son and whispered so his father wouldn't hear her words, "Simon, you're my only son, and I love you. I'll open the account tomorrow. Your father doesn't need to know."

Rose went to The Hilltop Sweet Shop the next morning. She paid for what would be a year's lunches for Simon as he watched from across the street. He waited until his mom drove away before he went inside the sweet shop and politely spoke to Mrs. Tyhanic. One small change was made. Simon added the name of Frank Bruno to his account. Mrs. Tyhanic said this was no problem, telling him that Rose had left enough money for two boys to eat at her place for at least six months, maybe a year.

The next day, Simon sought out Frank and told him what he

had done, adding a little white lie to the tale, saying, "My mother wanted to thank you for taking care of my problem with Red Hair. She opened a food account for both of us at the Hilltop. Eat all you want there, Frank. It's paid up in full for a long time."

Frank smiled and gave Simon a pat on the shoulder. I have no friends in this school except for this little guy, but one pal is better than none, even if this one is almost a dwarf. Who knows, maybe he has an "experienced" female cousin who's bigger and better looking.

Harold "Red Hair" Higgins never returned to school. He worked construction for his father and told anyone who questioned him about dropping out of New Town High, "School is for jerks."

CHAPTER FOURTEEN

New Town
High School Chaos

It was my sophomore year and just two days before Thanksgiving. I was excited because my dad and I planned to go back to Newark for a four-day visit. We'd stay with Uncle Louie and Aunt Marie. Dad had two full days of electrical work set up at M&M Candies for Saturday and Sunday, so I'd be free the whole the weekend. I'd look up some Romans and hang out with Mary Jo. Zan wasn't in my thoughts any longer. I'm sure she had a new boyfriend, anyhow.

Not much can happen in the two days left before I leave for Newark. At least that's what I thought as I packed my lunch of meatball sandwiches made from a leftover dish my Dad had brought home the night before. I called them "cellophane sandwiches" because that's what I wrapped them with. I grabbed a nice ripe pear and a couple of pieces of candy and was off to school.

I arrived early and sat in my usual seat in homeroom, near a window, and placed my lunch under my chair. During the last few weeks, Simon's friends, Donald Moore and Dave Nenninger, had become my friends too. Generally we all sat near each other. Today, someone I didn't know, except that his name was Tony and he was a wise-ass and about my size, sat on my right, in the seat Donald normally took. He was an older kid from some other country, with a reputation as one of the toughest guys in the school. I didn't pay him any attention.

Our homeroom teacher, Judy Norton, was a tall trim well-spoken woman who displayed her teaching degree from Trenton State College in a frame on the wall. A small picture of a man, who might be in his twenties, was inset in one corner. I assumed it was a special family member, but no one ever asked her. Miss Norton taught us every day practical things we wouldn't get in the regular classes.

This morning, she began by saying, "Today's subject is regarding how to provide directions." Miss Norton asked if anyone could give proper directions from his or her home to the high school. A smart girl, Dorothy, who always sat up front, raised her hand. Miss Norton nodded to her and told her to stand and proceed.

Dotty, as she was nicknamed, said, "You would exit the front door of our house and take a left until you get to Main Street. Cross Main and walk through the parking lot in front of you, and at the other end of the lot you'll be standing in front of New Town High School." The girl smiled confidently and sat down.

Miss Norton said, "Thank you, Dotty. If your house faces north, your directions would work just fine, but if your house faces south, you would go the other way and not come to this school. It would also help to identify the name of the street your house is on, and the parking lot, such as the Acme Parking Lot. But, overall, that was a good start." She gave Dorothy a quick

---

nod.

Another girl was called on, and I didn't even know her name until Ms. Norton said it was Vicki. The girl said that she lived quite a way outside New Town, but she stood and took her chance with the assignment. Miss Norton thanked her when she finished, but she pointed out several flaws in her directions, primarily that she'd also failed to identify all the streets.

Miss Norton glanced around the room and said, "Let's hear from one of the boys. She called on Simon, who stood and even stuck out his chest a little. Now that Red Hair was gone, Simon had gained some much-needed confidence. His directions were precise, and Miss Norton said so and thanked him. She was about to choose another student for the exercise when someone knocked on the classroom door. A hall monitor came in and handed her a note. She read it and said, "The assistant principal needs to see me. I'm sure I won't be gone long." She hurried out.

Simon, who was sitting right behind me, whispered, "When you were watching me give directions, Tony stole your lunch and passed it to one of his friends. It's probably somewhere across the room by now."

Without even thinking about it, I stood and grabbed Tony by his left arm and twisted it up behind his back. "Give me my lunch back or I'll rip your damn arm off," I yelled at him.

I assumed that Tony had heard what I'd done to Harold Higgins. I knew he probably had stolen my lunch to let his friends know he wasn't afraid to take me on. So far it had been a bad decision. He winced in pain and said, "I gave your lunch to the guy next to me." He pointed to a goofy-looking kid with a face full of freckles and braces on his teeth. "It was supposed to be a joke."

"You know where you can stick your joke, asshole. Now,

get my lunch back." I twisted harder on Tony's arm, and he cried out. "Get it back or I'll rip your fucking arm off." I pushed his forearm so high that Tony's hand touched his greasy hair.

I was certain my lunch bag was somewhere across the room, but whoever had it wouldn't give it to back to me. However, this wasn't about my lunch anymore, it was about who was who in this dung heap of a high school.

I twisted harder, not caring that Tony's shoulder might become dislocated or something might break. He screamed louder. Suddenly the screaming stopped, and tough Tony collapsed and hit the floor with a thud. He was unconscious when Miss Norton returned to the classroom.

One of the girls waved her arms frantically and yelled, "Tony passed out when Frank tried to twist his arm off." Miss Norton rushed to Tony, who still wasn't moving. She ran to the doorway and yelled down the hall for help. Soon the room was filled with other teachers. A minute later the school nurse arrived, followed by the principal.

The nurse straightened Tony's arm into a normal position and held a cloth with some type of smelly medicine under his nose. He came to slowly and grabbed his shoulder. Once the nurse determined that nothing was broken, Franny Large interrogated Tony and me in front of the entire class. Tony pleaded innocence, saying he didn't know what happened, only that I'd started it.

I told the principal what had really taken place, and Simon, Donald, and Dave, as well as several other kids, backed me up. After a few minutes of everyone now saying the same thing, it would be hard to dispute that Tony had stolen my lunch. I said to the principal, Franny Large, "He's a thief. You should expel him from school, or next time he might steal your pocketbook."

The principal ordered the room searched. The lunch bag was found, squashed under some books stacked on the floor in the back of the room. The principal held my lunch bag in front of me and demanded, "What is in this sack, young man?"

"A meatball sandwich wrapped in cellophane, a pear, and two pieces of candy. Now, thanks to this jerk, pointing at Tony, I have nothing to eat for lunch. I should twist his arm some more, and harder."

Fanny Large answered back in an angry tone, "You will do no such thing." Then she spoke to Tony, "I will see *you* in my office." I could hear Tony's buddies whispering to each other. They were saying something about this not going the way Tony had bragged it would. Two male teachers helped Tony up, and they took him to the nurse's office for further evaluation.

As a result of the incident, my reputation as someone not to mess with got another boost. It ended up that Tony wasn't expelled, but he did land five days of after-school detention.

Finally it was Wednesday, the last day of school before the Thanksgiving break. I walked up the steps to the building's ancient entrance and paused. *One day to go and I get out of this rat hole.* I entered the main hallway to find it blocked by dozens of students who weren't able to get into their classrooms.

I was told that three guys, who were cut-ups but not really bad kids, had nailed a couple of the classroom doors shut. "Another day at the zoo," I said to Simon, who was at my side. Two janitors arrived with crowbars and forced the doors open. The hallway cleared, and the classes scheduled in those rooms both started forty minutes late. The students were delighted and so was I, because it meant French class would be shortened.

French was the worst classroom experience ever, either here or in Newark. I was told that during the previous year six different French teachers had resigned, one after the other, because the classroom situation had proved too much for each of them. Because of the constant disruption, first-year French was a total disaster, with no one learning anything. So, now, instead of second-year French we were starting over at the very beginning.

Simon told me about one teacher, Mr. Le Tart: "He resigned when students openly mocked him by calling him Mr. Le Fart. Le Fart was so upset that he walked out after only three weeks, and for a while there was no teacher, so French class became a study period."

Today, another new French instructor appeared in front of us. We hadn't expected this, as the woman who was teaching our class, an older lady named Mrs. Hurley, seemed okay with us. This new guy was dressed very properly: nice gray suit, white shirt with a stiff collar, and a blue silk tie. Maybe he was trying to impress us with his fine clothes. It didn't work.

His name was Nathan Beleau, which he pronounced "bee-low." Five minutes hadn't passed before he became "Nothing Below." The kids wouldn't give him a chance, and it seemed to me that teaching anything to anyone in this dump was nearly impossible.

Mr. Nothing Below opened this time-abbreviated lesson with: "Our first word in the beautiful French language is the word 'oui' and it is pronounced 'wee.' It means 'yes.'"

One of the boys in the back shouted, "Can I take wee, or is that pronounced 'wizz?' Everybody laughed, with a few jeers mixed in.

He ignored the wizz comment and wrote 's'il vous plait' on the blackboard. Just as he finished, an eraser zoomed by his head and exploded with chalk dust when it hit the slate. He turned around, faced the class, and said, "S'il vous plait is

---

pronounced 'see-voo-play.' It means 'please.' Now, please stop throwing erasers when I write on the blackboard." He turned to write the next word on the blackboard just as another eraser zipped by his ear. He jumped to the side as if he'd been shot at. I felt sorry for this teacher, but it was funny and I laughed too.

Four boys were standing, gawking out of the window at a group of senior girls doing calisthenics on the grass playing field. Before long, none of the boys in French class were paying attention to what Nothing Below was saying. Except of course for Simon, who always took notes.

A kid hollered to the girls, and one of them yelled something back. But despite the noise and lack of respect, the man persisted: "Now, class, we are going to say hello. It is 'bonjour.' Let's try the pronunciation, which is 'bone zhure.'"

One of the boys hanging out by the window yelled, "I'm getting a *boner for sure*, watching all those boobs bounce around out there."

More noise from the class, but Nothing Below remained undaunted. "Listen to me, class," he implored. "The next word is spelled d-e-s-o-l-e. It means 'sorry' or 'I'm sorry.'" He wrote 'desole' on the blackboard, this time without a missile attack to impede him. He asked, "Would anyone like to try pronouncing d-e-s-o-l-e without my help?"

One kid said, "How about day-so-lay? So maybe this is the day so I get a lay." The class howled just as the bell rang. I had to believe Nothing Below was thrilled his twenty minutes of hell was finally over.

The final bell for the day rang at school. Thanksgiving break had begun at last! A girl I'd gotten to know from biology class, a cute brunette named Alice, who had dark eyes to match her jet-black hair, walked with me to The Hilltop Sweet Shop for an ice cream soda. I didn't think Simon would mind.

I walked Alice home and got a quick goodbye kiss. Really nice, considering I didn't know her that well. As I headed toward my house, I thought about her and why she'd kissed me on the lips like that. My day dreaming was interrupted when I noticed my dad's pickup already parked in the driveway. He must have come home early so we could make it to Newark before traffic got too bad.

An hour later, we pulled up to Uncle Louie and Aunt Marie's house. I had my Romans jacket with me, so after saying hello, I headed for The Paramount Sweet Shop. I swung upon the door and hollered, "Hello Romans." My old friends welcomed me back with hand-shakes and kind words, but it just didn't seem quite the same as before I'd left.

As I expected, Zan had started dating another guy. I saw the two of them, said hello and wished them well. I was happy she'd found someone other than me. I hoped this guy had better luck with her.

Joe Cheeks arrived a half hour later and greeted me with a bear hug. He filled me in with what was going on the neighborhood: the parties, the latest brawls with the Falcons, and a fight with an upstart gang who didn't concern the Romans. He also introduced me to two new gang members, who were both young kids.

No matter how much Joe shared with me, I felt like a visitor; like the guy who went into the Navy and came back after a year at sea. I played a couple of games of pool and decided to go to The Projects and see if Mary Jo was home. It didn't cross my mind that her family might have also gone somewhere for the holiday.

I knocked on the door to her apartment, and there stood Mary

Jo, the girl who always had my heart. I talked for a few minutes with her mom and dad, who had all sorts of questions about where I was now living. I made up a bunch of stuff to make it seem better, especially at school.

When Mary Jo and I left the apartment, we walked for blocks and I listened to her about what she'd been doing rather than my telling her about shitty New Town High School. Mary Jo was doing very well at West Side High School, and I was thinking I'd been too hard on the place, especially since I'd never attended any classes there.

Mary Jo was a sophomore like me, and a very good student. She said that she enjoyed her new school, especially civics class. "Civics," Mary Jo enthusiastically explained, "is really all about the government and politics and making a difference in the community and the world. It's all about making things better."

Mary Jo talked with more maturity than I remembered six months ago when I had last seen her. We stopped at the gate to Vailsburg Park. Mary Jo faced me and threw her arms around my neck. She gave me a long deep kiss. Alice's kiss had been nice, but nothing like Mary Jo's, which could always take my breath away—and did this time as well.

Mary Jo said, "I really miss you." She flashed her pretty eyes at me. "Frank, after high school, I want to join one of the political parties. Doesn't that sound exciting? Do you know what you'll want to do?"

"Really? Join a political party? You mean like being a Republican or a Democrat? All those politicians seem to do is pass laws that regular people have to obey and they don't. People like my dad and yours, who have to pay more taxes so those politicians can spend the money. Politics doesn't interest me, but to answer your other question, I'm not sure what I'll do after high school."

Mary Jo and I saw each other every day for the next four, as I knew we would. Lots of great kisses and nothing else, but I didn't expect it to be any different in this regard. Mary Jo was Mary Jo, and as I headed back to New Town with my dad on Sunday afternoon, I was happy with the time I'd spent with her but I hardly talked during the ride back. I hated New Town and thought about Mary Jo's question: "What will you do after high school?"

I didn't have the slightest clue about life after high school, but as we reached our driveway, I knew I had to do something to lift my spirits. I said to my dad, "Maybe I'll try out for the New Town High basketball team. They really stink, but it might be better than what I'm doing now, which is nothing but feeling lousy most of the time."

My dad said, "Might be a good idea, Son. You always liked the game, and you're pretty darn good at it, if I don't say so myself." I hopped down from the truck, got the mail, and picked up the newspapers scattered in the driveway. I was fine until I got in the house and realized that I was back in New Town. I was too depressed to even read the headlines.

———

CHAPTER FIFTEEN

New Town High School
The Toughest Kid

I hadn't lied to Dad. The New Town basketball team was terrible. So bad that I had second thoughts about playing with these guys. But after a ridiculously lopsided defeat, I couldn't take sitting in the stands any longer, and I talked with the basketball coach. "Coach" Milton was the woodshop teacher. He'd volunteered to coach the team because he liked being involved with kids, not because he knew very much about basketball.

New Town's record was miserable, five wins and ten losses, with only five games to go before Christmas. The son of the biology teacher had recently quit the team, so I knew there was an opening. Also, the boy who'd quit was a forward, just like me.

I'd gone to all of the home games, so I already knew the team. It had only one good player, the center, a 6-foot-5 inch,

230-pound moose from Poland named Wojokowski. Everyone of course called him "Wojo." From what Simon told me, the big guy was supposed to be the toughest kid in this school. Simon also said that no one had ever seen Wojo in a fight, which seemed really odd for him to be considered *that* tough yet he was never challenged to prove it. It's just not the way being a kid worked.

Coach Milton told me to come to the gym after school for a tryout. I looked away from him and rolled my eyes, wondering why I needed a tryout when the team was this lousy. But I agreed to the tryout.

The final bell sounded and I headed to the locker room. I was lacing up my gym shoes when Wojo came in and began changing into his basketball clothes. He said, "It's just us today. Coach wants to see what you do against me." He spoke with an accent, and I smiled at the big kid. I was three inches shorter and maybe thirty pounds lighter. "I hope you ready for me," he added as she stared down at me.

I said, "We'll just have to see, won't we?" I walked onto the court, took a basketball from a rack of worn relics—some so old they were missing pieces of leather—and I started warming up.

Wojo went to the basket on the other end of the floor and did the same. Five minutes later, Coach Milton blew his whistle and laid out the rules: "Each of you will have the ball ten times on offense, with the other man defending. Wojo, you take the ball first."

I got in my defensive posture. Wojo dribbled to his right and headed straight to the basket, no doubt planning to run right over me. I blocked his path and clipped him hard with my hip, just like I did on the outdoor court at The Projects in Newark. Wojo lost control of the ball just enough so I could steal it cleanly. I scored an easy layup, tossed the ball back to him, and said, "As you can see, I'm ready for you. But how about you? You ready for me?" I wasn't being friendly on purpose.

On his next possession, I defended him off the dribble and made him take a jump shot from outside the free throw line. He hit it, and the contest went back and forth, with me playing tough defense and Wojo pulling up and shooting over me now that he couldn't drive around me.

He was "on," and after twenty minutes and nine possessions each, the game was tied. One of us would have to win by two for a victor to be declared, but Coach blew the whistle and called it a day, I'm assuming because he'd seen enough. Also, he likely didn't want the game to go on for what could be quite a while since neither of us could pull away from the other.

"Good job, guys," he said, beaming. "Hit the showers. And, both of you, save some of that energy for the other teams."

As we were returning to the locker room, Wojo put out his hand and said, "Nice game, Bruno."

"You too," I replied, shaking his hand firmly. "Yeah... you too," I repeated, thinking that I might like the guy.

Wojo and I sat on benches, opposite each other, and started undressing. Since Wojo had a reputation as a tough guy, I kept an eye on him. I expected there might trouble because I had played a very physical game against him. Then it happened. He took off his shirt, and said, "Bruno, I hear you take care of yourself when it comes to fighting." *Shit. Just like always.* I was tired and didn't want a fight, but I jumped up so he couldn't come at me while I was in a sitting position.

"Yeah," I answered, "I can handle myself when I have to. Where I'm from, Outta Newark, you learn to fight or you're dead meat. So if you're looking for trouble, big as you are, Wojo, here I am." I balled my fists, and I raised my right hand as a distraction as I prepared to kick him in the groin with my left foot.

Wojo put up his hands, palms facing me, and said, "Whoa, you got me wrong, Bruno. I not looking for trouble, in fact, just opposite. I only have one fight in whole life, and that was way back in grade school. Kid kick me in the shin. I pick him up and throw him against tree. He out cold. I never even need to punch him in face."

I shook my head in disbelief and relaxed. "Wojo, it you want to be known as the toughest guy in this dipshit high school, you can have the title. I just want to play basketball. In fact, I'm going to tell everyone you challenged me to a fight and I backed off."

He laughed. "You not back off from anyone. I hear what you do to Tony and Harold Higgins."

"I only fight when I have to, or when some small kid like Simon Silverman is getting bullied. I feel sorry for little kids who get picked on. Assholes like Higgins really piss me off. He got what he deserved."

Wojo said, "Guy like Higgins sometimes come back after he convince himself other guy get lucky. Somehow, he justify why he lose fight. If he come back, it will be with weapon or with extra guys. Maybe both. But I think you know this. Anyway, welcome to basketball team." Wow! I had a new friend instead of another fight!

Wojo lived on the outskirts of New Town, but not that far way. He offered to practice with me on the weekend, and one of the guards on the team, who also lived close by, joined us. Some of the guys who sat on the bench had heard about us planning to play together, so they stopped by as well. On the very first Saturday we had enough people to play three on three. I knew more about basketball from the streets and from Stanton Prep than any of the guys, so I became the unofficial coach.

When we had decent weather, these informal practices went on until the Christmas break. We actually won a couple of games during this time, but the teams we played were awful. The current New Town High School basketball season would be impossible to salvage, but our returning guys would at least be better next year and the games more fun.

It was two days before Christmas, and my dad and I headed to Newark for another visit. I spent the first evening at Mary Jo's house. Her mom and dad were there, and all of us watched Elvis Presley make what was to become his final appearance on *The Ed Sullivan show*. We clapped and cheered as though it was a live performance instead of just a TV show, Elvis was that good.

Mary Jo and I talked and held hands, but her parents were home, which limited our affection for one another to sweaty palms. Even though she acted her usual self, and gave me a great kiss outside the front door when I left for the night, I sensed that something was different about the two of us. Maybe it was just because we had not seen each other since Thanksgiving; maybe it was more than that. We spent Christmas Day with our own families, which gave me time to think about her. Something was definitely not the same, but I couldn't figure out what.

It was December 27, 1956. I was up early and enjoying jelly donuts and coffee at Pantello's. It felt good, like the old days. I picked up a discarded copy of The Newark Star Ledger and read the sports news: Iowa beat Oregon State in the Rose Bowl, and a company named Wham-O had sold its first Frisbees.

Joe walked in, saw what I was reading, and gushed, "Look what I got for Christmas!" He handed me a Frisbee, the toy I'd

165

just read about. His was bright red. My buddy continued, "Plenty of room at Vailsburg Park to try it out, but first I need some coffee and a couple of Boston creams."

We talked while I read the paper and drank my second cup of coffee. "Listen to this," I said to Joe, in-between sips. "The first electric typewriter will be on the market in two months, and the Suez Canal will open on February 17th of next year. The world is sure changing."

Joe gave me his crooked grin. After breakfast, we went to the park and tossed his new Frisbee back and forth, starting at a distance of twenty feet or so and gradually backing farther away from each other. The Frisbee looked so simple, just a round plastic disk with curved edges. I spun it to Joe and said, "I wish I'd thought of this thing." Joe nodded and raised both eyebrows, as I'm pretty certain he was thinking the same thing.

We played Frisbee for an hour before heading to The Paramount Sweet Shop, where I was certain a bunch of Romans would be hanging out. We were less than a block away when Joe grabbed my shoulder and stopped me. He said, "Frank, there's something I have to tell you, and you won't like it. I'll keep my mouth shut if you want me to, but it's something you should know."

"If it's that big a deal, what is it? And don't worry, I can handle it, I'm used to trouble."

Joe didn't waste any words: "Rumor has it that Mary Jo is dating someone from the Young Democrats Club. I hear he's a nerdy bookworm type. Everyone knows about it except you, 'cause you weren't here, so I figured it's better to hear it from me than from someone else."

I took a deep breath. "I suspected that something was different with her. Since I'm not here much anymore, I guess it was bound to happen sooner or later." I forced a smile, like I was okay—which I wasn't—but I kept it together and added, Mary Joe is a special girl, with a whole lot going for her." I gave Joe a pat on the back. "Thanks for telling me."

That night, Mary Jo and I talked about it; no arguing, we just talked it through. I didn't blame her, and I certainly couldn't do much about her dating another guy. Beating the crap out of a nerd wouldn't solve anything except to make sure she'd never see me again. I asked her, "If I continue to visit Newark on long weekends and holidays, can you still keep some time free for me?"

"Sure I can, Frank. I knew you back in Scranton when we were kids, way before I met this fellow. You'll always have a special place in my heart." Mary Jo was being polite and friendly, but I knew better. And her not-so-passionate kiss goodbye told me it was over between us.

Newark and the Romans were things of the past. Now, so was Mary Jo. That night I asked my dad if we could head home the next day instead of staying any longer with Uncle Louie and Aunt Marie. New Town wasn't much, but it was better than nothing. Alice, the pretty girl with the black hair and dark eyes, was there. Perhaps we could have something together. She seemed to like me well enough.

The following Monday, after the ten-day break for the holidays, New Town High School was back in session. I skipped French class because it was a waste of time, but I went to the rest of my morning classes and had lunch at The Hilltop Sweet Shop with Simon. Dave and Donald joined us, and we talked about Christmas. Simon of course didn't celebrate Christmas, but he said Hanukkah was sort of the same thing.

I hardly discussed my visit to Newark and what had happened between Mary Jo and me. When Dave asked about

Newark, I switched subjects and told Simon that I expected to see him at our remaining basketball home games.

Wojo came through the doorway, which surprised me because I'd never seen him at The Hilltop. He ambled over to our table and said to me, "I was told I might find you here. I've got some news. Remember the forward who quit team? Well, he come to see me over holidays and ask if he can rejoin us."

"What did you tell him? And wouldn't that be Coach's decision?"

"I tell him team has changed. I tell him we don't want him if he going to be ball hog like always before. If he not pass ball and hit open man, he might as well stay home."

"What did he say to that?"

"That the funny part. He asked me if he really did that, you know, hogging ball? I told him, 'Yeah, you a ball hog, and it pisses me off. It pisses everyone off. You need pass the ball unless you have easy shot.' A few days later, he came to our weekend practice over Christmas holiday and apologized to everyone. Now, he only takes shots when wide open or has easy layup. You see at practice after school, Frank. He different guy."

Our next two games were at home, and we won both. The following game was three days later. Wojo asked the team, including the bench sitters, to meet him in the locker room after school. Coach heard about the team meeting and asked Wojo, "You want me there?"

"No, Coach, just us. I talk to team."

Coach shrugged his shoulders and said, "Okay with me" and he let Wojo have his team meeting.

Every player was there. Wojo asked me to stand next to him, and the two of us faced everyone else. He said, "This year almost over, but for first time all year we playing like a team.

Hit the open man. No gunning. Play tough defense. Now we have three games left. I expect to win them all." He pointed at each player, including me, going slowly from one player to another. When finished he yelled, "What you say, guys? Can we do it together?"

I clapped my hands and hollered back at him, no more than a foot away, "Yeah, we can win them all!" The rest of the team yelled the chant: "Win them all! Win them all! Win them all!"

And that's exactly what we did. Wojo and I played a rough-and-tumble game under the basket, and nobody could stop us when we went to the hoop. There were no ball hogs and no gunning from the outside unless a guy had a wide-open shot.

When the last game ended, I was sorry the season was over, and the other guys said the same thing. Wojo asked me to say something in the locker room—something to make our guys think about next season.

I thought about what to say as I showered, and afterwards I asked the team to stand together for a minute, and I said, "This year is history. We finished strong but have a long way to go if we're to beat the better teams next year. From here on, practice on your own and stay in shape. And don't smoke cigarettes. They suck the wind from you. In the fall we'll be a year older and a year better, and we'll kick some serious butt."

Wojo started clapping and whooping it up, yelling, "We can do it! And, if we do, some of you may get offer for basketball scholarship. Coach tell me that a friend of his is scout for Rutgers, and he at game tonight. Coach say he be back next year. We need to start strong, just like we finish up, and who knows how far we go? But for now we on win streak and should enjoy it."

It wasn't long before the locker room was empty. Only Wojo and I remained. Wojo didn't speak great English, but he was smart. I asked him, "What do you mean by getting a scholarship to Rutgers? I thought only Stanton University did that?"

Wojo slipped on a windbreaker. "Almost all colleges with basketball program give scholarship to best players. Rider College offers scholarship, so does Trenton State. Even fancy school like Princeton. My parents can't afford to send me to college, so my only way to get education is to play basketball. You can do it too, Frank. You really very good, and I not just saying this because you my friend."

My head was spinning at what Wojo had just told me. "You honestly think I might have a chance for one of those basketball scholarships?"

"Somewhere. Perhaps not at big school, but at good college. Maybe we both can get scholarship for basketball. Maybe we even go to same school. Who knows? All we have to do is improve in the off season. We both have two more years in high school, and we both can get better." He paused and peered at me. "You can play this game, Frank. Your problem is staying out of trouble when not playing basketball." He patted me on the shoulder and walked off, leaving me to consider everything he'd said.

I sat in the locker room and a tear came to my eye. Did I ever miss my mother. Mom, I think about you all the time. I might be able to get an education and keep my promise to you after all. I have to get good grades, practice basketball as much as I can, and stay out of trouble. The first two are easy. The third might be harder, but I think I can do it for you, Mom.

CHAPTER SIXTEEN

New Town High
Junior Year: 1957-1958

Just before school let out in the summer of 1957, I started looking for work. I wasn't having much luck, and I was talking with Mrs. Tyhanic at The Hilltop about the scarcity of jobs when she said that a man she'd known for years, who operated a TV repair shop in town, needed a delivery boy. She said, "The owner is from Hungary, same as me. His first name is Janos, but he calls his business John's TV and Radio Repair. You tell him that I sent you." She smiled at me as I ate another free breakfast, compliments of Simon.

She wrote down the address for Janos's shop, and I gobbled down my food. I went home and put on a clean T-shirt and combed my hair in a regular way instead of my usual duck's-ass. I walked to the shop, which was about ten blocks from The Hilltop. The business was a two story house, with a two-car garage the owner had converted into his repair shop.

I entered the shop from the door with the word "Open" on it

---

and found an older man bent over a massive TV cabinet. "Hello, sir, my name is Frank Bruno," I announced. "I'm looking for Janos, the owner." The man was working on an RCA Victor TV. He looked up but made no reply, so I continued, "Mrs. Tyhanic said you have an opening for a delivery guy. I've worked out a lot, so I'm used to heavy lifting. I have a driver's license, no tickets, and I can start right away."

"You say Helen sent you, right?" he asked.

I didn't know Mrs. Tyhanic's first name, but I assumed that was who he meant, so I nodded and after a short interview, which involved my lifting a TV cabinet that weighed at least 100 pounds. Janos hired me. I'd get $1.25 an hour. I was delighted, as I was hoping for just a $1.00.

Janos had a foreign accent, which I was used to with Wojo. He handed me the keys to a white Ford van with John's TV and Radio Repair painted on the side and said, "You drive. We go see customer. Pick up Magnavox TV. See right away if you can do job and be nice to customer."

I realized that my interview hadn't really ended, so I kept to the speed limit, signaled my turns well in advance, and listened as Janos directed me to a two-story gray-shingled house in a part of New Town I'd never been in before, with tall trees lining wide streets. The TV sat, like some sprawling beast, against a wall in the living room.

A huge console model, at least four feet long with a massive wood-grained cabinet and speakers on the sides, it also contained a record player. I checked to see if any records were on the player and closed the fancy wood doors over the TV screen, and I grabbed one end of the monstrosity while Janos picked up the other. The unit I'd lifted in the shop was nothing compared to this. This wasn't just a TV, it was a TV and a half.

I was impressed with Janos's strength for his age. I wondered how he'd possibly managed this work on his own. And I wondered if I could I do this without any help.

We loaded the enormous cabinet into the van and secured the home entertainment system, as the lady of the house proudly called it, with straps. I drove back to the shop as carefully as I had when we came out here, and we arrived without any mishaps. I'd even made sure to avoid potholes and slow way down for turns.

After two weeks on the job, Janos let me take the van home on occasion, especially if we had a late delivery or a pickup scheduled for the next morning. I arrived early every day and worked for however long he needed me, and he gave me a ten-cent raise before the first month was out.

One day, when we weren't too busy, Janos explained how he got his start. In his native land, Hungary, he used to fix his family's radio whenever it broke. He was just a young boy, but once his skill became known, it wasn't long before a slew of "friends" asked him for help with their radios. He volunteered to be a radioman when he joined the Hungarian army during World War II.

After the war, he immigrated to America with his young bride and repaired radios in the dining room of the same house he lived in now. The next part of his story made me laugh. In 1946, TVs became more available and Janos was the first person in town to own one. The first thing he did with his brand-new Philco television was to dismantle it entirely and inspect every single piece. And when he put it all back together, the TV worked! The following day, he changed his sign out front from Radio Repairs to Radio and TV Repairs.

He added his name to the sign a few years later, telling me that Helen Tyhanic suggested he use a common American name and not his own. He said he never understood why the painter made it John's and not just John. A year or so later he switched Radio and TV around, and the sign has read John's TV and Radio Repair ever since.

I worked in his shop all summer, made great money for a kid in 1957, and learned something new each day. For the first time since Mary Jo had asked me what I was going do after high school, I might have an answer. Television was the future, and a set would be in every home. Board games like Monopoly, and card games like pinochle and canasta, would be things of the past.

A couple of weeks before summer was over, Janos let me have the van for a whole weekend. I had been dating Alice but now that I had wheels, this date would be something special. Alice and I went to the movies. The van wasn't fancy but it was better than what I had before—which was walking.

We saw *Twelve Angry Men*. It was about a guy from the slums of New York City, accused of murdering his father and was now facing a jury. It starred Henry Fonda, Lee J. Cobb, E.G. Marshall, and Jack Klugman. All of the jury voted guilty except for Henry Fonda's character, only identified as Juror number 8 throughout the entire movie. After numerous votes, and lots of discussion in-between, the jury finally agreed on a not guilty verdict. Alice and I thought the movie was pretty good, and we both liked Lee J. Cobb in his role as Juror 3, but there wasn't much action.

After the show we went for hamburgers at a drive-in restaurant on Route 1. I was the only guy driving a van, and one with an advertisement on the side no less. But it was what it was, and all I had for now. Still, I envied the guys, some I recognized from school, who were driving early-'50s Fords with loud mufflers. There were even some 1955, 1956 and 1957

Chevys, and an older Mercury that was "nosed and decked."

A cute waitress, dressed in a really short skirt, roller-skated up to my window and tapped on the glass. I ordered a cheeseburger, Coke and French fries for both Alice and me. I liked Alice from the first day I'd met her in school, and after our first month of dating I bought her a silver friendship ring, and she wore it around her neck on a silver chain.

The next time we went to the movies we sat in the balcony so we could make out. The only problem was that people who smoked sat up there too. I remembered reading a story earlier that summer in The New York Times that said a just-published British study indicated that smoking caused lung cancer. Alice and I swore to each other that we'd never smoke, but a lot of kids we knew did smoke. They said that smoking made them feel cool, like the movie stars with cigarettes.

On the next to last Sunday before school started, I took Alice down to Asbury Park on the Jersey shore. At the entrance, a white metal sign told the history of the place: "Asbury Park was established by James A. Bradley, who made his fortune selling brushes to the Union Army during the Civil War. In 1871, the tea-totaling Methodist bought 500 acres of marsh and sand dunes and built this community called Asbury Park. Liquor was banned and a strict moral code applied to everyone. The rules included no undressing on the beach." I laughed at that last line and so did Alice.

Alice looked great in a bathing suit. Unfortunately, she and I got sunburned, which sort of ruined the day. When we got up to leave, I could hardly pull on my T-shirt, I was so sore. Later, the goodbye kiss was still sweet for me, but we were both in such pain that we couldn't tolerate being touched by each other.

The following Sunday, with each of us over our sunburn— and school starting on Monday—we made it farther south, to a beach called Point Pleasant. We enjoyed the waves, and later we ate sausage and pepper sandwiches, and chewed saltwater taffy. Despite its name, saltwater taffy didn't taste salty at all. We even tried cotton candy, another new thing for me. While I drove home, with Alice napping, my thoughts wandered and I realized that the girl I was thinking about wasn't Mary Jo. It was Alice.

My junior year of high school started off with a bang. Dave Nenninger was in the coatroom, making out with his girlfriend, super good-looking Pat Dohn, and they got caught. That damn kid, Tony, who'd stolen my lunch last year, saw them sneak into the closet before the salute to the flag started. Tony squealed to the teacher. I believe the only reason he did that was because he knew Dave was my friend. Dave and Pat each got an hour of detention. Dave told me he was going to get even with Tony. *Good for Dave.*

A week later, it was unseasonably warm for mid-September and all the 5-foot-wide windows in homeroom were pushed up to let in any breeze. Miss Norton was once again our homeroom teacher, and she assigned one student to read the 23rd Psalm aloud and another to lead the Pledge of Allegiance afterwards. But before anyone read anything, another teacher came in the room and whispered something to Miss Norton, and the two of them left together.

Everyone was standing for the Bible reading and the Pledge, but as soon as the door closed behind Miss Norton, Dave tapped Tony on the shoulder. Tony turned and Dave punched him hard in the gut and kicked him in the shin. Tony bent over to catch his breath, and Dave shoved him backwards. His feet slipped out from under him, and he started flaying his arms in an attempt to regain his balance. However, before he could right himself, and with his back to an open window, he started to fall over the sill—and outside.

I was standing nearby, and I grabbed Tony by his belt. Dave latched onto one foot, and we both began pulling him back into the classroom. Just then Miss Norton returned. It must have looked as if we were holding Tony out of the window instead of trying to save the jerk from plummeting to the sidewalk two stories below.

Miss Norton screamed at us, "Stop what you are doing! If that boy falls, he could be killed!"

It required Donald's help for Dave and me to haul Tony back into the classroom. As soon as he was safe, he crumpled to the floor and started sobbing to the teacher, "These guys are crazy. They tried to kill me. What's wrong with them? Just because I played a joke on Frank by taking his lunch and passing it around, it doesn't mean I should get killed."

Of course Dave and I explained what had really happened— well, sort of—and Simon backed up our story. Ms. Norton sent a student to get the principal. Some other teachers came with Fanny Large as she wiggled her way through the doorway and demanded answers. In this regard the scene was almost identical to the first time.

Most of the kids didn't see Dave slug Tony in the stomach, witnessing instead what was going on at the end, which was Tony going out of the large window opening. Dave got thirty days after-school detention, which meant he'd miss the bus each night and either have to hitchhike home or make the long walk.

The first time Dave came home late, he told me that his mom was really angry. It hadn't been that long since his detention for getting caught in the closet with his girlfriend, so he made up a story about the latest French teacher offering extra help after school—and this could take a while. Every parent knew about the revolving-door French teachers, so Dave's white lie went unchallenged.

New Town High football started a month after school opened. Alice and I watched the first game from the student section of a stadium that was as old as the school. Our guys were bigger and seemed faster than the kids on the other team, but we couldn't keep from tripping over our mistakes.

The series of downs at the very end of the game was typical of how they played. With the game tied, we scored a touchdown but the play was called back because the split end on the very far side of the field was offside. On the very next play, our tight end caught a pass right near the goal line. He was about to score but decided to show off by waving the football over his head. Of course he fumbled. A guy on the other team picked up the ball and ran it all the way back for a touchdown, with less than a minute left in the game. A river ran next to New Town, so the visitors taunted us, yelling, "River Rats, River Rats, River Rats." I hated it.

Alice and I went to the next couple of games and the results were the same, as stupid penalties killed our team. A few days after the third loss in a row, I was headed to biology class when the football coach stopped me in the hallway. "Bruno, I hear you're a pretty tough guy. But if you're so tough, why not try out for our football team?"

I could tell he wasn't being a smart-ass but just trying to get me to join the team, so I laughed and said, "Coach, I'm tough enough when I need to be. But from what I see, your players don't know anything about the rules of the game. This last game, there were more flags thrown against our team than what I saw at the Fourth of July parade. I think I'll just stick with basketball, but thanks for the invite." He nodded to me and I headed to biology class.

My seat was next to Wojo's. We had a few minutes before class started, and he said, "I hear you held some twerp out second-story window. I need you on basketball team. Why can you not stay out of trouble?"

I answered, "Trouble seems to follow me from one day to the next. But thanks for giving a damn."

"Well, if you think you find trouble, listen to what happened to me." Wojo shook his big head. "Saturday night, I go to the carnival in town. I was watching freak show, you know, the fat lady and the smallest man in the world, and I say hello to this girl who stands next to me. She smiled at me and says something in what I think is Russian, which I didn't understand. So I tried my Polish, which she understood and could speak some too. She tells me her parents are visiting relatives in Jersey City for weekend, and she is on her own."

"This is beginning to sound good."

"Just getting started. We went on tilt-a-whirl and merry-go-round and bumper cars. She tells me she wants a kielbasa and pepper sandwich from one of those greasy food stands, so I buy her meal too. She says she's having good time. It getting dark, so I ask her if she like to come over to my house, maybe have a beer, and watch the TV new show, *Wagon Train*. She say she know nothing about *Wagon Train*, but is excited about seeing TV because her parents didn't have one. So she walk home with me. It late when we get to my house, and parents already asleep upstairs.

This girl never drank beer before, and she get drunk after just two bottles of Rolling Rock. By third beer she so drunk she could barely walk. So I said she could stay in our extra bedroom and I'd see her home in morning. I carry her upstairs to the bedroom and pull off her shoes. I did not want to risk taking off her clothes, but she remove top and jeans on her own, then she collapse on bed and fall fast asleep."

"That's it?"

Wojo held up one of his big hands. "No, Bruno, here is where fun starts. About three o'clock in morning, I know time 'cause I hear a noise and look at my alarm clock, she got up and had to pee and searched for bathroom in the dark. Our old house has long hallway on second floor, with many doors. All look pretty much the same, especially with no light in hall. She found the bathroom, but a couple of minutes later I hear screaming and yelling."

"What happened, I asked?"

"What happened was that when she left the bathroom, she still very drunk, and wandered into the wrong bedroom and got in bed with my parents. She snuggled up to my dad, thinking it was me. Lights go on everywhere. My mom was screaming and my dad yelling and stormed into my room. 'What the hell is a naked woman was doing in our bedroom?' he ask me. The girl had taken off every stitch of her clothing."

"Wojo," I said, holding back tears, "that's about the funniest story I've ever heard."

That Friday, I picked up Alice and drove out to Simon's house to take him with us to the football game. Simon's modest home was now surrounded by a wire fence. Simon was waiting outside, and he rushed to the gate before I touched it. He did something on his side of the fence and opened the gate.

He said, "Sorry, my father sees Nazi soldiers at night, and he had this electrified fence installed. He gets crazier by the week. He's always seeing things and hearing voices telling him the Nazis are looking for him." Simon climbed in the van and said hello to Alice, and we headed to the game.

To our surprise, our team had only one penalty in the first half, and we held the lead by two touchdowns. Halftime always meant a stretch to walk around, but tonight a group of kids from the other school paraded past our stands with signs that read: River Rats Stink. I decided that a couple of them needed a good ass kicking, so I started down from the bleachers when Wojo, who was sitting just a few seats away, yelled, "Remember what we talked about, Bruno. I need you on the team." He was right. I sat down and let it go.

On the opening kickoff of the second half, our best running back broke loose around the right side of our line and scored. But while everyone cheered, one of our players was down on the field, holding his knee. It was the tight end who cost us the last game by showing off, and his injury looked like it might be serious. On Monday, the football coach came to me once more and asked if I'd join the team—the tight end's leg was broken. This time I accepted.

With adding football practice to working for Janos, dating Alice, and my studies, I was constantly doing something. However, I made time so the quarterback and I could practice on our own. I wanted to get a feel for the offense, learn the pass routes, and catch the ball from someone who could really fling it.

That next Saturday was my first game, and eight balls were thrown my way and I caught four of them. The fun part came after the catch. I was now 6 feet 2 inches tall, weighed 215 pounds, and I was stronger than ever from constantly lifting the very heavy TV cabinets. I bowled over two guys who tried their best to tackle me.

Our best play was a sweep to the left. Our right guard by the name of Bad Boy Bailey pulled from his position, swept to his left and the two of us demolished defenders and our half-back

---

had room to run. I loved the contact and, for the first time, when I plowed into someone and knocked them down, there was no one coming after me. Instead, I was cheered by everyone, including the coach. I scored twice that first game and told the coach after the game, "If all linebackers are as slow as those guys, I can beat them every time."

Of course some of the defensive players on other teams were just as fast or faster and some as big as I was, but the last six games were great fun for me, and by the end of the season we'd won half our games.

Basketball season started almost as soon as football season was over, and I was back to playing the game I liked most. With everything going on in my life, my grades had slipped a bit, but they were still pretty good overall.

Wojo and I played well together, and our guards had improved. To start the season, we ran off a streak of six wins. Then we played our rivals, New Brunswick. We held them close and had the lead several times, but they were loaded with seniors and had two outside shooters who couldn't miss. They beat us by six points.

We notched four more wins before the Thanksgiving break, but we lost to New Brunswick again, and when the season ended we finished second in the league.

Our chances to win the league in my senior year seemed really bright. We were all juniors and sophomores and getting better as a team with each game. Because we were doing so well, the stands were always full, with family, friends, our student body—and scouts from two nearby colleges.

In the locker room after the final game, Coach Milton congratulated us on a fine year and joked that he didn't know he was that good of a coach until this season. He got us all excited when he hollered, "Next year, we'll beat New Brunswick! You guys stay out of trouble, keep your grades up so you're eligible, and practice as much as you can, especially with each other!" He hugged each of us as we left the locker room. His eyes were glassy. I felt proud for him.

When I got home that evening I rummaged through the mail. To my surprise, there was a letter addressed to me. It was from Joe Cheeks.

CHAPTER SEVENTEEN

Senior Year: 1958-1959

I opened the envelope and read the message from my friend: "Frank, I've enclosed something from the West Side High School newspaper. When I saw the photo and read the article, I thought you would be interested in it because it's about Mary Jo. P.S. The Romans are not the same without you, buddy. I Hope everything is okay in New Town." He signed it: "Cheeks."

If not for Joe sending me the article, I wouldn't know that Mary Jo had been elected president of the Young Democrats Club. But there she was, in the picture, being presented with a plaque from the outgoing president, the same geeky kid she was dating. I thought about her as I drove the van to the TV shop, and sang along with Paul Anka on the radio: "Oh, please, stay by me, Diana." The shop came in sight, and I laughed out loud as I pulled in the driveway. *Mary Jo and Newark, who cares.*

My junior year ended uneventfully. I worked at the TV shop

the whole summer, had pick-up games with the guys from the basketball team on most Saturday afternoons, and before I knew it my senior year was about ready to start. Alice and I were now going steady, and we talked about what we'd do after graduation. Not really thinking I had much of a shot at the basketball scholarship Wojo had talked about, I thought I'd stay in New Town and work at the TV shop, at least for a little while.

Of course, neither Alice nor I really knew what the future held. Alice had even told me that her dad was talking about a job in another town, somewhere in the mid-west but it only sounded like talk so far. I remembered when my dad started talking about another job. I, too, thought it was just talk—and here I am in New Town.

In addition to making a lot of money working for Janos, picking up and delivering the massive TV cabinets provided me with a lot of exercise. But I missed the kind of serious training I used to get at Uncle Louie's gym. So I bought myself a set of weights and "lifted" in our garage. I was about as physically fit as I could be, and more than ready for my senior year of sports at New Town high. I expected the school year to be "quiet" otherwise.

My hope for a calm senior year was shattered on just the second day of school. Simon told me that two new kids, twin brothers from Germany, threatened to beat the hell out of him because he was Jewish. The next day, Simon pointed out one of the brothers to me. I walked up behind the kid, grabbed him by the hair, and spun him around. "No one picks on Simon Silverman," I said. "Touch him, and you'll pay a stiff price, pal."

The kid tried to get free of my grip, yelling at me in his heavy guttural accent, "He's a damn Jew. What the hell do you care if I kick his ass? In Germany, we know what to do with his kind."

I still had him by the hair, so I slammed his head into a metal hallway locker. "Simon's my friend, and this ain't Germany." I held him hard against the locker. "You've got your warning. Next time, we don't talk. Next time, I kick the shit out of you. Got it?"

I let him go and pushed him away from me. He ran his hand through his long hair. "You think you can take both me and my brother? If you do, think again, jerk. Maybe we take you out, Jew lover." I was going to finish him right there, but the bell sounded and kids starting running between us to get to class.

Simon thanked me for sticking up for him, but the next day, about the same time, there they were, the German twins, roughing up my friend. One twin had Simon against the wall on the opposite side of his locker. To my surprise, Simon kicked and fought, but he was no match for this big kid, let alone both of them. Simon saw me coming and yelled to me.

A sign above Simon's locker, in big black letters, read: "Men's Room." It was obviously the work of these two assholes. One brother was standing in front of Simon's open locker taking a leak inside it. I don't know when I've been madder. This wasn't just about Simon, it was a challenge to me personally, as I'd warned the one brother.

Without saying a word I ran up the kid who was using Simon's locker as a urinal and pushed him with my shoulder from behind so hard that I crammed him into the locker, and his own piss. I kneed him twice in his back, and he collapsed onto the floor and into another pool of his urine.

When the other brother saw what I did to his twin, he let Simon go and threw a roundhouse right at me, which I blocked easily. I kicked him in the shin, and as he bent over to grab at his leg I punched him in the face and rammed my knee in his forehead. He, too, fell to the floor. To be sure he understood my anger, I stomped his free hand with my heel. He screamed but stayed down.

The first kid was getting up, but I kicked him in the groin and he was on the floor again. I pointed at them as they lay outstretched and said, "You both fight like little babies. I warned you to leave this kid alone. If there is a next time, I'll put you both in the hospital. Now, you two Nazis give me your locker numbers and combinations to your locks. From today on, both of you will use this piss-smelling locker and Simon will use yours. I'll use the extra locker as my own." I glared at them. "Any questions?" All either of them did was whimper.

The students standing around us cheered me. I asked Simon if he was okay. He smiled and nodded, but he rubbed one hand and then the other. I wouldn't let the German punks leave until they gave Simon their locker numbers and combinations. I said to Simon, "Let's get your stuff out of your locker and wash off everything. Leave these Krauts where they are. And nice fighting back, by the way. Keep it up and one day no one will bother you."

Word of the fight spread not just among the students at school but around town as well. Everywhere I went that evening I heard the story of my beating up the Germans—often related to me as if I didn't know what had happened.

The same night, Simon told me what had occurred after he'd explained the fight to his parents. His father went crazy, ranting about Nazis continuing to track the family. Simon's dad screamed, "Nazis are everywhere. I see them in town every day."

Saul turned to his wife and said, "This is what I warned you about, Rose. They're searching for us. They know I tricked them in Germany." Then he spoke to Simon, "Be careful, Son, they're watching us. I'm sure these are the same ones who

188

followed me off the boat." The old man began walking in circles, wrenching his hands and shaking his head. "They will kill us if something is not done. And soon." He ranted well into the night, and Simon feared that his father had gone completely crazy.

Four days after the fight in the hall, both German teenagers were absent from school, and the next day their parents reported them "officially" missing to the police. Simon took me aside and whispered that his father had come home two days earlier—at six in the morning. Saul Silverman looked exhausted and had pine needles stuck in his clothing, and there was sand on the floor in the front seat of the family's Buick. Simon also told me that he'd checked the hiding place in the garage, where his dad kept the pistol he'd bought in New York City long ago, and the gun was missing.

Police were all over the school and questioning everyone, especially me, suspecting I might have had a role in whatever happened to those kids because it was no secret I'd beaten them up. However, the entire night before the kids disappeared, my time was accounted for by reliable sources: I'd worked at TV shop with Janos until 8:30. I left the shop and picked up Alice ten minutes later. We went to the drive-in for burgers, and the car hop remembered me and Alice because she'd seen us there often and knew the van. We were back at The Hilltop, having ice cream sodas and listening to jukebox music until Mrs. Tyhanic locked up, which was around 11 pm. With school the next day, I took Alice right home, and I was sitting in the living room, on the sofa with my dad, at 11:20 sharp. Together, we watched the late news, which had a story about the Ford Motor Company and a new car called the Edsel, with its weird-looking grill that the newsman referred to as a "horse collar."

With everyone swearing to my whereabouts, I was no longer

considered involved with whatever had happened to the German twins. Free of anxiety, I managed to enjoy the weekend with work, Alice, and a pick-up basketball game that Saturday afternoon.

Although Wojo scolded me harshly for getting into trouble again, I told him he'd have done the same thing if he'd seen those goons picking on Simon. He gave me an obvious reluctant nod, shook his head in disapproval, and that was it. A week later, it was as though the German punks had never existed, and they probably didn't any longer.

I worked hard during football practice and became a better tight end. I also played linebacker in three games. Other than a few pushing incidents that extended beyond the field of play I did okay at linebacker, which was harder than I anticipated. Overall, the team had improved and we had a winning year. Our record wasn't near good enough to take the league championship, but the coach was pleased with our effort and so was I.

In New Jersey, anyone turning sixteen could quit school and the parents couldn't do anything to prevent it. After football season ended, a number of the boys on the team were old enough to leave high school for good, and they did. Several guys took jobs in construction or in the factories. This work gave them spending money and cars for now, but no real future. A couple of kids joined the Navy or another branch of the service, but very few ever joined the Marines because of its reputation for being super hard. Me, I was determined to finish high school and *maybe* get that basketball scholarship Wojo kept saying was not impossible.

Few parents had enough money to send their kids to college.

I saw a dismal article in The Home News: "Only eleven percent of high-school graduates from 1959 are expected to attend college, and less than half of them will graduate." I wanted to be in the good half. As for Simon, he had plans to go to college *and* law school, all of which he told me his parents could easily afford.

Basketball season began, with Coach Milton telling us he expected to win a championship for New Town High.

Our first three games were easy blowouts, which allowed the second-string to get a lot of playing time. Edison High was next. They gave us a tough test but one we passed. After Edison, we had three more wins, beating Highland Park, East Brunswick and Sayreville. Our team was playing so well that the whole town was excited. Even The Daily Home News covered our games.

Fans filled the stands to overflow for every game, and at the halfway point of the season we were undefeated. Dad even promised to take off work early to make the New Brunswick game, which was next on the schedule and a big deal for me because of losing to them twice the past year, costing us the championship.

New Brunswick had graduated two key players, both of whom I'd learned from Wojo had earned college scholarships, one to Monmouth College and the other to Trenton State. As good as I was playing, with each ensuing game I became more convinced that I might get a scholarship someplace.

As for the game, with my dad cheering me on, I even scored on a dunk, my first ever in a real game. I knew where my father was sitting, so I looked in the stands to find him cupping his hands to his mouth and yelling his head off. I led the team in scoring that night, with eighteen points. I also had nine rebounds, just one less than Wojo. Oh, and we won! It felt great to beat New Brunswick and avenge at least one of last year's defeats.

After the game, three college scouts came to the locker room, and to my surprise they talked to me as much as they did to Wojo. I was feeling great until the scout from Rider College asked me about my reputation for getting into trouble off the court. He said, "Frank, Rider College is interested in you, actually very interested, but you have to stay out of trouble. If you can do that, we have a scholarship waiting for you. And before I forget, we just signed a friend of yours, Chuck Gallopo. He said he knows you from Stanton Prep."

"Wow, I sure do know Chuck! He's a great guy!" I smiled at the recruiter. "Tell Chuck I'll see him at college in the fall."

"Keep on playing like you're capable, and you'll join him on our new campus in Lawrenceville. But, Frank, you have to stay out of trouble." I nodded, feeling certain I'd be in Lawrenceville. I couldn't wait to tell my dad and Alice.

We ultimately won the league championship. The townspeople, the students, and even the teachers had something to be proud of. In May, with only three weeks left before graduation, the scout came to my house and presented me with the scholarship paperwork so I could attend Rider college. My dad was in tears as I signed the letter of intent, and all I could think about was Mom. I had a college education in my grasp, just as I had promised her before she died. I would cry later.

As it ended up, Wojo signed with Rutgers, so it seemed we'd be playing against each other next year. We joked about it, but probably wouldn't be laughing on the court when we faced off. I couldn't be happier, and I even discussed some possibilities for a permanent future with Alice. But, oh, how things can change at a moment's notice.

A week before graduation, a kid I barely knew, by the name of Bernard Hines, nicknamed "B-Hind" stopped me in the morning as I climbed the steps to enter the school building. B-Hind told me that Higgins was calling me out. He said that Higgins would meet me up on the hill in the New Town Cemetery after school. B-Hind said, "Face him like a man or be known as a chicken-shit, phony S.O.B. for the rest of your life."

Before I could answer, B-Hind ran into school and told everyone he bumped into that there was going to be a fight after school. It would be round two of Higgins versus Bruno! This wasn't what I wanted, but there seemed to be no way to avoid Higgins and keep my respect at school. *But damn! Respect or not, I could be jeopardizing my scholarship! Not what I wanted.*

By noon, it seemed that not one kid in New Town High School was unaware of the upcoming fight. Simon told me he was cutting French class to see if anything unexpected was going on at the cemetery. Wojo was furious with me for accepting Higgins's challenge, and he shook his head when I told him I didn't have a choice. "You never learn, Frank."

A bunch of kids followed behind me as I walked from school toward the cemetery. I was on the street when Simon came running toward me. "Stop, Frank!" he said, gasping for air. "You have to stop and listen to me. It's not just Higgins up there. There are two other guys waiting for you. And they're not kids. They're grown men from his father's construction company. I saw their pickups. I'll help you, but I don't think we have a chance."

"You have helped me enough already, buddy by telling me what to expect. Just stay clear of everything." I checked around me for anything I could use as a weapon, but all I saw was a little kid's bicycle leaning against a porch rail next to a house.

The bicycle would have to do.

"Come over here with me," I said to Simon and pointed to the bicycle. "I've got an idea. You sit on the seat and hold the bike down while I break the chain." Simon climbed on and kept the bike steady while I stomped my heel on the chain and snapped it. I picked up the chain, which was rusty in places, and wrapped it around my left hand.

"How will that work?" Simon asked.

"It's almost as good as a set of brass knuckles." I rewrapped the chain so it was good and tight and nodded to Simon. "Let's go find these tough guys." Just then I spotted a sandbox off to the side of the house. "You still want to help me with this fight?"

"After all you've done for me, I couldn't be more sure. I'm in this with you, Frank, no matter what… happens."

His words indicated confidence, but I could tell by his wavering voice that he was scared. I pointed to the sandbox and said, "Fill your pockets with a couple of handfuls of sand."

On our way up to the hill, I told him what I wanted him to do. To his credit, he didn't back away in the least. Regardless of the outcome of what was about to happen, his days of being bullied would definitely be over forever.

We reached the top of the hill, and Higgins and the two men stood a few feet apart from one another. The two older guys appeared to be in their mid-thirties, and they had their arms crossed. They were dirty from the day's work and wore tattered coveralls. I said to Simon, "Remember what I told you to do."

He said, "I won't let you down," and I gave him a quick nod.

I stopped walking and shouted, "I hear you guys are looking for me. Well, here I am." I glared at Harold Higgins. "You remember what I said about your front teeth if we ever met again. Well, yours will be missing in about two minutes."

———

CHAPTER EIGHTEEN

The Crooked Judge

Simon ran toward the workman to the left, as if he was going to fight him, which would have been funny under different circumstances, as the guy made about three of my little buddy. At the last moment, Simon circled around him. While this construction worker was huge, Simon was much quicker on his feet, and the ploy worked, as the guy chased after him and I had the other man all to myself.

Before reaching the top of the hill I pulled my shirt out of my pants letting it conceal my fist with the bicycle chain wrapped around it. The guy coming toward me was the bigger of the two men. Suddenly, I slammed him with a spinning back-fist to the side of his head. The chain did its work, as I heard his cheekbone crack. He went to one knee and yelled in pain. I finished him off with a hard kick to his skull. He was done, at least for now. *One down, two to go.* All the kids watching this fight let out a big cheer.

The other man who chased after Simon was way overweight

and soon got winded. He stopped to catch his breath, hands on his knees, which was a mistake because Simon circled behind him and kicked him in knee. As the guy turned around to grab Simon, he got a handful of sand in his eyes instead. He howled, wiped at his eyes, and danced around like he was doing the polka by himself. Simon kicked him in his groin and continued running around him in circles.

Higgins charged at me, his hands up to protect his face, which was stupid because this must have partially blocked his vision. I kicked his left knee and something popped, which stopped him cold. He cried out and I hit with a tremendous left hook with my chain-wrapped fist, smashing his face and breaking his nose. Blood ran all over his face, as if someone had turned on a faucet. He leaned over and blew one nostril, which made the bleeding worse.

The guy with the cracked cheekbone, and a very bloody face, staggered toward his truck, holding his left hand in the air. "You win, kid. I didn't want no part of this crap in the first place." Still wiping sand from his eyes, the guy who'd chased after Simon retreated along with the first guy.

I yelled to Simon, "Good work!" Now it was just Higgins and me, and I wasn't through with him even though he had a badly injured knee and a broken nose. I slipped off the bicycle chain and shoved it in my pants pocket. It barely fit, but no one could make out what it was unless they knew about it to begin with.

Higgins was in awful pain, moaning and groaning and holding his knee with one hand and his nose with the other. I circled him, pounding his face with right jabs and landing hard punches to his body, one after the other. He managed a feeble wild swing at me, but I ducked and kicked him in the groin. He went face down in the dirt. I kicked him in the ribs three times and said, "Just like last time, you fight like a girl." I shrugged and bragged, "I'll let you keep your teeth. You've got enough problems."

We left Higgins lying in the dirt and walked away. Two kids stayed to help Higgins get to the truck, but the rest walked off with Simon and me.

We decided on the sweet shop, but just as we started down the hill, Simon put out his hand and whispered, "Give me the chain buddy and I'll get rid of the evidence." I pulled the bicycle chain from my pocket and handed it to him. He put in under his shirt and dropped it under the same bicycle we borrowed it from. Simon told me that the chain now looked as if it might have rusted through from sitting out in the weather too long.

"You showed a lot of guts back there," I told Simon as we started walking again. You took a chance with this fight, but you did really well. Who knows what would have happened if you hadn't helped me." For the first time since I'd known Simon, he held his head high.

But that wasn't the end of my trouble with Higgins. No, far from it. His father filed a lawsuit in criminal court, and he got the case before an old political friend of his, Judge Harvey Peterson. The hearing was set to start in three weeks. The equally bad news, as I saw it, was that I was suspended from high school because of the assault and battery charge, and I wouldn't be allowed to take my final exams, which meant I'd have all incompletes and couldn't graduate with my class. Luckily for Simon, he wasn't charged with anything.

The judge handling my case had his staff look into my background, and learned that I was a member of the infamous Romans street gang from Newark. I found out that the information on me was sparse, so I was confident I wouldn't be found guilty of anything except defending myself against two adult men and a huge man-child in Higgins. However, the judge also learned from my school records that I'd had a number of fights at New Town High School, and he certainly knew of the first fight with Higgins. Then there were the stories that I'd had something to do with the Nazi brothers who'd recently disappeared.

On the plus side, the judge was told that I was regularly employed as a TV and radio deliveryman, had a clean driving record, played football, and was a star on the basketball team, the latter resulting in a full basketball scholarship to Rider College. And I had all A's and a few B's in all my courses.

What no one knew until much later was that Ralph Higgins, Harold's father, had secretly given thousands of dollars—in cash—to the judge for his re-election campaign. Higgins senior had made it known that anyone who worked for his construction company had better vote for Judge Peterson or that person would be fired.

My court date finally arrived. I don't know how Simon pulled it off, but he got his dad to hire an attorney to represent me, a guy named Cohen, from New Brunswick, and Saul Silverman footed the entire bill.

My dad and I were dressed in our best clothes, as we sat quietly and listened to the charge brought against me, which officially was aggravated battery with a deadly weapon. The weapon was alleged to be a set of brass knuckles used against Higgins and the two other men.

Higgins, whose face was a mess, limped to the chair and testified first: "Your honor, there's been bad blood between me and that guy"— he pointed at me but wouldn't look at me— "ever since the first day at school when he jumped me for no reason. Bruno later challenged me to a second fight and told me I could bring all the friends I wanted. I don't know why he hated me from the start, but he did. So I brought two friends, just in case I needed them. I would have taken him easily on my own, but he used brass knuckles, and he slammed me in the face with them before I could defend myself. He should be in Jamesburg Reform School, not in New Town High with normal kids."

Higgins's attorney showed the judge the medical bills. A loud gasp filled the courtroom when Higgins removed the bandages from his badly damaged face. The judge even sat back in his chair at the sight of Higgins's ridiculously swollen nose and the mass of cuts and bruises on the rest of his face.

After Higgins finished his testimony, with a lot of questions from my attorney, the man I'd hit in the knee took the stand. His leg was in a plaster cast, and he could barely walk, even with crutches. When Higgins's attorney finished, my lawyer got the man to admit he was sent to the cemetery—at his boss's orders—to make sure Harold Higgins won the fight. The other workman who'd been in the fight at the cemetery didn't show up for the hearing.

Now it was my lawyer's turn to present our side of the story, but Mr. Cohen told me he would not call me to the stand because I'd most assuredly be asked about my time in Newark with the Romans. So instead of me he called Simon to take the witness chair and asked him to describe what had "really" occurred.

Simon began: "Higgins has bullied me constantly since the fifth grade, and it continued into high school. He made my life miserable, so miserable that often I faked being sick so I wouldn't have to go to school and face him. It got so bad, that I'd get off the bus early and hide in the bushes until class started. I asked my parents to transfer me to a private school, but they wouldn't do it. I even thought about running away, but I didn't because there was no place for me to go."

Simon teared up and paused to collect himself. After a moment he took a deep breath, nodded to the lawyer, and continued, "The first fight between Harold Higgins and Frank Bruno only happened because Red Hair, Higgins I mean, hit Frank with a spit ball. Because Higgins was always picking on me, I told Frank who he was and Frank clobbered Higgins good. He quit school right afterwards. I hadn't seen or heard anything about him until some kid passed it around school that Higgins would be waiting for Frank at the top of the hill at the cemetery."

My lawyer asked Simon to describe the brass knuckles I was accused of using. Simon was quick with his response: "There are no brass knuckles to describe because there weren't any." He turned up to the judge. "Your Honor, troublemakers like Higgins always say there was some reason why they lost a fight. It's a way of saving face. Frank defended himself against Harold Higgins and two grown men, but here were no brass knuckles involved."

Simon looked to the crowd in the courtroom. "You can ask anyone who saw it happen, and you'll hear the same thing I just told you judge, there were no brass knuckles. The other man sent by Higgins's father to help beat up Frank is so ashamed of taking part that he didn't even show up for the trial today."

Mr. Cohen asked Simon about his role, and he admitted to throwing sand in the face of the construction worker who hadn't shown up for the trial. He said he did this so Frank would at least have some chance against the other guy and Harold Higgins.

Dave Nenninger was called to the stand, followed by Donald

Moore and six other students, all of whom backed up Simon's story. After the final kid testified, Mr. Cohen addressed the judge: "Your Honor, I can call another dozen students who witnessed the altercation. If I do, you will hear the same testimony. Your Honor, it happened the way Simon Silverman described, three adults against my client—a high-school student—and there were no brass knuckles." In a raised voice attorney Cohen yelled, "This is a clear case of self-defense. Your Honor I ask for the dismissal of the aggravated battery with a deadly weapon charges against my client."

The judge was quick with his response: "I accept that the rest of your witnesses will give the same testimony, but I am not ready to dismiss the charge. Do you have anyone else to call to the stand, Mr. Cohen?"

Mr. Cohen's face registered his disappointment that the trial was continuing, but he said, "Yes, I do have one more witness, Your Honor." Saul Silverman was called to testify. Simon told me that his dad had steadfastly refused to attend the trial, but his mom had somehow forced him to come to the courtroom.

Mr. Cohen had one question for him: "Mr. Silverman, have you ever paid Frank Bruno to protect your son, Simon? or act as his bodyguard in any way?"

Simon's father shook his tired face. "No, I never pay him a single dime for anything. He and my son are friends. That is all, they are just friends."

Rose Silverman attended the trial, too, and I glanced at her when her husband was testifying. By her look and the way she kept her hands, as if in prayer, it was as though she was thanking God that she'd never told her husband anything about Simon including me on his account at The Hilltop Sweet Shop.

Mr. Cohen had no more witnesses, and the judge announced, "I will make my decision in the morning. Court is adjourned for today." He banged his gavel and quickly left the courtroom.

Court resumed at 10:00 sharp the next morning. I saw Alice in the audience and smiled as I sat at the table with Mr. Cohen. I had a good feeling about the outcome. With so many people saying the same thing, there was no way I was going to be found guilty of anything.

Judge Peterson took his seat and pounded his gavel. I was told to stand, which I did along with my lawyer. "Mr. Bruno," the judge said and glared at me, "you are a member of the Romans, a street gang from Newark that is notorious for its brutality. And beyond the fight that brought about this trial, you've had a number of fights at New Town High School. It's all in your school records." He cleared his throat but kept a steady gaze on me.

"One decision would be to send you to reform school, but in your situation I also see good grades, athletic achievements, and a regular job. But this time your fighting has gone too far. With three men badly injured, I'm convinced a weapon of some type was used in this fight, even if one wasn't seen by anyone and nothing was found when the police searched the area later on." He paused and rose up a bit in his chair.

"As I said, I could send you to reform school, but I've decided to offer you an option. I will let you decide between joining the Marines or going to Jamesburg Reform School. You have two minutes to choose."

The courtroom was crowded, and screams of protest filled the air. My attorney and my dad stood and dad yelled at the judge, "This is unfair. There were three men against my son. You should send them to jail and dismiss the charge against Frank. Didn't you hear what everybody said who witnessed the fight? There was no weapon!"

People continued yelling and screaming even as the judge

repeatedly slammed his gavel. He ordered the courtroom cleared. Officers ushered the spectators from the room, but people continued voicing their outrage, many standing outside on the courthouse lawn and hollering.

Inside the courtroom, Judge Peterson pounded his gavel again. "Mr. Bruno, your two minutes are up. Choose between the Marines or Jamesburg. Make your pick or I will do it for you."

My dad stood and answered for me: "My son will join the Marines." I've never heard is voice so strained. "The people of this town will not forget this decision."

The judge turned to me. "I will have a copy of the paperwork with the Marine recruiter on my desk within forty-eight hours, Mr. Bruno, or you will be off to reform school. This case is concluded." He slammed his gavel one last time and left the courtroom.

After we got home, my dad hugged me and apologized for not being there for me more often during the past few years. With his working three jobs to pay off mom's medical bills, I didn't blame him for anything but being a great father. He certainly didn't cause my troubles.

I moped around the entire afternoon, finally going over to see Alice, who'd left the courtroom in tears after the ruling. She didn't wait for the courtroom to be cleared to get out of there. The next day I returned the van to Janos and told him what happened. We both had to hold back tears. He'd been like a second dad to me and had taught me a lot about electronics.

I had four days before I was off to boot camp. Alice and I spent as much time as we could with each other, and her parents even let me use their car, as I didn't have the van. For the first time, I had sex with her without using a condom. Alice didn't

203

care and neither did I. She said she loved me and I knew I loved her. The last "time" with her was perfect, and it certainly took my mind off of being forced to join the Marines. I didn't know then that her dad had accepted the new job he'd talked about, which would have them moving to the Midwest.

I hated facing Wojo, after all he'd done for me, and I apologized for not taking his advice. I wished him good luck in college, and I asked him to look out for Simon while I was away. I told him to tell anyone who bullied Simon that there would be hell to pay when I got back.

Just before I left for boot camp, I received a letter from my childhood friend from Scranton, Russell Brewer. He was joining the Marines and as it turned out, he would be riding the same train with me to boot camp!

Rider College was already aware that I'd forfeited my scholarship, but I also sent a letter to Chuck Gallopo because I wanted him to hear from me personally about what had happened.

I thanked Simon's father for hiring the lawyer. Mr. Silverman didn't say anything, so his agreeing to this probably came from Simon's mother, Rose. I couldn't possibly express to Simon and his mother just how much this had meant to me, regardless of the phony decision by the judge.

I had a particularly hard time saying goodbye to Simon. Like two brothers, we hugged each other for a long time. He managed to say in a choked voice, "Frank, we'll always be friends. I'll never forget you. Whenever you come home on leave, you better come and see me. In seven years, I'll have my law degree. Then, I'll be there for you."

Rose Silverman kissed me on the forehead and handed me a bag of her special apricot bakery rolls. She whispered in my ear, "I'll keep that account active at The Hilltop Sweet Shop, in case you come home and need it. Thank you so much for all you've done for Simon. If not for you, he wouldn't be the person he is. Even Saul knows what you've done for our son. We love you, Frank." Wow, I had to leave or I would've balled like a baby in front of them!

My dad, Alice, Simon, Wojo, Donald, Dave, and half the students from New Town High it seemed, were at the courthouse when I met with the recruiting officers who'd be escorting me to the train. I hugged Alice for one last time. Tears streaked her cheeks. My leaving was a lot harder on everybody else than I thought it would be—and for me as well.

I was driven to the train station in New Brunswick. A train took me on the short trip to Newark. At the Newark station, a number of guys boarded who were also headed for boot camp, so we were all sat together.

I found Russell Brewer in the second car. We babbled like little kids as the train rolled along. I learned that his family did move to New York City, and his dad had completed medical school and became a doctor. But it seemed that Russell was a lot like me, always in trouble and in need of direction. His dad had convinced him that the Marines were the best solution.

As the train rumbled south, after a couple of hours we'd both talked ourselves out and I closed my eyes. I'd been so involved with getting everything buttoned up before I left that I'd forgot about Harold Higgins, Jack O'Brien, Father O'Brien, and that stinking, crooked Judge Peterson, all of whom were on my revenge list. Payback wouldn't come anytime soon, not likely for many years, but at some point down the road I'd even the score—with all of them.

The train made a lot of stops, and we were told we'd get on a different one in Washington, D.C. Russell fell asleep and I spoke to a couple of officers, both lieutenants, who weren't that much older than either of us. I asked how they accomplished this at such a young age, and both said the same thing: "We went to college and took ROTC." I learned this meant Reserve Officer Training Corps. How I wished I could have done that.

Well, Marines, here comes Frank Bruno—the kid Outta Newark.

CHAPTER NINETEEN

1959: Boot Camp
United States Marines

I read a bunch of old newspapers while we rode the train. Fidel Castro had named himself premier of Cuba. Bob Cousy, a guard for the Boston Celtics, set an NBA record with 28 assists in one game, and the Celtics scored 173 points against the Minneapolis Lakers. Whitey Ford, who many were saying might be the best Yankee pitcher ever to take the mound, struck out 15 batters on April 22nd. *Some Like It Hot,* starring Marilyn Monroe and Tony Curtis, had opened on May 29th.

My mind wandered and I thought about Joe Cheeks and how busy he must be at the theater in Newark, and wondered when I'd ever see him again. I picked up a crumpled newspaper from May, and the headline read that the Soviet Union had invaded another country. *Maybe I'd wind up fighting the commies.*

After an hour or so, the conductor announced in a loud sharp tone, "Philadelphia, our next stop is Philadelphia." I woke Russell and asked him if he wanted to grab something to eat, should we have the time. He rubbed his eyes and grumbled a yes. The conductor told us we had *exactly* ten minutes.

A vendor with a cart right outside the station stop sold Philly cheesesteaks, along with fries and sodas. We each wolfed down a cheesesteak loaded with onions and peppers, and I bought two packs of Doublemint gum and we hurried back to the train. We weren't in our seats for thirty seconds when the train pulled away. Wow, were we lucky we'd paid attention to the conductor's warning.

Two guys sat in the seats across from ours, which had been empty. One fellow said, "I'm Gary Binder and this guy here is Neil Corona. We're both from New Jersey." Russell and I said hello and shook hands. They'd both graduated from Flemington High School the previous year. Each had held an okay job in a family business, but they wanted to see more than just their little town, and the Marines seemed like the answer.

Neil was a handsome guy and powerfully built, not too tall but tall enough, with big shoulders and arms that reminded me of my father. He'd worked at unloading trucks in his family's wholesale produce business in New York City, but he got tired of doing that, so he joined the Marines, along with his high-school buddy.

Gary was a tall kid, almost my height, maybe an inch below my 6 foot 3 frame, and he'd worked for his dad, driving a dump truck for the family-owned sand and gravel company. Both of these guys, like me, were in good physical shape. We looked forward to showing off in boot camp. However, the way the recruiters described it, I got the impression I shouldn't get too cocky.

As the time passed, I knew quite a bit more about them than they knew about me. I didn't tell them why I ended up enlisting—or had to enlist. I said I was "Outta Newark" and pretty much left it at that. One of the lieutenants I'd talked with earlier walked past, carrying a soda. He looked really sharp in his Marines dress uniform. I wondered if I might wear that same sort of uniform someday, or if that was only for officers.

He looked my way and I raised my hand. "Can I ask you a question?"

"Sure," he said and smiled. "Ask anything you want."

"When we get to Parris Island, will we report to you and the other recruiter on board, or to someone else?"

"You'll report to a Drill Instructor or 'DI' as these men are called. He and several others like him will train you for the next ninety days. After that you take an aptitude test, and then you'll be assigned to a job that bests fits your skills."

"Combat zone, right away," I asked?

"A marine might be ordered to San Diego or to Europe or to one of the hotspots. It depends on a lot of things." He nodded to me and walked on.

Neil looked at me in a weird way. "Frank, didn't you check into all this before you signed up? I went through everything, asked every question I could think of, and prepared myself for the physical part. Gary and I put both put in a lot of time at the gym. We also did a lot of running. Sounds like you just jumped right in."

I decided to tell them why I was on this train. "I had no time to ask anything, and I really had no choice other than joining the Marines. In fact, I only had a few days before I *signed up*." Neil and Gary both raised their eyebrows. "For me, the only two choices were the Marines or Jamesburg University." Both guys now stared at me as if not knowing what I was talking about. "I guess you guys never heard of Jamesburg. It's a reform school. Naturally, I chose the Marines."

I took a breath and explained what had happened at the

cemetery, but I left out the part about the bicycle chain. The more they asked, the more I told, including stories about the Romans and what had happened at New Town High and Red Hair Higgins. By the end of the trip, they probably wondered if becoming friends with me was such a good idea.

A half-day passed before the train finally reached its last stop in the small town of Beaufort, South Carolina. We all got off, and the recruiters led us to six huge green busses with "United States Marines" painted on the side.

"We'll be at Parris Island in a half hour," one of the officers yelled. "It'll be your home for the next ninety days."

The road from Beaufort was paved, but there were long stretches under repair. Strangely enough, there were guys— wearing what I did know were marine fatigues—shoveling asphalt and filling holes and picking up trash, with armed guards watching them. I wondered what that was all about.

In thirty minutes the busses entered a gate with a sign that read: "Welcome to Parris Island." I grabbed my small duffle bag of clothes and stuck a piece of Doublemint gum in my mouth. Everyone got off the busses, and I was happy to stretch my legs. I sang the Wrigley's jingle under my breath, "Double the flavor, double the fun," and pictured those cute twin girls who smiled their way through the advertising slogan.

Four marines, who said they were DIs, gathered us together and screamed commands as if we were deaf and dumb. The combined shouting finally stopped, and one DI hollered, "Fall in, you scum bags." I wondered what they meant by "fall in," but I learned soon enough. The order meant that you stood one arm's length from the recruit next to you—and exactly that.

The DI currently doing the yelling carried a very nasty look. His attitude and calling us scum bags really pissed me off. He appeared to be about forty. I wondered if this guy was as tough as he sounded, or if he was just using his rank to assert his authority.

He called out each recruits' name from a list he held, and when a guy answered the DI asked where he was from. Whatever the name, or wherever the guy from hailed from, he was ridiculed. If you were colored, Spanish, Italian, Irish, German or whatever, he had a name for you, and none of them were complimentary, calling us horse shit, dog shit, or some other type of shit.

He worked his way down the line, barking commands in our faces, calling us more names like scumbag, dirtball, and a bunch of other things, telling us what we were supposed to do next, like push-ups if we had a shirttail out. *Guys with attitudes like these back in Newark would get their asses kicked.* Each time he screamed at another recruit, he stood six inches from his face. One recruit after another, the DI got closer to me.

Just before he got to me, a different DI took over and screamed at us, "When I get through this list, you'll get your fatigues, shoes, haircuts, bunks, and two toothbrushes. You ass wipes might wonder why you get two toothbrushes. One is for your teeth the other is to scrub the floor of your quarters and the toilets." *This guy has to be kidding. What a jerk-off. Back in the streets of Newark, he would be lying flat on his back.*

This second DI worked his way down the line, without the name list, asking who we were instead, and getting closer to me. After saying his name, each recruit was told to answer him with "Sir" first and afterwards, no matter what the DI asked. He emphasized *Sir* as if addressing God himself.

The drill sergeant approached me. I read his name on his badge: Sgt. M. Jackson. The DI faced the recruit to my immediate right, and I couldn't help but notice that the kid was terrified. He shook so bad that he couldn't control himself and pissed his pants. The DI cursed him, and the kid started crying. He crumpled to the ground, rolled into the fetal position, and wouldn't get up. Two other DI's dragged him to his feet and took him away. Where he went, I wasn't sure, but I never saw him again.

I was next in line, and I was madder than hell the way that DI had cursed the poor kid. Although he was much older, his attitude reminded me of Harold Higgins and the other bullies I'd straightened out. *This guy's a prick, just like them.*

The DI stopped right in front of me, got in my face, and barked at me, "What's your name ass-wipe, and what shithole of a town are you from?" I smelled his breath from his last meal, particularly the onions.

I yelled back even though his face was just inches from me, "Sir, Frank Bruno, Sir. I'm Outta Newark, Sir."

"What's in your mouth, Bruno?"

This time I yelled back even louder than my first response, "Sir, it's fucking chewing gum, Sir." It was quiet except for the two of us, with the air became eerily hushed.

The DI broke the silence. "What do we have here, a candy-store gangster from Newark? You're not the first loser from that shithole."

"Yes, Sir, that's me, Sir. A candy-store gangster, Sir."

The DI stepped back a couple of feet and seemed to be taking a position as if he were going to punch me. I readied myself to kick the bastard in the groin. I raised my right hand above my head to distract him, and was about to let go with a hard shot to his balls when something hit me in the head and everything went dim. I barely remembered what had happened, and I had no idea how I was now on a bunk in a barracks. I lay there, dizzy as hell and hurting all over. *I guess I underestimated that*

DI. He had the bite to back up his bark.

I closed my eyes but opened them to Russell and Neil hovering over my bunk. Russell told me I had ten minutes to get my fatigues and a haircut. Neil helped me up, and the three of us got our fatigues.

The corporal cutting hair asked me, "You want it short or shorter?" I knew he was just bullshitting me, as I watched in the mirror as my perfect slicked-back duck's-ass fell to the floor with a few fast slices of his electric razor. When he finished and I checked out my "new" look, I shouted, "Holy shit, who the hell is that?" The jolt of seeing me virtually bald seemed to clear my brain.

The next step was a delousing shower. As I exited the shower, a different DI yelled, "Bend over, grab your cheeks, and spread them." I did this without the slightest lip. A country kid, who I later learned went by the name "Florida," not knowing what he was supposed to do, bent over, put his fingers to the sides of his mouth, and pulled his cheeks apart.

"Your ass cheeks, not your face cheeks, dipshit," the DI screamed at him. When he bent over, the light hit his behind and I spotted a birthmark in the shape of the state of Florida. So when I learned his nickname later, it made sense to me.

The next command to each of us was: "Grab your dick and pull it three times." Any recruit who had a yellowy discharge were sent to the doctor for a shot of penicillin.

After we were done with all this, I was still dizzy but managed to eat some chow with Russell, Gary and Neil. Talking wasn't allowed, but Gary leaned over and whispered, "Bruno, you must be out of your mind, saying what you did to that DI. Two DIs came up behind you and cold-cocked you. Keep it up, and you'll be out there working on that road with those other guys."

I nodded and said, "Yeah, maybe that wasn't very smart, but the DI reminded me of a pain in the ass from high school, kid was a bully." I thought for a moment and added, "It's been a long time since I lost a fight."

After "chow," Sergeant Jackson told us we'd be cleaning our barracks, adding, "Grab your extra toothbrush. You'll be on your hands and knees, recruits."

Six guys from our barracks were assigned to latrine duty, and rest of us were to clean the floor. Sergeant Jackson spoke for the first time in a little quieter tone: "Listen up, recruits, your day starts at 0500 hours and ends at 2100 hours. So don't waste the night talking. Get your sleep. Believe me, you're going to need it."

A half-hour before "lights-out," I inspected the floor and told Neil and Gary and Russell that we'd missed some places. The four of us went at it some more. Just before lights out, Sergeant Jackson inspected our spotless section of floor and nodded at me but said nothing. The floor was obviously perfect.

I washed up quickly, brushed my teeth, and gingerly touched the big lump that had formed on my head. I hit my bunk just before everything went dark. A short time later I heard guys whimpering like babies and pleading for someone to take them home. Other guys prayed aloud. In many ways the Marines were just what I expected, but in other ways much different.

CHAPTER TWENTY

90-Day Wonder

I couldn't believe it when the lights came on at 5 a.m., or 0500 as it was called. The first thing I heard was the sergeant yelling, "Good morning, ladies. You have one hour to shit, shower, and shave. Be prepared for bunk inspection. If one of you does not pass inspection, all of you fail. If you fail, all of you will run a quarter-mile before chow. This platoon does everything together. You have one hour."

My head was pounding and my stomach ached, as I'd apparently taken a few shots to the gut that I didn't remember after getting whacked on the noggin. I was sleepy as hell, but I got up anyway. Russell's bunk was next to mine, and I pushed him in the behind with my foot because he was still snoring. "Get moving, I yelled," and he only started to stir after I gave him another poke.

I hit the latrine, brushed my teeth, and took a quick look at my face. *Again, did I look different without hair!* But everyone else looked pretty much the same, except for the swelling on my head and the bruises on my belly, so it didn't matter. I dressed and made my bed, tucking in the sheets and blanket and smoothing out everything. Russell's bed was fine, as was Neil's, but Gary's blanket was loose so we helped him tighten it up.

As for the rest of our 80-man barracks, most areas appeared neat with the bedding tightly in place, but some bunks were just okay. I had a feeling we'd all be running a quarter-mile. Neil told me that we all had a Marine's Manual in the locker under at the end of our beds, so I found mine and began reading it in the short time left before morning chow.

I stood by my bed and read, but I had trouble concentrating because I was so sore from the beating I took. My body felt worse today than I did when I went to bed last night. A guy on the other side of me said, "Three of them did a job on you, Bruno. I'll give you this, you've got a big set of balls."

I groaned and said, "Thanks, but from the way I feel right now, maybe I'd be better off if my balls weren't as big." I was going to say something else when someone yelled, "Attention."

Four sergeants walked into our sleeping quarters looking for sloppy bunks. Of course, they found some. So off we went for a lap around the track. Some guys were pissed off, but I'd already decided that the lap was a forgone conclusion. After the run, we marched in columns of four to the chow hall, where I gorged myself on food that tasted like something from a basement cafeteria in Newark set up to feed the needy.

After chow we listened to an hour lecture on what we could expect over the next 90 days. We were promised plenty of running, drilling, marching, and calisthenics of every kind, with a thousand push-ups and sit-ups.

Our exercise program began right away. It was still dark as we followed a different DI on a well-used trail that ran through an old growth of pine woods. My ribs ached and I wanted to drop out, but I knew that wouldn't work. My mind went in many directions as time dragged on. I thought about Alice and how she had moved away and thought about high-school basketball and how that training should have helped me more. I was strong but I was away from the gym too long, and I was feeling it.

An hour later a small camp came into sight, and soon we were allowed to rest and get a drink of water. Gary, Neil, and Russell each had made the effort to work himself into shape prior to induction, and how I wished I'd had the same opportunity. But why was I complaining? The Marines were all about discipline, so I made up my mind to ignore my sore head and ribs. This was my life for now, and I was going to make the best of it.

Boot camp consisted of a "Twelve-Step Program." It was explained to us that each week we'd learn something new, and each day we'd practice some of what we'd learned from the earlier weeks. Like the lieutenant told me on the train, after twelve weeks we'd take an aptitude test. A career decision was predicated on how a marine did on the test. And as the officer also informed me, most who graduate boot camp are assigned permanent combat duty somewhere. A small percentage, however, are selected for noncombat rolls.

The first two weeks were all about getting us in shape. After three days, our barracks finally passed a morning bunk inspection, but the next day we failed again. The same few guys were the problem, so a dozen of us "talked" to them that same evening, but the next morning, they failed again. So we had a "blanket party" for those same guys. What happens at a blanket party is that someone throws a blanket over the head of the offender and holds them while the rest of the guys punch his body. Surprise, one blanket party did the trick. We passed from that day on.

I have to admit, after the first two weeks I began to like the workouts, the routine, the training, and the discipline. It also helped that I was pretty much healed from the beating I deserved. We learned how to fix a bayonet to our rifles, how to use it at its deadliest, and how to properly clean our weapons. During the fourth week we fired our rifles for the first time.

One recruit called his rifle a gun and Sergeant Jackson was all over him for using the term gun instead of rifle. From then on, every time the sergeant saw him, he made the recruit recite a poem: "This is my rifle, this is my gun, this is for killing, this is for fun." As he spoke the lines, the recruit had to point to his rifle or his crotch, accordingly.

We practiced the same things over and over. We even learned to take our rifles apart and clean and reassemble them with our eyes closed. Of course there was a purpose to this, should we ever need to do clean our weapons in the dark.

We were taught hand-to-hand combat, both offense and defense. When Sergeant Jackson called for volunteers, I stepped forward. The sergeant showed me some moves, most of which I'd learned from Uncle Louie and had already used quite often.

My unit cheered me on as I tried to take DI Jackson to the ground, but I never got him down. Several times I could have kicked him in the groin and maybe got an edge, but I knew better than that. Two other DI's stood nearby just in case, and I didn't need another thumping. When my time with him ended, I'm sure I did better than he thought I might, but he was definitely a whole lot better than me. This was his life, and it showed.

Today was the midpoint of boot camp or day 45. It was time to be tested on what we'd learned thus far. We fired our rifles at a range and then crawled through tall grass and stopped to shoot at various targets that were often hard to spot. Every challenge was scored in some manner. I think I did well with all of it.

On week ten, the drill sergeants introduced us to the obstacle course. It started with a quarter-mile run, followed by push-ups, sit-ups, and a long crawl under barbed wire just a few inches above our heads. The course continued through a 3-foot-diameter concrete pipe, and each of us had to carry a 40-pound backpack and our rifles.

We also had to cross a stream, using only our hands on the rungs of an overhead wooden ladder. If a DI saw water on your boots when you reached the other side of the stream, you failed and had to start the whole course over again. I was now in the best shape of my life, so even with the backpack and my rifle, I made short work of the ladder test.

On week eleven we faced still another test. Ten squads of eight marines each were trucked to different locations in a huge dense pine forest somewhere in the middle of the state. The time was 0300. Yeah, that's three in the morning. There was only a sliver of moon, so it was almost pitch black. The objective was to capture the other squads and take the flags. The squad with the most flags would be declared the winner.

Each guy had an idea of how to proceed, but when my turn came I said, "We don't know where anyone else is, and we don't know where we are so why don't we remain here. Let the other squads come to us but we need to keep very quiet." No one questioned my plan, we stayed put, and no one talked.

Sure enough, another squad, whispering and stumbling in the darkness, walked right into our location and we "captured" the team. I encouraged our "prisoners" to talk all they wanted. Within the hour, two more squads "sneaked" into our location, thinking they had easy pickings because of all the chatter. We took the flags from both squads.

We let the ruse continue and captured five squads in all. The exercise ended at daybreak, and no other squad had more than two flags. I was no longer seen as Bruno, the candy-store gangster. I was regarded as a leader, and later, with everyone from our barracks standing at attention, Sergeant Jackson acknowledged what our team had accomplished. I was proud of myself and our squad, of which I was just one part.

It was our last week of boot camp and the final test. Those of us who completed the obstacle course in the allotted time and passed the written examination would be promoted to the rank of Private First Class. Anyone who didn't either complete the course or pass the written test remained at the rank of Private. Sergeant Jackson barked his orders: "You'll depart, four men at a time. Fall in and stand at ease until your turn." Eighty men, who hoped to gain rank, lined up four-abreast and waited their turns.

I said to Gary, Neil, and Russell, "We can make this easier if we help each other, especially the part about getting over the wall." I pointed at Russell and Neil. "You guys have the strongest arms, but Gary and I are the tallest. So if we boost you guys up on our shoulders and get you to the top, you can then help Gary and me get up there too. The rest of the course isn't that tough."

"Sounds like a plan," Russell said, and Neil and Gary agreed.

I said, "One more thing. We cross the finish line arm-in-arm as a team, and all four of us win our new rank at the same time."

And that's what happened. We even beat the best time of

every quartet who ran the course. The four drill instructors, who'd pretty much been with us from the beginning, monitored our progress and clapped for us as we ran across the finish line, our arms interlocked. We came apart, pumped our fists in the air, cheered, and congratulated each other with handshakes and back pats. Again, it was a team effort, and I couldn't be more pleased for us as a unit.

After morning chow we were ordered to assemble for yet another lecture. Sergeant Jackson spoke: "I want to take this opportunity to explain a few things to you before you leave basic training. Some of you may think we're hard on new recruits, and I might agree with you. But there's a reason why we're hard on you. You're a team, a team that must be equally ready as one, a team that follows orders and executes them without question. In the field of combat, you have to be able to depend on each other. Yes, we're tough on you, but that's what it takes to be a marine. Now proceed to the written test. You are dismissed."

All four of us passed the written exam, but some guys in our barracks hadn't studied the Marine Corps Manual nearly enough and remained as privates. The only thing left in boot camp was the Marine Emblem Ceremony, which was held in front of the famous bronze Iwo Jima statue.

When Sergeant Jackson pressed the marine emblem into my palm and congratulated me, I was so choked up I could hardly breathe. I looked at the emblem with the anchor, the world, and the eagle and I felt like I was truly a marine. And not just any marine. I was Frank Bruno, Private First Class, 2nd Marine Battalion, Platoon 213. I couldn't help but think of Mom. This wasn't college, but she'd be as excited for me today as I was for myself.

Dad wrote that he was sorry he wouldn't be able to make the

ceremony, but he couldn't take off work the several days it would require to come to graduation. However, he'd certainly pick me up at the train station in Newark.

CHAPTER TWENTY-ONE

Two-Weeks' Leave

With boot camp completed, we were given two-weeks' "leave" before our next duty. I'd already seen my orders, and knew I'd be at Camp Lejeune, North Carolina.

I was packing up my belongings from my footlocker when Sergeant Jackson appeared before me. He said, "Follow me," and this concerned me because I didn't know if he was still angry with me because of my wise-ass attitude toward him on the first day of boot camp.

In his office, he told me to take a seat. I was nervous, figuring I was in trouble, but he said, "Private First Class Bruno, I want to congratulate you on scoring higher than every other recruit on the aptitude test. You and your squad also won the war-game's exercise, and you and your team had the best time on the obstacle course. You have accomplished as much as any recruit I've had during my time here on Parris Island, which is now more than twenty years. He stood and walked around to me. "You have potential, Private Bruno. But there are issues."

I was relieved but confused. "Sir, can I ask what you mean… about, uh, issues, Sir?"

Sergeant Jackson retook his seat. "Private Bruno, you and I and everyone else make decisions every day. Some are big and some are small; some are good and some are bad. In the Marines, one bad move can ruin you. An example would be attempting to assault a superior, meaning me, as you did on your first day. That decision had its consequences, as you know."

"Sir, I was a fool, Sir. I assure you, nothing like that will ever happen again, Sir."

"It takes deeds and not words, Private Bruno. I'm sure you've noticed those marines working on the roads around this base, filling potholes, and picking up trash. Those men made bad decisions—and probably always will. I could have put you out there with them and left you there, but I decided to give you a chance." He reached in his desk and handed me a piece of paper with my name, rank, and all satisfactory markings. "The other drill instructors and I have decided to remove that first-day bad decision of yours from your record, as you can see. We're doing this because of the good decisions you've made since then. You will move forward with a clean sheet when you get to Camp Lejeune. Don't screw this up. Am I clear, Private First Class Bruno?"

"Wow, what a break! Sir, yes Sir." I took a moment to compose myself. "Sir, my actions were stupid, and I apologize for my behavior, Sir. I assure you I've learned my lesson, Sir. Sir, thank you again, and please thank the other drill sergeants for me, Sir." He motioned for me to stand. I snapped to attention, clicked my heels together, and saluted. With that, I was dismissed.

On the bus taking me from the base, I looked out the window at the marines doing menial road chores, and I realized how very fortunate I was to have had Sergeant Jackson in charge of my barracks. His final advice was more like what I'd have gotten from my dad or Uncle Louie, and not a drill instructor that shouldn't care a lick about a guy like me. I swore to myself that I wouldn't let his faith in me be misplaced.

Before I knew it the bus stopped in Beaufort, and Gary, Neil, Russell, and I found seats facing each other on a train heading north, but there was a big difference on our return trip compared to coming to Parris Island. We were all dressed in our military khakis, so regular passengers knew we were marines and greeted us with respect. Businessmen offered to buy us food, drinks, and ice cream. Women, both young and old, were *very* friendly.

I plopped a fresh stick of Doublemint in my mouth and chewed away while Neil and Gary flirted with every woman under sixty. Russell fell asleep almost immediately and was snoring louder than the train.

We changed trains in D.C., as before, and in the predawn hours of the next morning I got off in gloomy, smoggy Newark and Russell continued on to New York City, which was the train's final stop. My dad was at the station to greet me, waving and yelling my name. Both of us were smiling from ear to ear as we hugged, and this time I lifted him off the ground instead of the other way around.

On my first night back, dad and I stayed over at Uncle Louie's and Aunt Marie's house, and she made my favorite dish, chicken parmigiana. At 9 p.m., all of us watched a new western named *Bonanza*, which was followed by another new show, *The Untouchables*, this one about gangsters and federal agents. It felt great to be with my family again.

The next day I worked out at the gym and later walked to The

Paramount Sweet Shop to see if any of the Romans were hanging out there. Luigi greeted me with a smile and a big hug, but the few Romans in the place were new, and I didn't know them except for their gang jackets. They didn't know me either, but they'd heard my name and said hello. I was in a different world and felt a bit out of place, especially in my military fatigues, when Joe Cheeks walked in.

He was now working fulltime at the RKO, making $1.65 an hour. He was buying a 1955 Chevy with a V-8 engine and stick shift. Other than the car, he was doing the same stuff as always. Joe was a day-to-day type of guy with no concerns about his future, but I didn't understand—with his good grades—why he wasn't going to college. He'd told me often that his parents couldn't afford to send him, but he was smart and deserved a better chance at life than working as an usher and cleanup guy in a theatre. I never did figure this out.

I asked him about Mary Jo and learned that she had graduated from West Side High School with honors and was attending Caldwell College. Joe had seen her only once since graduation, and all she talked about was college life and the Young Democrats Club. *Oh, well, it's her life now.*

Joe and I walked the streets and talked for hours, but it wasn't at all like before. We were in different worlds. I was lucky in mine. I was a United States Marine.

After dinner with Uncle Louie and Aunt Marie, dad and I headed back to New Town in his pickup. Dad told me that this next week he was taking time off from his two main jobs. "We can spend some time together," he said and smiled wide. "I'll only be doing some residential projects right near our house, so the truck will be free if you want to use it to visit old friends."

I slept in. It was 0600 hours when my internal alarm clock

went off, as everything for me was now on military time. Just like when I was at the base, I showered, shaved and dressed in my fatigues. I walked the short distance to The Hilltop Sweet Shop. It was 0700 when I entered, and Mrs. Tyhanic ran up and gave me a big hug.

I ordered a huge breakfast of ham and eggs and potatoes, but when I tried to pay she smiled at me and said, "Simon asked me to keep the account open in case you came home on leave and needed something to eat. Actually, this breakfast is on me." She smiled again, but it was different this time. "You look great in that uniform, Private First Class Bruno. You'll soon find out that you're a hero in New Town for how you stood up to those three lying bullies, despite the corrupt judge."

Mrs. Tyhanic was right. Several people who stopped in for breakfast came up to me and said how sorry they were for the judge's actions. I told them that becoming a Marine was the best thing that could have happened to me. The judge was so hated because of the way he'd decided my case that he quit the bench and moved out of Middlesex County and opened a law practice.

Several more customers came in and greeted me while I ate. Each person thanked me for my service. One man offered to buy my meal, but I told him that Mrs. Tyhanic had already taken care of it. Another man, who must have heard the conversation, came by as he was leaving and tucked a couple of dollars next to my plate and told me to use it for the tip. I smiled and thanked him.

I drove over to the TV shop and said hello to Janos, who was delighted to see me and also told me how sharp I looked in my fatigues. As he did so, he patted me on the shoulder. "You make a fine marine, Frank. I'm proud of you, my boy."

He asked if I wanted to work for him on Thursday or Friday

or Saturday, to pick up a little extra cash. I definitely wanted the money, so I told him I'd work all three days if he needed me that much. He hustled me out to the garage and showed me his new van. He offered me his old one, parked out front as usual, to use while I was home. I said, "Thank you, sir." He laughed and raised his bushy eyebrows as if to ask why I'd called him *sir*. The word had become a part of me, and now I said it with pride.

I continued to drive my dad's truck that day, but that evening he rode with me to the TV shop so I could take the van. The moment I got in the van, I thought about Alice. I drove to her house, but she and her family were gone. I'd learned about this earlier in the day from a letter she'd left with my dad. I parked the van I front of her house, wondering why Alice had never written to me directly. There was no forwarding address, and a neighbor could tell me only that they'd moved somewhere in the Midwest. There was nothing I could do but shake my head. *Too bad she's gone. I really fell hard for that girl.*

The next day I went over to Simon's house to see if by chance he might be home from college for some sort of break or whatever. As I drove up, two huge attack dogs were now guarding the Silverman property. Apparently the electric fence wasn't enough to satisfy old Saul. These monster hounds growled and drooled spit as I stepped from the van.

I pressed a button in a box on a fence pole, and Saul Silverman came out of his house and pointed a shotgun at me. "Who the hell are you, and what you want?" he hollered in his heavy German accent.

I took off my hat and smiled, "It's me, Sir, Frank Bruno. I'm Simon's friend. Don't you remember me?"

A glint came to his nervous eyes. "Oh, yes, I remember you now. You are good boy, but you have no hair, and with those clothes you wear, I think you are a Nazi. They look for me. I see many of them, just three nights ago." Rose, hurried out, tied up the dogs, and invited me into the house for a piece of her apricot coffee cake. I'd have fought through the dogs for this.

They asked me what it's like in the Marine Corps. I was telling them about life at Parris Island when Saul thought he heard a noise outside. He grabbed his shotgun and stood behind the front door, ready to fire away at whoever might try to break in. Rose said that her husband was slipping more all the time, something I didn't need to be told.

I learned that Simon was still planning to attend law school when he graduated. Rose said he might be through with his undergraduate studies in just three years. She talked on and on about her pride and joy, her Simon: "He's at the top of his class, and he has made many friends at college, even has a girlfriend, if you can believe that. Every night, I thank you in my prayers for what you did for him. Without you as his friend, who knows what would have happened to him in that awful high school." I smiled and she served me another piece of apricot coffee cake.

"Simon was my friend just as I was his," I replied. "So it worked both ways, Mrs. Silverman. You should have seen him fight alongside of me against those three bullies at the cemetery. He was really something. Very brave."

Simon's mom and I reminisced for some time as old Saul wandered around the house, his shotgun at his side, ranting about Nazis. Before I left, Rose told me the name of Simon's dorm and gave me a number to a hall phone in his building, but she had no idea what his class schedule was like. I'd look up Simon as soon as I could get away.

But first I had three days' "duty" at the TV shop. As I picked up and delivered TVs and some big radios, one customer after another told me what they thought of the judge's treatment of me. Some prominent townspeople had made certain that the governor got wind of the judge's decision, and it hadn't been long before stories about potential corruption surfaced. The rumor was that the attorney general of the state of New Jersey had planned to prosecute him, but some kind of a deal was made and the case went away.

On Monday, I tried to reach Simon by phone before driving to New Brunswick, especially not knowing my friend's class schedule. It took a while to get through to his dorm, as the line was always busy, and when I finally reached Simon he sounded excited to hear from me. But he was studying for finals the next week, and there was no way he could take time to meet with me. We pledged to each other that we'd get together the next time I was back in New Jersey, but I of course had no idea of when that might occur.

Since I couldn't see Simon, the next day I decided to look up Gary Binder, who lived in Hunterdon County in Ringoes, a town in which a lot happened back in the days of the Revolutionary War. Dad gave me directions, and part of the trip would take me on Route 69. I laughed when he said Route 69. Dad looked at me and said, "Yeah, Frank, Route Sixty-Nine is the real name of the road. College kids steal the signs all the time. I read a while back that the state is considering changing the route number because of all the sign thefts."

Dad had told me to take his truck rather than Janos's van, and his directions were very good. He'd written the words "Somerville Circle," and he said I'd pass Ortho Pharmaceutical, part of Johnson and Johnson, the parent company beginning way back in 1886 when it first sold Band-Aids. Dad knew all this because he'd done some work at that plant a long time ago and remembered the date—and Band-Aids.

As I drove west the terrain soon changed to more open land,

with farms along both sides of Route 202. In fifteen miles I reached the Flemington Circle and stopped at a diner, as I needed a restroom break. I was about to leave when I spied a cherry pie with a thick crust sitting on a tray with a glass top covering it. I couldn't resist, and I was glad I took a seat at the counter when a cute blonde came through a swinging doorway and waited on me. The girl was very friendly, and her nametag said she was Diane. If I was staying around here any longer I would've asked her for a date.

I left and it wasn't long before I was in Ringoes. Had I known it was this close, I wouldn't have stopped at the diner. But then I wouldn't have met the blonde. Oh, well. I made a right-hand turn that took me into the town, and I put on the brakes to read a sign. The gist of it was that Ringoes was settled in 1711, centered around the John Ringoes Tavern, a stone building that still existed. The Sons of Liberty had gathered in the tavern and formulated their plans to battle the British.

At a filling station, I asked for directions to Gary Binder's house. My military fatigues made it clear, without my saying a word, that I was a friend of Gary's, and the two guys at the gas station couldn't have been more pleasant or helpful with directions.

No one was home when I got to the house, so I waited at the end of what was a long driveway. A lady came up to me and said that father and son were at the family's sand pit, off Route 69. I had nowhere to go, so I drove to a small grocery store I remembered passing and bought a local newspaper, The Hunterdon Democrat, which I soon learned came out weekly and not daily. I drove back to the Binder house, but it was several hours before Gary and his dad showed up. If it had taken them much longer to come home, I'd have had the entire paper memorized word for word.

Gary was super happy to see me and said all kinds of good things about me to his father. For some reason I thought Gary's dad would be much younger, as he appeared to be at least sixty. The lady who'd greeted me earlier brought dinner to the house, which I learned was the daily routine. I didn't know that Gary's mom had died three years earlier, and this woman, who lived in a farmhouse down the road, did all the cooking for Mr. Binder.

Gary's dad was a pleasant man, and I talked about the Marines and made jokes about some of the "duties" his son and I performed around the base. His dad asked me if I'd like to work with him for a few days. I would learn how to operate heavy equipment. He also said he'd pay me $1.75 an hour. That was money I couldn't refuse, and I called Dad that night to tell him what I was planning to do. He was fine with it, so for the next three days I drove an enormous dump trunk that constantly required shifting gears, and I learned the basics of how to operate a front-end loader. These big machines had a ton of power, so they were right up my alley.

At the end of my three days, Mr. Binder paid me in cash. With what I'd already made from my time at Janos's shop, I felt rich. I was ready for a good-night's sleep before a lazy drive home the next morning. Gary had another idea. He told me about The Rendezvous Bar, just outside New Hope, Pennsylvania, a joint Neil Corona and he had gotten into because no one checked IDs. Gary said, "There are has plenty of good-looking girls who like to dance, and a house band that plays great rock-and-roll." How could I refuse that combination?

Neil met us there around 7 pm, and Gary was right. The girls were pretty and the band kept the place jumping. A cute brunette danced a fast song with me, and she stayed on the dance floor for a slow number that followed. She told me she'd had a fight with her boyfriend that same day. We stood by the bar and I drank beer while I bought her a couple of drinks. She drank stuff I'd never heard of. When she finished the last one, she took me by the arm and led me to *her* car, and we had wild sex.

Afterwards we both needed another drink, so we headed back into the bar. As we walked through the main room, I noticed a guy watching us. Before I could order drinks from the bartender, the same fellow came up to me and said, "You ain't gettin' shit from her, pal. She's my girl." I shrugged my shoulders and smiled at the idiot, knowing I had already gotten "it" but she did leave with him that night. I had a few more beers and danced with more pretty girls. It was a great night all around.

I headed home to New Town the next morning, my head a bit aching from all the beer, but I didn't need a hangover as an excuse to stop at the diner in Flemington. The blond waitress was still as cute, and the piece of cherry pie I ate for breakfast was also as good as I remembered from a few days earlier. As I drove off, I glanced back at the diner. *Maybe Flemington is where I'll wind up after the Marines, but that's a long time from now, isn't it?*

CHAPTER TWENTY-TWO

War Games

Returning to military life, I'm getting my first lecture at Camp Lejeune, which is the history of this place. It began operation in September of 1941 when the 1st Marine Division set up camp, just a couple of months prior to the U.S. formally entering World War II. The first stage of the camp's construction was completed in 1944. Today, Camp Lejeune covers 246 square miles, has 14 miles of beachfront on the North Carolina coast, and remains the primary Marine base for amphibious training. The compound houses 35,000 regular marines, plus officers, support staff and their families.

Camp Lejeune comprises over 3,000 buildings, including churches of every denomination, and 130 miles of paved roads and 85 miles of unpaved roads. There are several recreation centers, two water-treatment plants, and a shopping center. The lieutenant conducting the lecture went on for an hour, quoting one boring statistic after another. His monotone voice created a solid din by itself.

As determined by the scores from our aptitude tests at the end of boot camp, we were assigned to one of a variety of training positions, everything from postal clerk to helicopter pilot. I would learn combat communications, meaning I'd become a radio operator, which was what I requested and seemed a natural fit for me.

Overall, the new marines at Camp Lejeune became components of regiments, battalions, companies, platoons and squads. I was part of a radio team consisting of four marines. An experienced radioman instructed us. Unlike the other three trainees, I already knew a lot about the technology and parts of a radio, so I could concentrate on learning how to operate the equipment.

Everything came easy for me, and after a year I was promoted to corporal and became the leader of a squad of eight men, which included Neil, Gary and Russell. It took some officers I'd become friends with to pull some strings to get the three of them with me, but it happened.

We were to practice what were referred to as war games. Training included every conceivable scenario we might face when deployed for actual combat. It didn't matter to me where I went for combat, what mattered was that I'd be ready to go when called. The guys in my squad all felt the same, so for the next year we practiced attacking and avoiding the enemy in every possible situation, whether in brightest daylight in summer, darkest night in fall, blinding snow in winter, or flooding rain in spring.

At the end of our war games training, I got a three-day pass and went home. My dad asked a lot of questions. I explained how we'd "invaded" Virginia Beach and captured the town. Both of us had a good laugh, but I assured him that my commanding officer took how my team performed very seriously.

Dad told me over and over how proud he was that I'd made corporal, and we had three great days together. Simon wasn't home, and it wasn't practical to go to see him at school, but we had a good talk on the phone. The little shit had a girlfriend—and it sounded serious.

My three days' leave ended much too fast, and I was now back at Camp Lejeune. Combat training, and the physical exercise that went with it, was a huge part of our daily lives, but on weekends we often had "liberty," which was a pass to go off the base for a specified amount of time, usually 24 to 48 hours.

In the city of Beaufort, on Fridays and Saturdays, the Elks Club and the Moose Club put on dances for the marines at the base. Females of all ages came to these dances. These women weren't just locals. Many officers at the base had daughters who enjoyed these dances on weekends, because they were looking for husbands. They often found one. As for me, I was only interested in a lover and not a wife, regardless of a potential father-in-law's military rank.

One Saturday night, I was slow-dancing with a colonel's daughter, who I'd "seen" for four months, when she whispered in my ear, "Frank, I'm twenty-three, and I want to settle down and have a family." That stopped me cold. I was still nineteen, and nowhere near ready for married life, so to be fair to her I told her the truth. She left me that night for a sergeant.

My next "leave" allowed me four full days at home. The first morning in New Town, I ran into Pat Dohn at The Hilltop Sweet Shop while I was having breakfast. She looked great as ever and was still as always, very friendly. There was, however, one difference, as she wore an engagement ring. I complimented her on the sparkling diamond and asked, "So when is this big event?"

Pat gave her long blond hair a shake and said, "We haven't set a date yet." Pat had hesitated with her reply, which was odd for her because she always acted sure of herself and very mature about things. She changed the subject and asked if I'd heard anything about Dave Nenninger. I told her that Simon had said he did pretty well at his new high school and might be going to Rider College.

After breakfast I stopped at Simon's house, and this time he was at the gate to greet me. I'd written him with the dates I'd be in New Town, and he wrote back that he'd be certain to be home this time.

College had made Simon a new person. He was using the Rutgers gym regularly and it showed as his arms and shoulders had developed, and he projected an overall level of confidence I would never have believed possible. He wore stylish clothes, and a late growth spurt had added a couple of inches to his height. His teeth were straightened by braces made of clear plastic that weren't noticeable unless you were specifically looking for them. He wasn't at all the same guy I knew from high school, except for academics, the one area in which he had always excelled.

On this visit home, I didn't even go to Newark. I wanted to see Uncle Louie and Aunt Marie, as well as Joe, but I decided I was officially Outta Newark and hardly thought about Mary Jo.

The next year in the Marines was more of the same until new orders were announced just before the onset of winter. A thousand men were being sent to Cuba by ship, which sounded like a vacation to me. But before we were let loose to explore what Havana had to offer, while still aboard ship we were given the history of the 200 mile-long island and a stern warning to avoid trouble.

Cuba's politics were interesting. Fidel Castro had taken over Cuba in a bold coup in January of 1959. Batista, now the deposed dictator, had fled in terror on New Year's day, thinking that Castro had a much larger army than he actually controlled.

Castro was seen as a hero by most Cubans and elsewhere. He was invited to visit the States in 1960, and he was greeted by thousands of Americans upon his arrival. Tourists from both North and South America soon visited Cuba, and Havana became a cesspool of brothels and casinos supported by drunken foreigners.

For most of us, the lecture we heard while on ship had gone in one ear and out the other, and the warning to stay out of trouble ignored. Thousands of marines, looking for fun descended on Havana like a swarm of locusts wanting to devour everything in its path. Neil and I wanted to try what we were told was Havana's best restaurant, Gato Tuerto, while Gary and Russell headed straight to the wildest bars, searching for the hottest women the island had to offer.

The interior walls of the Gato Tuerto were painted mild yellow and plastered with poster-size pictures of Fidel Castro and Che Guevara. A five-piece conga band played while we dined on a fantastic meal of pork, black beans and rice. After a strong expresso coffee, Neil and I walked the streets. Fords and Chevys rumbled past us, blowing smelly exhaust.

It was a pleasant evening, perfect for taking in the sights. We came to the Great Theatre of Havana, which housed the Cuban National Ballet. A half-block away, a group of street musicians played a 1930's favorite "Guantanamera" while locals sold hand-rolled cigars and just about anything else a person could think of. And of course prostitutes sold themselves.

As we approached an area heavily populated with nightclubs, we saw Gary Binder come out of a bar not far down the street. He stopped, opened his fly and took a leak on the base of some kind of statue. He zipped up and went back inside, laughing at what he'd done. A moment later an argument started and then I heard "Semper Fi," meaning "always faithful," shouted by Gary, which was a call for help to any marine within earshot. I learned afterwards that Cubans inside the bar were insulted at Gary's pissing on a Cuban national monument.

Neil and I ran to the doorway to find both Gary and Russell up against a dozen angry Cubans, one of whom had a knife pressed against Gary's throat. I saw a trickle of blood coming from my friend's neck, so there was no time to think about what to do. I raced inside and grabbed a wooden chair. It was back to the days with the Romans. I slammed the chair against the floor and two legs snapped off. Neil and I now each had a "cudgel."

The Cuban who was threatening Gary screamed his words in Spanish, sounding both drunk and angry as hell. He was focused on Gary and didn't see me coming. I hit him on the side of his head with my club, and he fell like a ton of bricks and the knife flew from his hand. I kicked it under a table and Gary yelled, "Bruno, I owe you man!"

The fight now began in earnest and bar patrons screamed and ran in panic, as everyone in the place was now aware that a brawl was in the offing. The band stopped, and the guys took their instruments and rushed out a backdoor while the waiters hid behind the bar.

Gary, Neil, Russell and I bloodied a few of the knife-wielder's buddies, and the tussle was over in short order. The four of us scrambled out the same backdoor where the band had exited from, wanting to get a good head start before the MPs arrived. We took to the alley and didn't stop running until we were a good distance from the bar, and we made it back to our ship without being caught. The four of us talked about our shore leave in Havana, for years afterwards.

In April of 1961, the CIA sent a small group of poorly trained Cuban exiles and few CIA agents to invade Cuba and overthrow Castro. The covert maneuver became known as the Bay of Pigs Invasion. It failed miserably. Over the next months, Fidel Castro made a secret pact with Nikita Khrushchev of the Soviet Union, and in July of 1962 missile-launch facilities in Cuba were detected by U.S. spy planes. Ballistic missiles were now just 90 miles from Florida! President John F. Kennedy would forever be associated with the Bay of Pigs failure, but he couldn't let Russian missiles remain in Cuba.

JFK announced that the USA would enforce a naval blockade of the island nation. This began a series of intense negotiations, resulting in the Soviets withdrawing their missiles from Cuba in exchange for our removing some missiles in Europe that we had aimed at Moscow. During this entire time, our central command had us on high alert. I believed that the order to invade Cuba would be coming at any moment, but it never happened.

With no need to invade Cuba, new orders arrived for our regiment, which assigned us to a place called Vieques for advanced amphibious training. I'd never heard of Vieques, but I was happy to learn it was an island in the Caribbean, twenty miles east of Puerto Rico. The island had an average temperature of 75 degrees all winter, and an old sergeant told me that the 6th Marine Division always drilled there because of the good weather. "Sure better than freezing your ass off in

Camp Lejeune," the sergeant told me and laughed.

A week later we boarded the all-too-familiar green busses, which this time took us to Morehead City, North Carolina, a port town that wasn't too far from Camp Lejeune. On the way out of the base, I saw those marines picking up trash alongside the road and filling potholes. I shook my head, all too aware that I might have been one of them.

As we approached the docks, ships came into sight, which were to be our homes for four or five days, depending on the wind and weather. I watched while dozens of military vessels were loaded with weapons of all types, along with jeeps, tanks, and tons of foodstuffs and other supplies. A short while later I was one of four-thousand marines boarding a ship.

Upon arrival in Vieques, we set up camp and trained daily for an amphibious assault on a beach. When the "invasion" finally occurred, we dug ourselves in, infiltrated enemy camps by stealth, and took prisoners. When the one exercise was complete we returned to camp, and started the next. When that was done, we marched and practiced more war games. To break the routine, Gary and I volunteered to drive bulldozers and other heavy equipment.

The days and weeks wore on. In my free time I learned to play pinochle. It was a difficult card game to figure out, but I eventually caught on and won quite a bit of money, even playing for just a penny a point. I also wrote letters to my dad and to Simon. I even wrote one to Alice at her old address. I figured it would probably never get to her, but I dropped it off at our base post office anyway.

War games ate up many months before our training was completed, and at the end the officers held a huge celebration for our regiment. Camp photographers took pictures of each of us in action poses, and every marine received a hardcover book documenting all of our experiences at Vieques.

My picture as a radioman in a combat setting made me proud to be a Marine. I'd come such a long way since that first day. Even though it wasn't possible, I wished I could go back and do that day over.

On the return trip to Camp Lejeune, I was on troop ship Number 103, along with Neil, Gary, and Russell. *So what's next in store for us I wondered?*

What came next was a major surprise. We were notified that our active duty in the Marines would be completed as of December 15, 1963, which was several months sooner than what we had anticipated. It was revealed that we'd been trained to be the first assault force to invade Cuba, but since this mission never occurred we were being discharged early. Our time in the Marines after the announcement was easy and relaxed, with every weekend off the base.

A lot had happened in the world since I was a marine. In 1961, John F. Kennedy, at 43, was the youngest man to become President, OPEC was formed, and the United States sent 3,500 "advisors" to Vietnam. That same year, Yuri Gagarin of the Soviet Union became the first man in space, followed by Alan Shepard of the United States one month later. And the Berlin Wall was built.

In 1962, a rock band from England, called The Beatles, released a song titled "Love Me Do."

In 1963, Martin Luther King gave a speech in Washington, D.C., called "I Have a Dream." Marilyn Monroe, who many people suspected of an affair with JFK, was said to have died of an overdose of barbiturates, but an autopsy revealed that no drugs were found in her system. JFK was assassinated in November of 1963 by Lee Harvey Oswald. It was during this year that the United States started using something called ZIP codes to help streamline mail delivery.

On the day of our discharge, Neil, Gary, Russell and I packed our belongings, said our goodbyes to the other marines we'd become friends with, and boarded the train heading north. My dad would be there to pick me up at the station, as always. But I had no idea what I'd do once I got home.

Other than my dad's living there, New Town had little to offer. Alice was gone and Simon was in law school. I thought about returning to the TV shop, at least for a little while, but it held no future for me unless Janos retired and sold me the shop. Even if he did, TV repair wasn't what I wanted to do forever.

I thought about going to college. I'd earned my GED in the Marines, but in truth I no longer had any enthusiasm for a formal education. People like Jack O'Brien, the always-blessed Father O'Brien (who'd died of old age) and Judge Peterson (who'd committed suicide) and Harold Higgins and his weasel of a father, had ruined my opportunity. Two of them were dead, but O'Brien and Harold Higgins were still out there.

Gary sat across from me as the sound of the train's wheels droned on, and my deep concerns must have registered on my face. He gave me a light tap on the shoulder and said, "Hey, buddy, I know my dad can't run the sand pit much longer. I was wondering if you might want to join me and help me take over. The work can be damn hard at times, but the money is way better than what most other jobs pay. What do you think?"

I sat back and placed both my hands behind my head, recalling Flemington and its rural atmosphere and friendly people. I smiled and thought about my friend's offer.

"You know what, Gary? It sounds like a good idea to me. When do I start?"

CHAPTER TWENTY-THREE

The Dirt Merchant

It's February 28, 1972, and I just celebrated my 32nd birthday. Times flies, like everyone says, and a lot has happened in the years since I left the Marines and began work at the Binder Sand Company. I've kept up with news with a subscription to The Trenton Times, and I read the Star Ledger when I eat breakfast at the Flemington Diner.

Neil Corona was in town this past weekend, visiting his parents. Gary and I met him at the Ford dealership on the Flemington Circle just as a shiny new red Mustang convertible, with a hot new engine and a standard transmission was being pushed onto the showroom floor. By the time we left the building, Neil had signed the paperwork and left a deposit on the floor model, which he planned on picking up the following weekend.

Over the years I learned all I could about operating a sand and gravel business. I not only knew how to run every piece of heavy equipment at a skilled level, I could also repair most of the machinery. I became familiar with our customers and them with me, and I understood the ways to get along with the unions in North Jersey and New York City, which basically meant paying bribes in cash to whoever was in control of the various construction sites.

I had a nice feel for the business, and everything was going pretty well until Gary's dad passed away from heart failure last week. He'd never really turned the sand and gravel pit over to Gary completely, even though his health was bad for a long time. As sick as he was, he'd hung on until this year. Frankly, I didn't believe he'd live much beyond a year or so from when Gary and I started to work fulltime at the pit, but he'd fooled me and his doctors for almost a decade.

Gary's dad had always lived a frugal life. The family house was old and falling apart, our four dump trucks were so worn out that Gary and I had to retire two trucks and use their parts in order to keep the other two running, the front-end loader leaked hydraulic oil like a sieve, and our bulldozer sounded like the engine was ready to go at any moment. But while it appeared that the place was always on its last legs, we made do and things managed to work themselves out.

This didn't mean that Gary hadn't often asked his dad if we could upgrade our machinery, even if this meant buying used equipment. The requests didn't matter—regardless of their frequency—as Gary's dad always said he didn't have the money for improvements, and we'd have to go on with what we had.

When the old man passed away, Gary went through the company's books, something he'd never been allowed to do when his father was alive. All Gary expected to find was a thin balance sheet and little money in reserve, which is exactly what he discovered to be the case.

I was with Gary in the office as he finished examining the

---

ledger. He tossed aside the big green book and told me he was unsure if there would be enough money to keep the company going. I wasn't expecting this kind of news, and I had to take a seat to let what he'd just said settle in my mind.

The only hope remaining was what might be in the safe. Gary said, "We're in this together, Frank, so get up and look in here with me. There's either something in here or there's not, and you have a right to see exactly what I see."

At first glance all we saw were a lot of papers and folders. But there was also an old White Owl cigar box, which was stuffed with tens and twenties, and when we were done counting it came to more than three-thousand dollars! Gary let out a whoop at the total. "At least we've got enough operating cash to keep going until we can figure out what to do next."

But there was more. Gary discovered two bank-deposit books, one for the Flemington National Bank and another for The Somerset Savings and Loan. The sums in both accounts were staggering. His father had also invested money in stock mutual funds. In addition to all this, a thick brown envelope tied shut with a string was crammed with hundred-dollar bills, so many we didn't even count them, but it had to be more than ten grand. I'd never even dreamed of seeing that much money in one place.

As it ended up, the safe contained all sorts of investments, and it didn't take my friend much longer to realize he was a rich man. He leaned his chair back against the wall and laughed out loud. "Not only am I rich, I've been working at the sand pit since I was twelve, and now I'm finally free of it."

Gary was soon sitting on the dirty office floor, pulling out stock certificates and bearer bonds from envelopes, and throwing the valuable documents in the air. He laughed like a crazy man and said, "Look at this fortune scattered all around me. Why the hell would my dad live like he did when he had so much money?" Of course I had no answer, but I was happy for my friend.

Gary turned to me, his face suddenly very serious. He sniffled and said, "If you hadn't come to my rescue at that bar in Cuba, there's little doubt in my mind that I wouldn't be here to see this. Frank, you saved my life, and now I've got more money than I'll ever need. So if you want this business, you can have it for a hundred bucks, lock stock and rusted barrels."

My throat got tight but I managed, "Wow, I'll take it, rusty barrels and all!" The deal of a lifetime had come my way, and I pulled out my wallet and gave my friend five $20 bills and shook his hand. Later that week we used Simon as our attorney and made the sale official.

By Monday of the following week I'd physically assumed control of the business. Yep, I owned a sand and gravel pit, the barely serviceable machinery necessary to dig up and haul the materials, and the customer list. I asked Simon to suggest an accountant, which he did, and I was surprised to learn that the sand and gravel business actually made a pretty decent profit. The accountant prepared a detailed financial statement that I could take to a bank.

Gary used Simon to transfer the deed for the family home to the spinster woman who had cooked for his dad all these years. Gary had spent a couple of days going through his dad's personal belongings and loading his truck with what personal items he wanted to take with him, and this morning he stopped by the old sand pit office to say his final goodbye.

We hugged each other for the last time, and he said. "Have a great life, buddy. And if you ever get to South Carolina, stop in a town called Green Earth. That's where I'll be." I watched as he drove off to follow his dream, which was building hot rods.

A few days later I went to the Flemington National Bank, spoke to the manager, a Mr. Fowler and secured a loan based on my excellently prepared financial statement. I bought two brand-new Mack dump trucks, each weighing 44,000 pounds and each capable of hauling 26,000 pounds of sand and gravel and still remain within legal limits. I had "Dirt Merchant" painted on the side doors and on the tail gates, along with my business phone number in huge print. I got the bulldozer overhauled, and all the hoses, belts and even tires on the front-end loader replaced. I owed the bank a lot of money, but I was ready for serious business.

I was proud of my Mack trucks, and I hired three reliable drivers who'd worked off and on for the sand and gravel company over the years. With four trucks hauling dirt, I was heading in the right direction. But I was frugal, too, so to save money I lived in a room in back of the office. Then I got lucky. Really lucky.

My biggest competitor, a sand pit in Jamesburg, New Jersey—the same town where I might have attended reform school—went out of business. Their supply of "select fill" was depleted. In simple language, they'd sold all the usable sand and gravel they could extract from their pit. Upon learning this, I immediately raised my prices by twenty-five percent—yet I had to turn away business.

I was driving one of my new dump trucks to a delivery in north Jersey and listening to a radio talk show as the host was interviewing a writer who had chronicled the Kennedy dynasty. The conversation turned to how fabulous Ted Kennedy was as a senator. The thought of this coward made my blood boil, as all I could think about was Mary Jo, my first girlfriend.

Mary Jo Kopechne had drowned while she was a passenger

in a car Kennedy drove off a bridge after attending a campaign party on Martha's Vineyard. Kennedy climbed out of his car but left Mary Jo to fend for herself. He made it back to hotel and went to bed, failing to report the incident to authorities until the next morning. Ted Kennedy later pleaded guilty to leaving the scene of an accident—and received a two-month suspended sentence.

People with fame and fortune have different rules from the rest of us. Ted Kennedy attended Mary Jo's funeral, as if that were enough. *That was really big of him to attend Mary Jo's funeral. Yeah, what a fabulous man. He let a woman die, and all he got was a citation. He wasn't even charged, no less put on probation. Mary Jo deserved so much better out of life, and I will always believe it should have been him and not her who'd perished during that ill-fated night.*

I started to think about my other girlfriends, wondering about Zan, the Romanette, and what had ever happened to Alice. I didn't have a steady woman in my life. Just dates. Lots of dates.

Money began rolling in, and I begged my dad to move to Flemington and help me run the business, which he agreed to but only after a lot of pleading on my part. I'd helped him pay off the last of mom's medical bills, so there was no reason for him to stay in New Town.

The following year I tore down the old office and replaced it with a new structure altogether. I also built a house with four downstairs bedrooms and a loft with an extra bedroom area upstairs for my dad. The new house had a large kitchen with granite countertops and plenty of cabinets. I owned a Sylvania color TV with the biggest screen I could buy so I could watch the New York Giants football team. It was hard to believe it, but the "candy-store gangster" had made it. I wished my mom were alive and here to see how I'd succeeded financially despite not having a college degree, but at least now I had my dad with me.

The sand and gravel pit had to be closed during the peak of harsh winters, so plowing the Hunterdon County roads proved to be a great diversion from sitting around and doing nothing, and I got paid good money for doing it. I loaded a dump truck with salt and gravel, put chains on the rear wheels, and faced the blizzards, often plowing the roads all night long.

I wasn't the only independent contractor hired to augment the county's small fleet, as there were many of us, and every truck was outfitted with an identical massive yellow snow blade, making our vehicles virtually indistinguishable from one another from the front. The County also provided us with walkie-talkies that were similar to what I'd used in the military.

When I finished plowing, I generally stopped at the Circle Diner, where the friendly blonde, Diane, had worked years earlier. I learned she wasn't just a waitress; she was the manager. She'd moved to Metuchen or Edison, according to the guy who now ran the place, to start a business of some sort with her father. I'd asked around about her, but no one knew anything else, so I gave up on the idea of looking for her. She was likely married by now, anyhow.

One Saturday night early in the summer of 1973, I stopped at the Rendezvous Bar outside of New Hope, where I still met up with Neil Corona when he was in town. This was the guy who had so many beautiful women waiting in line that he could hardly make time for all of them, but tonight his mind was somewhere else, as he didn't dance with a single girl. We walked to the parking lot at closing time, with neither of us finding a girlfriend. Neil hadn't even tried.

I asked him, "What's going on? You're not yourself tonight. Is something wrong with your business or with your parents? If you need some money, maybe I can help you out."

In the glow of the parking-lot lights, I watched a smile come to his face as he said, "Frank, I've met someone in New York City, a woman by the name of Carole." He placed his hand on my shoulder and added, "It's been great fun partying with you all these years, but I doubt I'll be around very much in the future, and definitely not here. I'm buying a house in Newtown."

I couldn't imagine Neil settling down in my old community. I raised an eyebrow. "New Town?"

"Sorry, I mean Newtown, New York. It's near the Tappan Zee Bridge."

Regardless of the exact name or location, I was in a bit of shock. Neil getting married! "I'm going to get invited to the wedding, I hope?"

"For sure. I'll let you know in plenty of time. We just haven't set a date yet."

As Neil drove off, a great many thoughts raced through my mind. *Wow, Neil met someone... someone special enough to marry!* I'd often considered that I should lighten up with "recreational dating" and look for someone to get old with. But here I was, the very next weekend, following the same pattern at the same bar and ending up the same as always, with no concerns about finding someone beyond a night of pleasure.

It was after 2 a.m., and my mailbox's reflective decals showed clearly in my headlights when I made the turn into my driveway. My dad was away, visiting Uncle Louie and Aunt Marie, so no one was home and only the outside lights were on. I got out of the car but had the strange feeling that someone had been at the house. The driveway was paved, so there was no way to see any fresh tire tracks, and the front door hadn't been jimmied. The house had several other doors, and they were all fine, too, but something didn't seem right, and the next morning I'd find out that my suspicions had been correct.

The doorbell rang at 9 a.m., and two figures, who were about the same height, stood next to one another as I squinted through the peephole. They were both too far away to make out. I was in my underwear, so I said through the door, "Who is it?"

"It's Alice," a voice responded, "and this boy next to me is your 14-year-old son, Frankie."

"What? Alice?" I wondered if this could really be the same Alice from high school. Did she say *your* son? I wasn't sure. How could this possibly be true? I told her to wait a minute so I could throw on proper clothes.

CHAPTER TWENTY-FOUR

Simon's Advice

I was so overwhelmed that I fumbled pulling on a pair of pants and a shirt. I threw some water on my face and ran my hand through my hair and rushed to the door and invited Alice and the boy inside.

It was Alice for sure, as she looked almost the same as she did years ago. She took my hand in hers and I kissed her on the cheek and told her I was really glad to see her. I was so surprised by her appearing in front of me that all I could do was stare at her for what I'm sure was a long time.

The boy, who Alice said was fourteen, stood at his mother's side. He broke my concentration when he said, "Like my mom said, I'm Frankie. Are you really my father?"

His facial resemblance to mine was obvious. Also, like me when I was fourteen, he was big and tall for his age. "From what your mom just said, I think I must be your dad, but I promise you, I didn't know it until just now. Let's all go sit in the living room."

I got Alice some coffee and the boy a soda, and I introduced Frankie to a gentle old Golden Retriever I owned who wouldn't even bark at strangers. I joked with people that I kept the dog inside for her own safety, and this wasn't far from the truth. I asked Frankie if he'd take the dog out for some exercise, and he was all for it.

Once the boy was with the dog, Alice continued her story: "So my father could take his new job, we all left New Town and relocated just outside Akron, Ohio. The area was nice enough, but it seemed that everything in the community centered around the Catholic Church, which meant that nothing ever happened without the priest's knowledge—and requiring his blessing."

Alice took a sip of coffee and continued, "When I learned I was pregnant, I had to tell my parents but dreaded this because of my overly religious father. My stomach began showing at four months, so I went to my mom and told her first. She was sympathetic and caring, but she was also fearful of what my father might do. Instead of telling him right away, she took me to see the priest. He wasn't any help. All he said was, 'Bless you my child... God will provide.'

"The next day my mother told my father, and he exploded, just as I'd expected. He ranted and raved for hours: 'What will the parishioners think? We'll be the center of gossip. This is terrible. Terrible, I say.' He walked around the kitchen in circles, talking to himself about what others might say instead of thinking about me, his daughter or his grandchild."

"I'm so sorry," I said, never feeling sadder about anything in my life.

"Don't beat yourself up about this," Alice said. "You didn't know. But let me go on." I nodded. "My father's next words changed my opinion of him forever. He said to my mother, 'Alice will have to leave here. She can live with your sister in

---

256

Michigan. I cannot be the center of gossip for the rest of my life.' And that's what happened, Frank. I was sent to Michigan, where I lived with this aunt on my mother's side, a woman I barely knew. I was fortunate because she treated me well. A few months after Frankie was born, I found a job in a factory that made recapped car tires. I paid my aunt room and board, and she took care of Frankie while I worked."

"Did your parents come to see you and their grandson after he was born?"

Alice shook her head. "Only at Christmas. But to be sure to avoid any 'family embarrassment,' my father insisted that he and Mother always drive up to Michigan rather than the two of us going back home. My father said the same thing every year, 'It's more important to be a good Catholic than for me to play childish games with your son.'" She added with anger, "He never called Frankie his grandson. Not ever!"

"Wow, if I'd only known." I got up and poured us some more coffee.

"For fourteen years I worked at the factory and raised Frankie." Her eyes welled up. "The plant closed last month, so I was in trouble. There's no work in Akron right now, and I certainly couldn't go home and ask my father for help. I did some checking at your old address and learned that your dad had moved. One thing led to another and I found out that he was here—and working with you in your sand and gravel business. I packed my car and came here, hoping you might find it in your heart to help Frankie and me."

I was about to break down, but I held it together and said, "You and Frankie will never have to worry about anything for the rest of your lives." It was then that Alice lost it and both of us got up and held each other in a long embrace.

After we both finally sat down again, she said, "I have to tell you the truth, Frank, I did ask around to find out if you were married. I'm just so sorry to have to come to you like this."

My heart was breaking for this woman. I took her hands in mine. "Alice, you've come to the right place. I only wish you had come to me a long time ago."

Alice reached at her neck and pulled out a thin silver chain with a ring on it from her blouse. "Remember this?" It was the silver friendship ring I gave her when we were in high school. I was amazed that she still had it after all this time. Just then Frankie burst through the front door, with the dog following him.

He nodded to the dog. "Sure is nice. Slow walker though." He noticed his mother fondling the ring on the chain and glanced at me. "So, Mom, *that's* where that ring came from." *Smart kid.*

Alice said, "Yes, your dad gave me this back in high school."

I helped her and Frankie with their clothes and other stuff and gave them each a separate bedroom. I also called my dad to tell him we had company, and these people would be here for a while. It was the strangest thing, but he seemed to know what was going on, as he never questioned me at all, even when I said it was Alice and her son. Maybe he somehow knew, but I wasn't about to ask Alice if maybe she'd talked with my dad. If so, this would be one secret they would always have between them.

It was unnecessary, as it was obvious by Frankie's face—and everything else about him—that he was my son. Still, Alice showed me a birth certificate, and it documented that the boy was born three days shy of nine months from the night we'd had unprotected sex. He was definitely my son.

I made us all a big breakfast and told Alice and Frankie that I had to leave but would be back later that afternoon. In the meantime, they should treat the house as their own. I drove off, thinking about all that had just taken place, as so much had changed in my life in the course of just one morning. I called Simon on the payphone at the diner and told him I had a problem and needed to see him right away. Since it was Sunday, I would catch him at home. He pressed me but I wouldn't tell him what it was about. He said he was planning to take his family to the park, but he'd see me instead and told me to come right over.

Simon and I had remained best friends after all these years. To no one's surprise who knew Simon, he was valedictorian of his class at Rutgers, and after three years of law school he passed the bar exams for both New York and New Jersey, each on the first attempt. The New York exam had a reputation for being particularly difficult, with many law-school graduates failing it initially, but it was no problem for Simon. He passed easily and signed on with Newman and Myers, one of the biggest law firms in New York City.

Newman and Myers took only the top law graduates, working them to death but paying them well. Simon did what they asked of him for three years. After that he opened his own office in Somerville, New Jersey, specializing in clients in construction and commercial trucking.

Just as I finished my phone call at the diner, out of the corner of my eye I thought I saw someone I knew from a long time ago. I walked over to a man dressed in a dark pinstripe suit and a striped tie. He was reading a paper, and I took a hard look at him to be sure I was right. I said, a bit louder than I intended, "I know you." I'd startled the guy and his head jerked up. He was my old basketball teammate and friend from prep school, Chuck Gallopo.

His face lit up. "Frank Bruno, well, I'll be damned." He

smiled, stood, and shook hands with me.

I had a cup of coffee with him while he told me about his life. He'd played basketball for Rider, graduated with high marks and a degree in finance, and was hired by Johnson and Johnson to work in the accounting department. It wasn't too many years before his career took off and he was promoted and making good money. However, he decided to take an offer from a private accounting firm because he was given part-ownership.

Chuck looked great and we talked for some time. I gave him the short course on my time in the Marines and how I got into the sand and gravel business. We shook hands and promised to keep in touch, but as it ended up we never saw each other again. We lived in different worlds, his of suits and ties while mine was Blue Collar, Mack trucks and dirt.

As I drove off to meet Simon, I thought of how Jack O'Brien had forced me and Joe Cheeks out of Stanton Prep and destroyed any shot at college for both of us. I wasn't jealous of Chuck's white-collar success, but I never got over what Jack O'Brien and Father O'Brien had done to me, as they stole my chance for what should have been a clear path to a college education and who knows what beyond that.

At 34, I owned my own company and was probably making more money than Chuck, but it was not the same thing. I always wondered what I would have become with a college degree hanging on my wall. The whole thing made my pulse race, as if everything had happened just yesterday.

Simon greeted me with a hug. He was a different man compared to when we first met. The little guy who was terrorized by bullies was now a prominent lawyer. His house was big and beautiful, and the neighborhood where he lived was one of the most desirable in Somerset County. He and his wife had two children, and Mrs. Simon Silverman was expecting their third child, I was immediately informed. I was happy for him after what he had gone through in high school.

Simon welcomed me into his study and closed the door and said, "I hope this isn't another problem like the last one when the brakes failed on one of your trucks and it ran over that guy. I was very lucky to save your butt that time."

The accident in which the worker was crushed had happened a few months before my dad took over the paperwork for the business. I'd let my truck insurance lapse. I had the money, I just forgotten to pay the premium, so at the time the accident occurred I was uninsured. If not for Simon, the incident would likely have ruined me.

One of my men had delivered nine tons of gravel to a construction site, which was a muddy quagmire because it had rained steadily for the preceding three days. He'd set the parking brake at the top of a slick ramp, but the truck slid backwards and crushed a man working at the bottom. The poor guy died. Simon hired an engineer to investigate the site, and he proved that the grade for the ramp was far too steep to meet state regulations, and the jury cleared my company, which meant me, of any blame.

The jury found the general contractor at fault, who, of all people, was Harold Higgins, the bully who'd tormented Simon back in high school and the same guy who'd laughed in my face when I was forced to join the Marines. Simon's win in court was a long overdue victory for him—and for me.

The jury award put Higgins in deep financial trouble. He had to "fire sale" his equipment or file for bankruptcy and get nothing in return. He sold his machinery for about a quarter of what it was worth, the buyer none other than Jack O'Brien, the asshole from Stanton Prep who now ran the construction company his father had started. In this twist of events, Higgins

261

became Jack O'Brien's employee.

Simon interrupted my thoughts by saying, "So, my friend, on the phone you said you had a problem?"

"I may have misspoken when I said 'problem,' but here's the story." I related everything as it had occurred that morning. When I finished, Simon, who'd been taking notes, nodded.

"So your old girlfriend, Alice, showed up with her son, named Frank, and you saw the birth certificate. As a lawyer, you know my next question, which is how much time elapsed from when you were *with* Alice last, and the date when her son was born?'"

"She has a birth certificate that shows that the boy was born three days short of nine months from the last time I saw Alice. He's fourteen, Simon, and he looks just like me when I was his age. There's no doubt he's my son. I really doubt that Alice could have moved to Ohio, which is at least a two-days' drive from New Town, found a serious boyfriend, and got pregnant all within the same week from when I last saw her. She was a virgin when…."

"I know you, Frank, and I'm certain you don't want to deny this boy is your son."

"No, Simon, that's not me. Besides, I'm still fond of her and I want to do what's right. I just want to get your advice as a friend and not a lawyer. I thought I loved Alice back then, but it's been a long time. So my question is, what do I do from here?"

Simon rubbed his chin and took a sip of some tea he'd brewed for himself and said, "There are several ways to think about this. Alice raised your son all these years on her own and never asked for any help from you until now. And this is out of desperation, if what she says is correct."

"I don't think she's lying," I said rather aggressively, and

Simon gave me a "cool it" smile.

"I don't either," he said. "I'm just talking like a lawyer, but let's say everything is exactly as she says. Alice could request child support for the last fourteen years. A sympathetic court would most likely give her what she asked for if it's within reason. Child support alone would come to a hefty sum. Could be as much as a hundred grand. And if the boy had medical or special school expenses, it could be a lot more."

"So what should I do?"

"Take care of both of them. Find them a place to live, buy her a decent car if she doesn't have one, and give her enough money so she can get on her feet. I have a few favors I can call in, and I'm sure I can get her a job. You say she worked in a factory, but I remember her being smart back in high school. If she has other skills or can be trained, I can probably see that she lands a position with good potential. My advice as your best buddy and not an attorney is to be a friend to her and a father to your son. See where things go. Think how lucky you are. You have a son you didn't even know you had. And he sounds like a strapping boy."

I considered Simon's suggestions and how it all might work out. One thing for certain, my dad would be as happy as hell when he got home and found out he had a grandson. I couldn't see why I wouldn't take Simon's advice on all accounts.

Before leaving, and solely as a friendly parting remark, I asked Simon how everything else was going with him. He sat back in his chair, hesitated and took a deep breath. Deep concern showed liked shadows on his face. "Since I won the lawsuit that cost Harold Higgins his business, I've had a problem... a serious problem with him. And it involves Jack O'Brien too."

263

CHAPTER TWENTY-FIVE

The Blizzard

I ended up staying for over two hours as I listened intently to what was happening. With Higgins driving and Jack O'Brien riding in the passenger side of a pickup truck, before heading to a construction site in the morning, they have routinely stopped somewhere near Simon's house and waited for him to leave for his office.

On his normal route to get to work, Simon turns right on County Line Road, which leads to Route 22 and an intersection configured like a T. A concrete barrier is constructed in the middle of Route 22, which forces all drivers to make a second right-hand turn. Route 22 always has heavy traffic, especially at rush hours, so County Line Road backs up while drivers wait for an opening at the T. Every morning, Higgins has been following right behind Simon's car. At the intersection, he blows his horn incessantly and makes obscene gestures while Simon has no choice but to remain where he is until there's enough space between cars to proceed.

The harassment hadn't escalated beyond horn blowing and raised middle fingers until just this past Friday morning. Higgins tapped Simon's bumper with his truck, as if daring him to get out of his car to see if there was any damage. Because it would incite Higgins further, Simon didn't want to get the police involved, but he decided to call me if anything else happened. I reminded him that Higgins was a miserable, mean sonofabitch, and O'Brien was no better, so I doubted the situation would go away. In truth, I suspected it would get worse.

"Let me give this some serious thought," I told Simon and patted his shoulder, "but for now vary the times you leave for work—early on some days and late on others. And sometimes take your wife's car and leave yours in the garage." As I was talking, an idea came to mind, but I quickly dismissed it. "I've often thought about what I'd do for payback against those two, but I haven't had many ideas that wouldn't get me a front row seat in the electric chair." I sighed. "If we can keep these two idiots at bay for a while, I promise I'll come up with something, and something that will fix their clocks for good." I had to take care of my friend, but I also I wanted to get back at Higgins and O'Brien for what they did to me.

Simon took my advice and left his house for work at different times each morning, but in a few weeks Higgins and O'Brien figured out what was going on, including Simon using his wife's car. Now they arrived early and waited until Simon drove off, regardless of the time or vehicle.

By the end of the second month, it was now a full-scale assault by Higgins and O'Brien. Higgins was banging into Simon's bumper with his truck, and with increasing force. It was this activity that gave me an idea of a way to take care of both Higgins and O'Brien for good—and not land myself on death row. But I needed a good snowstorm, actually a blizzard, for my plan to work.

When such an event might occur was of course impossible to predict, but if weather patterns during the past several winters were any indication, the first big storm would be a couple of months out. I suggested to Simon that he take a vacation, even if it was just for a week, as this would frustrate the jerks and also make them lose time at work.

Simon liked my suggestion, and he rented a house on Lake Hopatcong not for a week but for a month, and he commuted to work from there. When he returned to his house, it didn't take long for Higgins and O'Brien to get back to their antics, but another month had passed, and really bad weather wouldn't be that far off. While all this was happening with Simon, a lot was going on with my life, but in much different ways.

As Simon suggested, I found Alice and her son a nice place to live. It was a spacious old home converted into apartments, and close enough that I could see her and Frankie by making just a short drive. Simon had a contact help Alice get employed at Mack Trucks, and she was hired as a manager trainee in quality control. She liked the work, and the job paid her a lot more than she'd made at the tire factory, even after fourteen years. I never asked, but I had to believe that Simon had somehow orchestrated her pay grade as well.

Frankie adjusted amazingly well to his new school, making friends right away and going to sock hops and other activities. I had him work for me on Saturdays, which provided him with spending money and the opportunity for us to get to know each other. Alice had done a wonderful job of raising him, and I had a great kid. No, we both had a great kid. Frankie made me feel like a proud father, and my dad didn't have to tell me that he loved having a grandson. When Frankie asked questions about me and his mom, I answered him honestly. Alice told me that Frankie really liked me, and I believed this to be true.

Over the next few weeks, the more Alice and I talked about Frankie, the closer she and I became to one another. This past Saturday we went to a bar in Flemington called "Jakes," and we ordered the house pizza. A trivia game was organized in the lounge area, and it was set up so couples could compete against one another—and keep drinking. Because we worked as a team and "helped" each other with the answers, Alice and I were really good, winning several matches until two "Brainiacs" beat us. We laughed throughout the evening and enjoyed each other's company, and I was feeling good about her. One date led to another and another and it wasn't long before the flames from our high school days were a roaring fire again.

In mid-December I asked Alice to marry me when winter was over. She jumped into my arms and said, "Yes, yes, yes, but why wait until winter is over, let's get married for Christmas."

"I have something I have to do before I can get married... something important."

Her face dropped. "More important than getting married?"

"It's something I can't talk about right now, but please trust me. And don't worry, spring will be here before you know it, and we'll be husband and wife."

Alice put her arms around me. "Frank, I trust you. I can wait a few more months if that's what you want. But you can't tell me why we have to wait?" I didn't say anything, and after a long pause she nodded and we left it at that. I would have told her if she'd pressed me, but I was relieved she hadn't, as I was certain she wouldn't have liked my response.

Simon called me the week before Christmas, his voice

fluttering. "Frank, it's gotten worse. Higgins and O'Brien smashed into the rear of my car this morning, hard enough to crunch part of the trunk. Higgins ran up to my window and demanded that I give him money for causing him to lose his business."

"How much does he want?"

"Fifty thousand. He told me to pay up or they'd put me upside down in a ditch the next time. I don't want to go to the police. It's my word against theirs, and then they'll come after me for sure, whether or not the case ever gets to trial. Frank, I hate to admit this, but I'm really scared and I'm scared for my family. Even if I pay them, how will I know this will end?" I told Simon to stay calm and to drive his car that evening to my garage at the sand pit. He'd been to my business before, so he knew which building to go to.

That night, Simon and I temporarily traded vehicles. My dad and I had been working on my pickup, reinforcing both the front and rear bumpers, something I'd wanted to do for some time. I'd just put the finishing touches on huge bumpers both in front and in back. My pickup was formidable, like it was ready for a war zone and not for the street. I said," This truck will serve you well. You just have to hold on until we get a big snowfall, then we'll turn the tables on Higgins and O'Brien."

"What if they damage this truck?"

"It's insured... I think."

It was nice to see Simon give me a slight grin, even if it was obviously forced.

Simon wasn't bothered while in the truck, but just after the first of the New Year, Higgins and O'Brien found Simon's wife coming out of grocery story in Flemington and followed her on foot through the parking lot. She opened the trunk to her car and bent down to set her bags of groceries inside the trunk when

Higgins rushed forward and pushed her up against the vehicle. He yelled in her face, "Tell your husband to pay the fifty grand he owes me or next time this'll go a lot worse." Both were gone before she could collect her senses. She'd left her kids with a sitter, which was the only good thing, as they'd have been scared out of their minds. She thought about contacting the police but decided to hurry home and tell Simon instead.

Simon phoned me immediately after his wife told him what had happened. I said to Simon, "I'll call my Uncle Louie in Newark, and he'll have two bodyguards at your house before morning. He'll send tough men who are used to dealing with trouble a lot more serious than this. They'll follow your wife everywhere. Stick with me on this just a little while longer, and you and your family will never have to worry about Higgins or O'Brien again."

"I don't know how much more of this I can take... and now my wife."

"I know I keep saying this, but just a little while longer, my friend." *Please, God, send us a snowstorm!*

I called Uncle Louie in Newark and told him what had happened. He knew that Simon was my best friend and had even met him years ago. Uncle Louie said, "Simon won't have to wait until mornin'. I'll have two gorillas at your friend's doorstep before midnight." We talked for a little longer, and I asked about Aunt Marie and he asked about Dad. With all that was going on, I didn't tell him about Alice and Frankie. This would have to wait for better timing.

Two rough-looking men in their forties, Romans well before I was a member, arrived late that night. Uncle Louie had told me they were "muscle" for the Longshoremen's Union. Simon told me later that his wife put each man in a spare bedroom, and she'd never acted more relived about anything in her life.

A week later, the weather forecast called for snow—heavy snow. This is what I was waiting for all this time. I drove to Simon's house, was greeted by the two men at the door and now I told them my plan. I thought Simon might argue with me, but he didn't register the slightest complaint. The threat to his wife was the last straw. When I finished, I told him to come out to my truck, and I handed him a walk-talkie and showed him how to use it.

Per my instructions, he called Higgins by phone and told him he'd had enough and was throwing in the towel. His wife was terrified, and he was ready to pay the fifty grand to get O'Brien and him off his back. "Follow me to my office tomorrow morning," Simon told Higgins. "I went to the bank today, and I've got your money in cash in the safe at my office. The building will be cleared out tomorrow because of the snowstorm, so no one will see you go in with me or when you leave. But if you're not outside my house tomorrow morning, I'm going to the police. I've had it!"

"Don't worry, Silverman," Higgins replied. "We'll be at your house bright and early, snow or no snow. And make damn sure those bodyguards you got hanging around stay inside. That's right, we know all about them. And in case you're thinking of trying anything, those goons can't guard you and your family forever."

I watched the weather report on TV, and the message that ran across the bottom of the screen which kept repeating: MASSIVE SNOWSTORM HEADED OUR WAY.

Simon called me just as I was going to phone him. "Good news," he said. "Higgins and O'Brien are confident that I'm scared to death and ready to make the payoff. I'm positive they'll show up, regardless of the weather."

271

I smiled as I said, "I'm sure that they think tomorrow will be their payday. And it will be, but just not quite what they have in mind."

We reviewed every detail of our plan one final time. I reminded Simon to install the snow chains on the pickup, which he told me was already done. As I walked out to the garage to get in my dump truck, I felt the first snowflakes brush against my face. The sky was cold and gray. A bad storm was indeed coming our way—in more ways than one for some people.

I climbed inside my truck and drove it to the gravel pit, fired up the front-end loader, and loaded the Mack's bed with "winter mix," a combination of sand, salt and light gravel. I filled it to overflow and watched as the excess spilled on the ground.

My dad was with me, and he helped me line up the truck so I could attach the huge yellow snowblade. Not much snow would accumulate for several hours, but I casually said that once the storm started I expected to be salting and plowing all night. He nodded, as he understood what keeping the roads open entailed.

The snowblade was an exact duplicate of what the county had in its own fleet and provided for every independent driver. I maneuvered my Mack dump trunk into the right position and got down and helped my dad set the heavy pins in the slots to secure the blade. We hooked up the hydraulics, and I tested the controls from the cab. Everything was set just right. Dad had worked quietly and asked no questions, yet I couldn't help thinking that he knew something was different tonight but didn't want to ask.

I attached a wooden horse with blinking lights to each side of my truck. I'd installed new batteries in the lights the night before. I dropped my dad at the house and drove off. I called Simon a few minutes later on my walkie-talkie to make certain the unit I'd given him was operating correctly. It was, and

Simon responded on the first buzz, telling me that he was ready. I told him to try and get some sleep, and I'd be calling him in the early morning.

The snow started just after midnight and fell as heavily as if God had opened a giant pillowcase full of goose down. At 5 a.m., the wind started blowing hard.

At 7 a.m., a foot of snow covered the roads, and in some places the drifts were three feet or higher. But the snow presented no difficulty whatsoever for my dump truck and I was certain that my pickup, with chains on all four drive wheels, would cause Simon no problems.

My walkie-talkie buzzed and Simon said, "Frank, I sent the guards out to wait for you by the side of the road, a half-hour ago."

"Roger that."

"What?"

"I got it, Simon. You did great. Now let's see this through and your nightmare will end." *Yes, everything was in place!*

I drove toward Simon's house and listened to radio chatter between the other snowplow operators, most of whom I had known for years. I didn't respond to any of the banter. I was responsible for keeping Route 202 and its side roads open but with the swirling snow, roads were treacherous.

From Route 202, I turned onto County Line Road and stopped my truck. As I stepped down from my cab, blowing snow made it almost impossible to see as I untied the wooden horses and set them up in the roadway, blocking both lanes. I turned on the bright yellow blinking lights and they flashed bold "ROAD CLOSED" lettering. For good measure I gave the ice-covered lenses a good wipe-down not wanting any vehicles to be able to follow me.

The wind was so strong that I had to struggle to get back into my truck. Once inside the cab, I could hardly see the road. The defroster wasn't doing much, so I cleared the windshield with a scraper I kept on the front seat, revved the engine, put the transmission in gear, and headed my beast of a truck toward Simon's house. I wasn't on the road for five minutes when my walkie-talkie buzzed. It was Simon. "The assholes are here," he said.

I said, "Take your time about leaving your house. I'm not more than a mile away. Hesitate before you make the right-hand turn on County Line so I can pick up those two guys Uncle Louie sent, but don't look for my truck, just know I'm there. My lights will be off because I don't want Higgins and O'Brien to see me."

"I'm ready," Simon said.

I proceeded, keeping my blade well above the pavement so the snow-covered road would be impassable for any standard vehicle. I had to open my window to scrape ice from my outside mirror. As I did this, snow blasted me in my face. It was just as the weather report had predicted: a major blizzard. Perfect!

It wasn't long before I came upon the union muscle Uncle Louie had sent. Both of them were covered with snow and couldn't climb up into the cab fast enough. As they got in and rubbed their gloved hands by the heater vent, I put out my own gloved hand and said, "Welcome, from one Roman to another."

"Morning, brother," was the response the bigger man gave as the other gave me a quick smile. Nothing more was said by either man as they continued to warm their hands.

With my truck lights off and the engine idling, we waited in the dark by the side of the road. A few minutes later, I made out a set of headlights and watched as Simon's car made the right hand turn towards Route #22 with Higgins and O'Brien in their pickup right behind his vehicle.

I kept my gaze on their truck to see if either of them might glance in my direction, but both of them kept their heads straight ahead, watching Simon, probably seeing dollar signs with nothing else concerning them. When I thought about it later, why would a snowplow raise the slightest red flag, because what else would anyone expect to see in a blizzard like this?

At the T intersection, Simon signaled his usual right-hand turn, but he came to a complete stop and Higgins had no place to go but to wait behind him, his truck exposed. I watched as Higgins's driver's-side window came down. He waved his hand erratically, so intent on giving Simon hell for stopping that he didn't pay the slightest bit of attention to my massive snowblade fast approaching.

I lowered my snow blade and hit Higgins's pickup, and in a natural reaction he pressed his brakes hard when he felt the impact. When he did this, my snowblade slid right under his truck, and I lifted the back half of his vehicle off the road. His front wheels barely touched the snowy road surface and his rear wheels were "locked" in my snowblade. I had them!

With no way to drive off, Higgins and O'Brien forgot all about Simon as he made his right turn and disappeared. Both of them opened their windows and waved their fists, screamed and cursed at me, but they didn't know who I was or what was happening. Every other day they were the predators; today, they were the prey.

I gave my monster truck the gas and it charged forward, carrying the pickup as though it were a toy. I laughed as Higgins revved his engine and tried to steer to escape. There was little Higgins or O'Brien could do except jump from their truck and run for their lives, but I wasn't going to give them that option.

I had my gas pedal floored, and my fully loaded Mack dump truck carried their smaller truck at 20 miles per hour. The cement barrier that separated Route 22 was just ahead. Higgins's taillights indicated he still had his foot on the brakes. One of the two thugs in my vehicle yelled "You have to press your brakes harder you fool."

I looked to my left for oncoming traffic on Route 22, but with blinding snow swirling in front of my windows, I couldn't see anything. I doubted anyone else would be out in a storm like this, but from chatter on the county radio I learned that other snowplow drivers were coming from the west on Route 22. They were only minutes from my location, but I had plenty of time.

I slammed Higgins's truck into the concrete divider and watched as his truck rolled over. The crash left the pickup in a heap of twisted metal and glass. All the pickup's lights were out, and hot water shot out from the radiator as the steam from it mixed with snowflakes, creating a weird picture in the semidarkness.

Nothing moved inside the truck. I told Uncle Louie's guys to pull Higgins and O'Brien from the destroyed pickup. I got down from the cab and watched as they dragged the two bastards who'd plagued Simon to the side of the road. Higgins and O'Brien were in bad shape but alive. Both bones in Higgins's right arm protruded through his jacket. He must have hit the steering wheel with his mouth, as all the teeth I'd told him I'd knock out way back in high school, were now gone. O'Brien's head had hit the windshield and punched a hole in it. His face was a mass of blood, his lips and eyebrows destroyed and his teeth in fragments.

Higgins was moaning but conscious. One of the union enforcers said to him, "Youse assholes ever bother Simon or his family again, next time I put a slug in both youse brains. Don't make me come back lookin' for you two punks. Ya understand what I'm sayin'?" Higgins, his eyes closed, could only nod. "And if that punk buddy of yours survives, make damn sure he knows what I just told ya." Higgins nodded again and grunted something before he passed out.

The two union guys and I climbed back in my truck, and I drove off a distance and pulled to the side of the highway where I turned my lights off. Tree branches hanging low from being weighed down with snow gave me cover. I was pretty certain that my truck couldn't be seen from the "accident" site, but by peering through the limbs I could make out what was going on.

Before long I spotted the flashing lights from a truck pushing a wall of snow down route 22. The truck's snowblade caught the smashed pickup and rolled it over. The excited driver yelled into his radio, "I hit something... something big! It might be a car. Oh, shit, now it's burning! I'm eastbound. Can anybody help me? I need to see if I can find anybody alive! Oh, shit, I hope I didn't kill anyone!"

Someone came on the radio and said he was driving a county snow truck and would be there in a matter of minutes. I decided I'd seen and heard enough, and I eased my truck onto the highway, lights still off and drove away. I was confident that my truck had gone undetected. As I listened on my county radio, at no time was there any mention of a vehicle leaving the scene. The first snowplow driver had found Higgins and O'Brien, unconscious and barely alive, and requested an ambulance. I wouldn't have minded if he'd not found either of them and they'd frozen to death in the snow and ice.

With a snowblade and a half-load of "mix" still on my truck, I drove the two union "helpers" to the train station in New Brunswick and handed over the money Simon had promised them, which was $1,500 each. I said, "Thanks for your help and keeping Simon and his family safe. That guy means a lot to me."

The big one who had done all the talking, said, "No problem, Frank. You're a Roman, just like us. Them bums will probably live. Ya ever want 'em dead, call Louie and he'll get ahold of us. I don't like them and what they were doing so next time, two grand will cover it, and that's for both of 'em." I told him I'd contact my Uncle Louie if I needed help again, hoping that would never happen, and we shook hands. The other guy nodded at me as I shook his hand but still never uttered a word.

I drove away, listening to the news reporter on my regular radio: "A pickup apparently lost control in the snowstorm and hit the center barrier at the intersection of County Line Road and Route 22. A plow hit the truck afterwards and it burst into flames. Two men, apparently thrown from their pickup, whose identities have not been released, were found in a snowbank on the side of the highway. The conditions of those men are listed as critical, but that's all the information we have at this time. Now back to the Blizzard of 1975."

Simon and I purposely didn't talk to each other over the next two months. I wasn't worried that our scheme would be discovered, and Simon said that he wasn't concerned either, but we decided to avoid contact, just in case.

I finally had a reason to get in touch with him and called his home. I invited Simon and his family to my house for dinner, and with Alice and my dad and Frankie at my side, I said to Simon, "Alice and I are getting married next month, and I want you to be my best man."

With tears in his eyes, my best friend replied, "It will be my honor."

Simon and I took a walk alone after dinner. Well away from the house, I said, "Those bastards got what they deserved. After what we did to them they won't bother you again, not ever. Higgins is never going to use his right arm again and from what I hear, he's lucky he didn't lose it entirely. O'Brien never fully recovered from his head injury and he's selling out and moving. You okay with what happened?"

Simon's only words were, "Frank, my friend, I've never felt better about anything in my whole life."

I smiled and placed my arm on his shoulder. That evening we agreed never to talk to anyone about what we did and from that point forward, we never did.

Alice and I were married on the 20th of April and honeymooned in the Poconos. On the third day we drove to Throop and ate dinner in Scranton. Our marriage was perfect and seemed as though we'd never been apart. I felt like the luckiest man alive and was very happy about the way my life had turned out. I'd like to think that the sergeant in the Marines who gave me that break and my mom would be proud of me. I know I was.

Author's Note. Frank Bruno has been my friend for almost 50 years and I'm pleased he chose me to tell his "story." He was and is a Marine and did operate his own sand company for many years. Frank retired from the Operating Engineers Local # 825 after 50 years, and at age 80, designed his own clothing line and launched his idea in the fourth quarter of 2017. He was a Blue Collar guy and that is exactly what his clothing line is: Blue Collar USA. Great looking denim shirts. See his Web Site: www.bluecollarusallc.com

Although Frank Bruno is a real person, many of the events portrayed in this book are fiction from the author's imagination. One thing for certain, he is OUTTA NEWARK.

Author's Plea. If you enjoyed this novel please write a reader's review on Amazon, Barnes and Noble or another site. Five stars is the best rating. I hope I have earned your approval.